CHASING STARS

HELEN DOUGLAS

BLOOMSBURY

LONDON NEW DELHI NEW YORK SYDNEY

With thanks to my lovely family, Julia Churchill, Martin Philp,
Chris Higgins, Becca Stuteley, Lauren Cumes, Leanne, Tamzin,
Sarah, Becky R, Becky W and the whole team at Bloomsbury.

Bloomsbury Publishing, London, New Delhi, New York and Sydney

First published in Great Britain in June 2014 by Bloomsbury Publishing Plc
50 Bedford Square, London WC1B 3DP

A CIP catalogue record for this book is available from the British Library

ISBN 978 1 4088 2870 0

Typeset by Hewer Text UK Ltd, Edinburgh
Printed and bound in Great Britain by CPI Group (UK) Ltd, Croydon CR0 4YY

1 3 5 7 9 10 8 6 4 2

www.bloomsbury.com

Praise for AFTER EDEN

'Once I started reading I couldn't put it down. I took it everywhere!' **Chioma**

'This book is a masterpiece . . . It takes you on a roller-coaster ride of love, secrets, deadly discovery and time travel.' **Grace**

'*After Eden* is absolutely amazing . . . and has everything which you could want: romance, action and so much more!!' **Aadya**

'"Light-hearted", "fun" and "plain brilliant" are the words I would use to describe *After Eden*. It leaves you starry-eyed and with questions that keep you up at night. This is definitely on my favourite books of the year list.' **Nawa**

'Adventurous, exhilarating, plot-twisting, heart-warming book! You love each and every character. A Must-Read!' **Ella**

'This book is about planets and literally took me out to space because I forgot what was around me as I was so interested in the book.' **Beth**

'A very thrilling story with twists you never expect and an element of romance. This all comes together to make a perfect book you can't put down until you've turned the last page. I read it all in one night!' **Regan**

By Helen Douglas

After Eden
Chasing Stars

For Harry, with love

PROLOGUE

Then

She ran, her long red hair billowing behind her. The harbour wall was high and narrow, its surface slick from the recent rain. Yet still she ran. As she neared the end of the wall, she risked a look behind her. He had slowed to a walk. She had nowhere to go. Below her, the swollen sea churned.

'Wait, Eden!' he shouted. 'I'm not going to hurt you.'

She hesitated, throwing a quick glance over her shoulder, before launching herself into the air. Arms flailing frantically, she fell. The sea sucked her under.

Travis stopped and studied the surface. The sea was too rough to tell where she had landed. He kicked off his shoes and tugged off his jacket, all the while watching patiently for her to surface. The moment her head bobbed among the waves, he dived in.

It could have been worse. His forehead just scraped the jagged rocks concealed beneath the water. Blood streamed from the wound, but he was pretty sure it was just a graze. He surfaced and searched around him, the high rise and fall of the waves making it difficult to see much of anything.

As he floated to the top of a large wave, he saw her, swimming in a splashy front crawl towards the opposite headland. He dived beneath the surface, where the water was calmer and the wind less of a problem. Opening his eyes in the grey light, he began to swim in the same direction. He would catch up quickly. Her trainers and her clothes would weigh her down and she was not an accomplished swimmer. This would be easy.

He saw her feet kicking up and down in front of him, almost within reach. One strong push from him and he was able to reach out and grab her shoe. She jerked to a stop and kicked out at him, but he simply grabbed the other foot. He'd got her.

Her frenzied kicking and thrashing reminded him of a fish out of water and he smiled to himself at the strange irony of his imagination. He surfaced briefly for a lungful of air, saw the wild panic in her eyes, the realisation that she was going to die.

It didn't usually happen this way. Travis preferred to kill people unexpectedly, so they didn't have time to feel fear or fight back. He wasn't a sadist. He liked to imagine that those he killed had a happy thought in their mind at the end – or failing that, nothing more disturbing than a plan to pick up toothpaste on the way home or take the dog for a walk.

It was different with Eden. She'd been clever enough to

realise that he was going to kill her and she had run. Nearly got away with it too.

He reached forward and placed one hand on the top of her head, forcing her under the water. She was surprisingly strong for a young girl, though he knew that the survival instinct made people discover hidden reserves of strength. He began the methodical counting – training told him two minutes was enough in most cases – and began to formulate his story. Eden was helping him take photos of his restaurant when she fell in. He dived in to save her, but the sea was too rough. He couldn't find her until it was too late.

Suddenly he was dragged from his reverie. Her hand grabbed at his shirt and pulled him under. He hadn't expected this, hadn't prepared his lungs for a lengthy spell underwater. She was trying to hit his head, but the water took all the force out of her punch. He could tell she was weakening, that this had been the last desperate attempt of a drowning girl.

He admired her, actually. She had spirit. In another time she would have made a good agent.

He watched as her mouth opened and she sucked water into her lungs. Bubbles made their way towards the surface.

Grabbing her arm – if he let go of her now it could take hours to find her again in this unsettled sea – he swam towards the beach, grateful for the onshore wind.

When a big wave finally crashed him on to the sand, he felt a huge wash of relief. This had so nearly gone wrong. Had she survived, had she lived for several more decades, chances were at some point she would have inadvertently said something about the future. But now the timeline was safe once more.

He checked her pulse, made absolutely certain that she was dead, before heading into town to call the emergency services.

The tunnel wobbled. Ryan focused all his concentration on keeping the ship centred. It threw a sudden curve to the left and his heart jerked. He'd only ever encountered curves like that in time-travel simulations. It usually meant the imminent collapse of a portal.

This had to work. He had to make it. Everything – nine months of anguish, of begging, borrowing and stealing – had been about this.

The tunnel was narrowing. He swore. If it collapsed, he was space dust. A quick glance at the control panel told him he needed just ten more seconds. There was a chance it would hold that long. There was nothing more he could do anyway. It was too late to alter course. He squeezed his eyes shut, afraid to face the end with his eyes wide open.

Counting backwards in his head, he wondered each moment if this second would be his last. When he reached zero, he unpeeled his eyelids and saw the green of the farm-house garden.

He'd made it.

The question was: had he made it in time?

He released the hatch and ran down the steps to the garden. Rain fell in torrents, bouncing off the ground and forming streams on the hard surfaces. Turning to the house, he quickly observed that there were no lights on. There were no cars in the driveway. He was either too early or too late.

She had drowned in the harbour in Perran. Five miles

away. It would take him the best part of an hour to run there. Too long.

He raced up the lane to the hamlet of Penpol Cove. He could see nothing but the flickering blue glow of television screens behind curtains and a row of neatly parked cars. The residents were all locked safely away in their homes, out of the storm. This was a tiny dead-end place. Someone would have left their car unlocked with the keys inside. He tried the car doors. The fifth one opened. He checked the usual places – sun visor, glove compartment, CD storage area – before realising the keys were in the ignition.

Gunning the engine, he raced along the bypass into Perran. Squinting through the rain and into the darkness, he searched for any sign of her, but there was none. He jumped out of the car when he reached Perran and ran towards the harbour.

There she was. He could see her standing at the end of the harbour wall. She threw a look over her shoulder at Travis, who was walking – with the confidence of someone who knows he doesn't need to hurry – towards her. He would reach her in twenty seconds, at a guess. Ryan would need a minute.

How had it come to this? How had nine months of planning and plotting brought him to a place where he was perhaps forty seconds too late? He sprinted harder, trusting his feet to find the right place on the narrow wall, hoping that he'd find traction on the wet surface.

She jumped.

'Eden!' he yelled, unable to prevent himself.

Travis turned.

'No!' yelled Ryan, pounding the distance between them.

Staring at the water, Travis removed his jacket and shoes, then dived in.

Was he too late? How long did it take to drown? He was nearly there. Pulling off his jacket as he ran, he tried to remember what Eden had told him about the rocks near the wall. Which side were they? He knew he needed to throw himself far out if he was to avoid them. Pausing just for a moment, he used the toe of one foot to hold down the heel of the other, as he kicked off his shoes.

He could see them, struggling together about ten metres from the wall. He launched himself into a dive, aiming as close to them as he could.

Visibility was low. Opening his eyes, all Ryan could see was churned up sand and seaweed. He pushed to the surface and got his bearings. Travis had one hand on Eden's head. He was pushing her under. Blood poured from a cut in his forehead. Even so, Travis was strong.

Ryan threw himself into a powerful front crawl, while the high waves tossed him up and down. Travis and Eden disappeared and reappeared from view as the sea rose and fell beneath him. Once he was within striking distance, Ryan swung his fist and made contact with the bloody cut on Travis's forehead. Travis's head snapped back and then recovered. Ryan swung again. This time with power. Travis fell beneath the waves.

Ryan wasted no time.

7

He held his breath and kicked down below the surface. Eden was slowly floating downwards, one hand clutching Travis's shirt. A ribbon of pink rose from Travis's head.

She was sinking fast. He kicked harder and reached for her, grabbing her waist and pulling her hand free from Travis. He had her now. Clutching her to him, he kicked hard for the surface, his lungs burning.

He had to get her to shore as fast as possible. On his back, he floated her next to him and held her under her armpits. The onshore wind helped. He reached the sand and pulled her up the beach.

Water trickled from the side of her mouth, but she was breathing. He'd saved her.

CHAPTER 1

Cornwall – June 2012, three days later

It was no ordinary cemetery. There were no white granite headstones sparkling in the diffused light, no ancient cracked tombs, no parish church. Just a deep, green woodland tumbling down the steep side of a hill to a stream.

'First she had you cremated and then she buried your ashes next to a tree down by the stream.' He looked at me. 'An apple tree.'

'My favourite. Blossom in the spring, apples in the autumn.' I couldn't keep the shakiness from my voice.

Three days ago I had been dead. Three days ago I had drowned in the swollen waves of the harbour during a storm. Three days ago, Travis, my aunt's boyfriend, had pushed my head under the water and held me down until my lungs burned and I opened my mouth to let the water in. But now I was alive.

'Are you sure you want to do this?' Ryan asked.

I nodded.

We made our way down the hillside, stepping over

gnarled and twisted roots, past hawthorn and beech trees, plums and cherries, to an ancient apple tree whose knotted, weather-beaten branches reached across a small stream.

I ran my fingertips down the rough bark of its trunk. 'So this is where I was laid to rest.'

'Yes. She buried your ashes next to this tree. I saw it in your file.'

The nearby stream gurgled and the air was sharp with the scent of English apples. As final resting places went, this had to be one of the best. Miranda knew me well. I wouldn't want to be buried in the ground, trapped under the weight of a granite tombstone. But my ashes nourishing the earth was a cool way to end up.

'I should be dead,' I said. I couldn't shake the feeling that I was living on borrowed time, that eventually Fate would catch up with me and it would all be over.

Ryan reached for my hand, twining my fingers through his. 'No, you shouldn't. That should never have happened. And now it didn't.'

We left the darkness of the trees behind and followed the stream until it emerged into the sunshine. We were less than a mile from the sea; I could smell the salt on the air.

'I just worry about the future,' I said.

'What do you mean?'

'You coming back and changing time works out great for me. I get a second chance. But what if you coming back to save my life sends ripples of change through time? What if we bring death and destruction to the future? What if the price of saving one life is too great?'

Ryan smiled. 'You're talking about the butterfly effect. When a butterfly flaps its wings in the Amazon, it helps to create a hurricane on the other side of the world. Small actions lead to great consequences.'

I nodded.

'It's a beautiful theory. I studied it in pre-college science and philosophy class. Completely wrong, though.'

'What do you mean?'

'It's just not helpful when applied to time travel.'

'When you visited 2012 for the first time, you stopped Connor from discovering Eden and saved the future of the Earth. That was a pretty massive change.'

'How can I explain?' said Ryan, half to himself. He pointed at the stream trickling through the orchard. 'OK, where do you think this stream runs to?'

I shrugged. 'Probably to a larger stream or a river. And then eventually to the sea.'

'Right. And there are millions of little streams just like this all running into the sea.'

'What does that have to do with time travel?'

'Think of the timeline as a giant ocean. It is fed by millions of tiny streams. If one of those streams runs dry, what impact do you think that will have on the size of the ocean?'

I shrugged. 'Not much.'

'Exactly. But if the Amazon or the Nile runs dry, it will have a significant impact on the ocean. Connor was an Amazon. His life changed the course of human history. But you're just a little stream, Eden. No one in the future will notice whether you run dry or carry on.'

'I guess.'

'In any case, Travis changed the future when he killed you. If you're concerned about the integrity of the timeline, I'm just putting the future back on course.'

We reached a wide section of the riverbank, where the ground was green and mossy. Ryan stopped suddenly.

'What is it?' I asked.

'I want to dance with you.'

I looked around. 'Here?'

'What's wrong with here?'

I laughed. 'Well, there's no music.'

'I don't care about music.' His voice was quiet.

He opened his arms and I walked into them, resting my head on his shoulder as he held me. I'd never felt so alive. I felt the thudding of his heart against my chest, the blood racing through my veins, the mad tingle of electricity in every place his skin touched mine. I'd never felt so aware. Of the stream gurgling and sloshing alongside us, the honeybees, slow and drowsy, buzzing around like sleepwalkers, the soft ground yielding beneath our feet. I'd been given a second chance at life and I was going to make it count.

'I've been waiting for so long to dance with you again,' he said.

I laughed. 'It hasn't been that long. You danced with me last Saturday night at the Year Eleven Ball.'

He shook his head. 'It's been four days for you; it's been nine months for me.'

I knew that of course. He'd already explained to me that he had left me four days ago, after the Year Eleven Ball, and

12

portalled back to his time. It had taken him nine months to find a time-ship and enough fuel to get back to 2012. But he had come back just one day after he had left. Nine months for him. Four days for me.

'I want to dance with you at night, under the stars,' he said.

'We can do that.'

He pulled me closer to him and then we were tumbling slowly backwards on to the green moss. I fell on top of him, our legs tangled together, my head against his chest. His fingers were in my hair and the sun was warm on my skin. I breathed in his scent, the lemony soap he always used, the metallic smell of his jacket, the warm, clean smell of his skin. Things were going to be different between us now. We hadn't even kissed until the night he left. Because we knew he would leave and we would never see each other again. Because we knew we couldn't be together. Because we knew how much more it would hurt if we allowed ourselves to fall in love.

But now he was here. For ever.

And he was here because of me.

He kissed me, his lips brushing mine softly, as though we had all the time in the world. This was for ever. Limitless. A slow, lazy kiss, our lips and tongues slow-dancing. He rolled on top of me and I slipped my hands under the hem of his T-shirt on to the smooth, warm skin of his back, feeling my way up to the wings of his shoulder blades. He lifted his lips from mine and kissed my chin and my jaw and then my neck. I shivered although my body was filled with warmth.

This was what it felt like to be alive.

By the time we stopped kissing, my lips felt bruised, my face rough from the faint stubble along his jaw.

Something occurred to me. 'You turned eighteen while you were gone.'

'Am I too old for you now?'

I pushed myself up. 'Did you have a party?'

He sat up beside me and laced his fingers with mine. 'I wasn't much in the mood for celebrating. But my friends insisted. They rented a party boat and dragged me out for a night on the lake.'

'That sounds fun.'

'I spent the whole time wishing that you were there with me.' He glanced at me. 'I think you'd have liked it. I think you'd like Lakeborough.'

'What's it like?'

He described it in detail, from the shape of the landscape to the best place to eat. The last time he had described his home, it had been a small town bordered by miles of waste-land. Now it was a vibrant city surrounded by miles of forest-covered mountains.

'It sounds beautiful,' I said. 'I wish I could see it.'

'One day we'll go and see what it's like now. In my time it's one of the wealthiest cities in the country. It's where the Guardians of Time are based. My favourite part, though, is the waterfront. There's a boardwalk by the lake with a statue of my great-grandfather, Nathaniel Westland, smashing a huge clock. And my favourite bar – the Watering Hole – is there. It's too bad I can't take you there. I think you'd like it.'

'It sounds like you miss it a lot.'

He shrugged. 'I miss my family and friends more.'

'What were they like?' I realised I was using the past tense, as though they were dead. In a way they were – even though they hadn't been born yet.

'I'm not supposed to talk about the future. I've already said too much.'

I nudged his shoulder with mine. 'It can't be dangerous to talk about the people you know. We'll both be dead long before 2123, so it's not as though . . .'

His face stopped my words in their tracks. I wished I could take them back. 'I'm sorry, I didn't mean . . .'

'It's OK. I know I'll never see them again.'

'That must be so hard.'

Pain flashed across his face, but he forced a smile. 'I have some photos. You want to see?'

I squeezed his hand.

He pulled out his wallet. Inside were several photos, slotted into clear plastic sleeves. The first photo was of a man and a woman, sitting in a restaurant, smiling at the camera.

'My parents,' said Ryan. 'This was taken on their twenty-fifth wedding anniversary. Just a couple of weeks ago.'

I stared hard at them, trying to find some resemblance to Ryan, but he didn't really look much like either of them. His dad had the same colour hair and his mum had the same smile. He was a mishmash of the two of them.

Ryan flipped the wallet to another photo; this one was a group of friends sitting laughing on a dock on a lake, their feet dangling in the water. Behind them was a sign that said *The Watering Hole*.

'My friends,' said Ryan. He pointed to a tall, dark-haired boy with a manic smile. 'That's Pegasus, my best friend. Best pilot I know. Far more courage than common sense. If you want someone to do something crazy and stupid – like help you steal a time-ship – he's your man.' He pointed to the other people in turn. 'That's Antoine and his sister, Belle. And that's Lyra. We all grew up together.'

'They look like fun.'

He nodded and turned to the final photo, one of three boys. 'Me and my brothers.'

I took a closer look. 'You're the youngest?'

He nodded. 'Jove is twenty and Jem is twenty-two.'

'They must miss you so much. Where do they think you are?'

'I don't know. I couldn't tell them I was moving time.'

He snapped his wallet shut and pulled me close to him.

'You've given up so much to save me,' I said.

He drew back far enough to look into my eyes. 'I'd do it ten times over. And I think you'd do the same for me.'

CHAPTER 2

'Where have you been?'

I was about to defend myself – it was only three in the afternoon after all – but the worry was all over Miranda's face.

'I went for a walk with Ryan. I left a note.'

'We have a visitor.'

She stepped aside to let me into the hall and I braced myself. We'd had lots of visitors in the days since my near drowning and Travis's death. Neighbours we'd been on little more than nodding terms with had shown up with shepherd's pies and lasagnes, and there had been a steady stream of Miranda's friends and colleagues come to pay their condolences.

'She's in the sitting room,' said Miranda.

A tall woman dressed in a smart black suit stood in front of the unlit fireplace. Her shiny brown hair was wound into a slick bun and her hands clutched a briefcase.

'This is my niece, Eden,' Miranda told the woman. 'Eden, this is Lauren.' She paused and then added, 'Travis's sister.'

For a moment, I was confused. Travis, obviously, didn't have a sister in 2012, because he was from the future. He was a cleaner sent back to 'clean up' anything the time agents left behind. Which meant that anyone who knew

17

anything about Travis was either an imposter or from the future too.

The tall woman, Lauren, smiled at me and held out her hand.

'Eden,' she said, her cold hand shaking mine stiffly. 'How lovely to meet you. I'm just sorry that it's under such unfortunate circumstances.'

Adrenalin raced through me. I took my hand back. 'Travis never mentioned a sister.'

'My brother was estranged from most of the family. However, he and I had always been close. It saddens me that he never mentioned me to you.' She unsnapped the catches of her briefcase and removed some papers. 'I have identification with me. And rest assured, I have no interest in any of Travis's material possessions. I would, however, like to claim his body.'

Dread gripped me. I took a step backwards. This wasn't some con woman come to steal Travis's possessions. This was someone from the future who knew about Travis's mission. Did cleaners have cleaners?

'But the funeral is tomorrow,' Miranda was saying. 'Everything's arranged. The body is with the undertaker in Perran and I have a plot in the churchyard.'

'I'm sorry,' said Lauren. She smoothed back her hair. 'This must be very hard for you. But Travis always made it clear to me that he would want his body to go home in the event of his death overseas.'

Miranda looked stunned. 'Can I see your identification?' she asked.

'Yes of course,' said Lauren. She handed her paperwork to Miranda. 'Here.'

Miranda flicked through each document in turn and then passed them to me. The passport was blue. I flicked it open to the photo page. Lauren Deckard, the name said. Date of birth: 8th August 1982. I picked up the birth certificates. One read Lauren Deckard, born Oakland, California, 8th August 1982. The second read Travis Deckard, born 3rd March 1980, Oakland, California. The parents of both children were Scott and Heather Deckard. They looked real enough. I handed the documents back to Lauren.

'This is just such a shock,' said Miranda. She sat on the edge of the sofa, shaking her head.

Lauren smoothed her hair back again. 'This must be dreadful for you. I don't want to upset you. But you should take a look at his will. It spells out clearly his wishes for his body to be repatriated.' She passed the other document to Miranda.

Miranda glanced over the document and looked at me. 'We'll need to cancel the funeral arrangements.'

'I'll take care of it.'

'I'm going to need to take a look around his flat to see what personal effects he left there,' said Lauren.

'Of course,' said Miranda. 'Eden and I will drive you there.'

'I have my own car. I'll follow you.'

'I'm just going to nip to the bathroom,' I said, backing out of the sitting room.

I ran up the stairs and into my room, almost tripping

19

over Katkin, the neighbour's tomcat who seemed to think my bedroom was his second home. I dug my mobile phone out of my bag and speed-dialled Ryan. He answered on the first ring.

'Missing me already?' he said.

'Ryan, listen. There's a woman here claiming to be Travis's sister. She wants his body.'

Ryan swore. 'Are you at home?'

'Yes. She showed up about five minutes ago. She wants to go to his flat. Miranda and I are going to take her there in a few minutes.'

'I wasn't expecting this yet. Has she asked about me?'

'No. Just Travis. What's going on, Ryan?'

He hesitated. 'This woman will be Travis's cleaner. There's nothing for you to worry about . . .'

'The last time a cleaner showed up, I ended up dead,' I whispered angrily. 'I'm worried, OK? Really worried. You need to tell me what's going on.'

'Travis died on the job, so the Guardians have sent another cleaner to clean things up. She'll want to erase any trace of him. That's it. When she's done that, she'll leave.'

'Did you know this would happen?'

'Yes, but I didn't expect anyone to show up yet.'

'Why didn't you tell me?'

'I didn't want to worry you.'

'Well, I'm pretty worried now, Ryan. If you'd told me, at least I would have been expecting her.'

'I'm sorry. I didn't want you to worry needlessly. I thought we had time. It's only four days since we portalled out. She took a real risk travelling back so close to when we left. I thought we'd have a few weeks at least.'

'Eden!' Miranda shouted up the stairs.

'Miranda's calling me,' I said to Ryan. 'I have to go.'

'OK. She's not here for you or me, just Travis's body and anything personal to him.' His tone was soothing and reassuring. 'There's no need for you to be anxious. Call me when she's gone.'

I hung up, pushed my mobile in my jeans pocket and ran back downstairs.

Travis's flat was above his seafood restaurant in the middle of Perran. The restaurant had been closed since he drowned the previous Sunday. The white blinds were down on both the windows, resting against the black slate windowsills like two shut eyes. Miranda pulled into the small parking space in front of the restaurant. Lauren parked behind us.

'Are you OK?' I asked.

Miranda's face crumpled. 'No, I'm not. I'm about as far from OK as I've ever been in my life. And you know what makes me feel even worse? People asking me if I'm OK. I'm not OK and I'm not going to be OK for a while because that's the way it is when someone you love dies.'

She wiped her hand across her eyes, smudging black mascara across her cheekbones.

I grabbed a tissue from the box in the glove compartment and passed it to her. 'I'm sorry. I just don't know what to say.'

'So don't say anything. Accept that this is horrible, but we'll live through it because people do.'

Lauren was standing outside the restaurant, peering at the menu posted in the window.

'Miranda,' I said. I paused, choosing what I said next carefully. 'I don't trust this woman.'

'We don't have a choice, Eden. From the look of her documents she is who she says she is. We could refuse to let her in and make her go to a lawyer and all that, but then Travis wouldn't be laid to rest for weeks. Nothing is going to bring him back.'

'Let's just not tell her any more than we have to. Let's get rid of her as fast as we can.'

Miranda nodded silently and reached for her door handle.

'Is this his restaurant?' asked Lauren.

'Yes. It's very popular,' said Miranda. 'Travis was an amazing chef. But I'm sure you don't need me to tell you that.'

'My brother was a man of many talents.'

Miranda unlocked the black door next to the restaurant and we climbed the stairs to his first floor flat in single file. Halfway up the stairs I realised that Lauren was behind us and my heart began juddering in my chest. Was she corralling us into Travis's flat so she could finish us off? I stepped aside at the top of the stairs to let her in first.

'After you,' I said.

I had never been to Travis's flat before. The door opened on to a large living room with views over the harbour. It was sparsely furnished, with just a single couch, a coffee

22

table and a lamp. It reminded me of Ryan's farmhouse – furnished just enough to be comfortable for a short stay.

'We'll go home and give you some privacy,' said Miranda. 'You can just drop the key at the solicitors' office when you're done.'

'I won't be long,' said Lauren. 'And I might have a few questions. Would you mind waiting outside?'

Miranda and I walked back down the stairs and into the hazy sunshine. We crossed the road and sat on a bench with a view over the harbour.

She dabbed at the corner of her eyes with a tissue. Neither of us said anything for a moment. I watched a seagull swoop down and snatch an ice-cream cone from a child's hand.

'I can't stay around here,' she said suddenly.

'What do you mean?'

'You heard what the woman said. She's taking Travis's body back to America with her. There won't be a funeral or anything.'

I wished I knew what to say.

Miranda dabbed her eyes again. 'I don't want to sit around the house thinking about him. I have to get away.'

'OK. Where do you want to go?'

'I think I'll drive up to Bath and stay with Tanya for a few days.'

I felt a weight lift from my shoulders. I loved Miranda to bits. She'd raised me ever since my parents died in a car crash ten years ago. But Tanya was Miranda's best friend. She'd know the right things to say. She'd be much better at helping Miranda through this than I was.

'When do we leave?'

Miranda put a hand on my arm. 'Do you think you could manage a few days here alone? I need to get away from . . . everything.'

My heart constricted. Did she blame me for Travis's death? He'd been trying to kill me, but Miranda believed he'd been trying to save me.

'I'll be fine,' I said. My voice croaked.

'You've never been on your own before.'

'I'm nearly seventeen.'

'I'll ask Mrs Grady to look in on you.'

'You don't need to do that.'

Miranda managed a small smile. 'It's OK for Ryan to come over, but promise me that you'll be careful.'

I felt my face heat up. 'OK,' I said, turning my head in the opposite direction, just as Lauren began marching across the road towards us.

'My brother didn't collect many possessions, did he?' said Lauren. 'I take it the flat and the restaurant are rentals?'

'Yes,' said Miranda. 'The only item of value he owned was his car.'

'I will arrange for the car to be sold and any furniture to be given to charity. Unless you want any of it.'

Miranda rubbed her eyes. 'No.'

Lauren held out a photo of Ben – the leader from Ryan's original mission. 'Do either of you know who this is?'

'Let me have a look,' said Miranda, reaching for the photo. She shook her head slowly. 'Never seen him before. Perhaps he's one of Travis's employees?'

'What about you?' Lauren asked, holding the photo to me.

I tried to think quickly. Ben's cover story had been that he was Ryan's father, an American scientist who had relocated to Penpol Cove to write a book. In reality he had been the mission leader on an assignment to 2012 to prevent my friend, Connor, from discovering a planet.

'I don't recognise him,' I said, handing the photo back.

Lauren passed a small card to Miranda. 'Do you know what this is?'

'It's a passenger ticket to the Isles of Scilly,' she replied.

'Where is that?'

'Just off the coast of Cornwall,' said Miranda. 'This is a return ticket to the islands on the *Scillonian*, the ferry that sails between Penzance and the islands. Funny, I never knew Travis had been there.'

'Did my brother leave anything at your house?'

'He spent most of his time at my place during the last few months,' said Miranda. 'But it's strange. There's almost nothing of his in the house. I have his pyjamas and a tooth-brush, half a pack of the cigarettes he smoked and some spare socks. But no photos or anything that really reminds me of him. It's as though he never existed.'

Lauren nodded. 'That sounds like Travis.' She pursed her lips. 'What is the name and address of the undertaker who has my brother's body?'

'Wakfer and Williams. They're the only undertaker in Perran. Located on Bread Street.'

Lauren nodded and began to walk away. She stopped

halfway across the road and turned back to us, smoothing her hair with one hand. 'I'm sorry for your loss.'

Ryan opened the farmhouse door before I knocked and closed it quickly behind me.

'Were you followed?' he asked.

'Nice to see you too,' I said. 'I don't think so.'

'Stay against the wall.'

Warily, he peered through the glass of the front. It hadn't even occurred to me that Lauren might follow me. A frown creased his forehead and I realised his calmness on the phone earlier had been an act. He was dressed in his boots and jacket and a backpack leant against the wall. He was ready to leave.

'She never asked about you,' I said. 'Didn't even mention your name.'

'Good. Come in, I think we're OK.' He put his arm around my waist and led me into the kitchen.

And then I remembered the photograph.

'There was a photo of Ben at Travis's place,' I said. 'She asked if we knew who it was. We both said no. Do you think that means anything?'

'I don't think so. But I can't take any risks. If she's here for me, this is one of the first places she'll look. I'm going to need to disappear for a few days. Until I'm sure she's gone.'

'Where will you go?'

He shrugged. 'Away from here. Just until the week-end. If she's here to clean up Travis, she'll only need a

26

couple of days. If she's still here next week, then I'll know I'm in trouble.'

I walked to the sink and poured myself a glass of water. It wasn't fair. I'd only just got him back and now he was going to leave again.

'I'll be all alone,' I said. 'Miranda is going to Bath to stay with a friend.'

I didn't tell him that the thought of being the only one around with Lauren in the area terrified me. There had been something detached and robotic about her. Travis, although he was a psychopathic killer, had at least shown signs of humanity from time to time. But Lauren had no warmth. I smiled to myself.

'What's funny?' asked Ryan.

'I was just thinking that at least the man who tried to kill me could make me laugh occasionally. Whereas this Lauren woman just creeps me out,' I said. 'There must be something seriously wrong with me – clocking up Travis's good points.'

Ryan came up behind me and slipped his arms around my waist. He nuzzled my neck; my skin prickled and my pulse accelerated. I still wasn't used to this.

'She's a cleaner,' he said. 'She's not here to make friends.'

I turned around in his arms. 'Now it sounds like you're defending her.'

He shook his head. 'When is Miranda going away?'

'Tomorrow morning.'

A smile appeared in the corner of his mouth. 'So she won't miss you if you come away with me?'

'I like what you're suggesting,' I said. 'Have you any-where in mind?'

He ran a hand through his hair. 'What I'd really like to do is whisk you away to a deserted island. But right now I don't have a passport. Or a whole lot of money.'

'What about all those credit cards?'

'I was on an official time mission back then. The credit cards were supplied to me. And of course they're totally traceable. If I used a credit card now, they'd be on to me in no time.'

'You spent all that time in the future and you didn't memorise winning lottery numbers?'

'Lottery winners attract publicity. I need to keep a low profile.'

'I have some savings,' I said.

'I have enough to cover a few days away.' He slipped his hand back around my waist. 'We just need to decide on a place to go.'

I had a sudden flash of inspiration. 'Hang on a second. I know just the place. It won't be tropical temperatures, but it has deserted islands, beautiful beaches and doesn't require a passport.'

CHAPTER 3

The woman at the reception desk smiled apologetically. 'It's almost impossible to get a room here in the summer without a reservation.'

'Oh,' I said, feeling foolish. Had I really dragged Ryan across twenty-five miles of stomach-churning sea to the Isles of Scilly just so we could turn around and make the same journey back home that afternoon?

'Do you know of anywhere else on the island that might have a space?' asked Ryan.

The woman pressed her lips together tightly and looked at us in turn. 'I might be able to sort you out a room. But I warn you, it's not really ready for letting. We only finished painting it yesterday. You'll need to keep the windows open until dark or you'll suffocate on the fumes.'

'I'm sure it'll be fine,' said Ryan. 'We just need a room for a couple of nights.'

The woman gave us a look. 'It is a double room.'

I looked at the floor.

'Double is fine,' said Ryan.

'And the name is?'

Ryan and I looked at each other. He couldn't risk using the name Westland.

'Shall we book it under my name?' I asked.

'I'll need both names.'

'Right,' said Ryan. He hesitated.

The woman cocked her eyebrows. 'Will it be Mr and Mrs Smith?'

'Yes,' said Ryan. 'Mr and Mrs Smith.'

We followed the woman as she led us to a room at the back of the guest house.

'The air should be clearer by this evening,' she said, as she unlocked the door and stood aside to let us enter.

The room was simply furnished with two wooden bedside tables, an armchair, and a large double bed made up with crisp, white bedding. I looked quickly away from the bed and focused instead on the doors that looked out on to a small enclosed patio with views of the sea beyond.

'This is perfect,' said Ryan.

'The bed is made up, but I'll need to go and get you some towels,' the woman told us. She strode across the room and opened the patio doors. 'I'll leave the doors open to clear the air. The room is perfectly secure. I'll be back in a couple of minutes.'

We stood awkwardly in the centre of the room until she'd left.

'So, what do you think?' asked Ryan.

'It's great,' I said, trying to ignore the big double bed that took up most of the room. My voice trembled. 'Perfect.'

'Hey,' he said, closing the space between us. 'What's the matter?'

I shook my head. 'Nothing.'

'We're safe here,' he said, running his fingers through my hair. 'The cleaner is back on the mainland dealing with Travis. She'll be gone soon. There's no need to be afraid.'

But it wasn't the cleaner that I was scared of. It was everything else. Here we were. After months of wanting this, we were together. A room of our own. No adults conspiring to keep us apart. No friends to gossip and stare. No Fate to get in our way. Just Ryan and me.

And then we were kissing and all my fear floated away. I fell softly backwards on to the bed, Ryan beside me. My heart drummed against my ribs so hard that the bones ached. My limbs were tangled with his, my fingers in his hair. We were going to spend the whole night together. And then the whole of the next day. And then after that . . . for ever.

There was a knock at the door.

Ryan sighed. While he collected the towels, I jumped off the bed and walked through the doors on to the small patio, letting sunlight and warmth flood over me. The water was choppy; white foam sprayed and danced playfully above the waves. I breathed in deeply. The briny smell of the beach lingered in the air.

'Where were we?' he asked, as he pushed open the bathroom door and chucked the towels inside.

'Let's go and explore the island,' I said. 'Those paint fumes are still strong. I think we need to let the air clear.'

We hired bicycles from a shop overlooking the harbour beach. Dozens of boats were moored in the harbour, their masts clanging musically in the light breeze.

'How come you never told me there were a bunch of subtropical islands a couple of hours away?' Ryan said, as we set off along the seafront road.

'It never came up,' I said, wobbling as I tried to get the bike moving.

'Eden, have you ever ridden a bicycle before?'

'No.'

'How can you get to sixteen without ever riding a bike?'

'I don't know. I just haven't.'

'The first few seconds are the hardest,' he said, pulling alongside me. 'Once you get going, it's easy. Push down and start pedalling hard.'

I grimaced. 'One day I'm going to discover something that I can do better than you.'

The bicycle gained momentum and I was off. The warm air blew my hair back from my face and I breathed in the scent of flowers and seaweed. We left the harbour behind and began climbing a steep hill, past a blur of tall, green hedgerows and fields of cows. My thighs burned with the effort.

'You're doing great,' Ryan said, looking back over his shoulder at me.

'Don't patronise me,' I yelled back at him.

It bothered me that I had no real skills. I wanted to be prepared for everything and anything. Ryan might be convinced that now that Travis was dead we were safe, but I wasn't so sure. And if Lauren posed no danger to us, why had Ryan decided to run and hide until she'd left?

The narrow road that encircled the small island took us

past farms and fields, a couple of duckponds and craggy beaches framed with brown granite. We were never very far from the sea and the gritty combination of salt and sand hung in the air, a constant reminder.

After a while we came across a sandy cove with a small slipway and a couple of sailing boats tied up above the high water line. Ryan pulled off to the side of the road. 'Do you mind if we lie down and rest for a while?' he asked, yawning. 'I'm still suffering from time lag.'

I hopped off my bike and laid it carefully on the ground. 'What's time lag?'

Ryan rested his bike next to mine. 'You know what jet lag feels like, right?'

I shook my head. 'Sorry. I've never been further than Paris.'

'You're even more sheltered than I thought.'

'It's not like I don't want to travel,' I said.

Ryan held my hand in his and we walked down the slipway to the beach. It was a rare sunny day, the air hot.

'I wasn't judging you,' he said. 'I'm glad you haven't done much travelling. We'll get to see the world for the first time together.'

'Anyway, I know what jet lag is. So tell me about time lag?'

'The human body isn't designed for time travel. It throws your body clock completely out of whack. For the first few days, you get these sudden bouts of sleepiness. It's a bit like narcolepsy. The best cure is to have a short nap.' He yawned again as if to prove his point. 'I'll probably only need twenty minutes.'

We strolled along the shoreline, shoes in our hands, feet just in the water. The helicopter from the mainland buzzed across the sky. A mother and her two young children were walking across the wet sand, collecting shells in a bucket. We waited till we'd passed them before looking for a patch of dry sand to sit on.

I laid out my hoodie and sat down. Offshore lay two other islands, rising from the ocean like turtles just breaking the surface.

Ryan squinted out to sea. 'These islands don't look that far apart. I wonder if it's possible to rent a sailboat for the day. We could go and explore the other islands. Maybe dive on some shipwrecks; I bet there're loads of wrecks around here.'

'So you can sail and scuba-dive?' I said with a dramatic sigh.

'I grew up by a lake,' said Ryan as though that explained everything.

I didn't remind him that I'd grown up by the sea, but still didn't know how to dive or sail a boat.

'And when I come from, the sea levels have risen,' said Ryan. 'Lots of towns are underwater. My friends and I liked to scuba-dive in the drowned cities. It's eerie, swimming along what were once roads, seeing fish swim in and out of the windows of buildings that were once apartment blocks and offices.'

He scrunched up his hoodie to make a pillow and lay back, an arm over his eyes to block out the sun, his muscles bunching and lengthening beneath his skin. I wondered what it must be like to be able to do so many things, to feel strong and capable.

'I want to learn something new,' I said. 'I feel like I'm not good at anything.'

'You're good at Scrabble,' he said sleepily. 'And chess.'

'Great. Next time I come up against one of your cleaners I'll challenge them to a game of chess.'

He rolled on his side and opened his eyes again, narrowing them slightly against the bright light. 'You're good at running.'

'That's just the problem. I don't want to run away from things. I want to be able to fight back.'

Ryan raised an eyebrow. 'Like a ninja?'

'Don't make fun of me. It bothers me that if you hadn't risked everything to travel back through time and rescue me I'd be dead. I should have been able to defend myself better. And now Lauren is here and once again I'm relying on you to protect me. I want to learn new things so I can take care of myself.'

Ryan smiled to himself. 'You're what – about a hundred and twenty pounds? Travis was about two hundred pounds of pure muscle. You could be a black belt in every martial art going and you still wouldn't have had a chance against that sort of bulk. Running was the right thing to do. It's what I would have done too.'

'Really?'

'Yes. And you managed your encounter with Travis brilliantly. You outsmarted him. You understood when to play along with him and when to run. And you outran him! He

35

was a trained killer, but you managed to drive away from him, outrun him and then you had the smarts to lead him to his death. You did ninety-nine per cent of the job – I just came in at the end to take the credit.'

'Don't patronise me, Ryan.'

He sighed. 'I'm not patronising you. Having your wits about you and the intelligence to think on your feet is worth a hundred black belts.'

He rolled on to his back again. I watched his breaths grow slower and deeper, the small shadow his long lashes cast beneath his eyes, the faintest hint of stubble under his skin.

He opened one eye. 'I can't sleep if you keep staring at me.'

'I wasn't staring at you,' I said. I bit my lip. 'I was just thinking.'

'Thinking what?' He yawned loudly.

'What are you going to tell everyone else about coming back to Cornwall? What will your cover story be?'

He closed his eye again. 'I'm not going to tell them anything.'

'But they'll think it's odd. A few days ago you told them you were moving back to New Hampshire with your family and now you're back again.'

'They can't know I'm here. You'll need to tell Miranda that I've left again. Tell her that our departure was postponed by a couple of days if you need to. And don't tell Connor or anyone else that I'm back.'

'They'll find out in September when you enroll at college,' I said, confused.

'I'm not going to college, Eden. I can't. I can't appear as myself anywhere. I mustn't leave a trail to the future.'

'So what will you do?'

'I'll find a job. Something casual like flower-picking where they won't ask to see identification to start with. I'll get some fake ID, but I will still have to keep away from anyone who knew me as Ryan Westland. Once you're at university in a town where no one has ever seen me before, I'll be able to come out of hiding.'

'You can't hide away for two years!'

'I can and I will. If I start appearing as myself, the Guardians will pick it up and send a cleaner straight back to get me. I have to become someone else, and I can't do that until we move to a place where no one has seen me before.'

It had never occurred to me that Ryan wouldn't just slot back into his old life. I'd pictured him hanging out with the old crowd from school, studying for his A Levels alongside me, going off to parties together. Not hiding away at the farmhouse and working on the land.

'But you're missing out on your education.'

'I can read books,' he said through a yawn. 'In any case, I'm already eighteen. I've had a pretty good education.'

'You'll be living like an outlaw.'

He smiled sleepily. 'I'd sooner spend a lifetime living as an outlaw with you, than a single day of freedom without you.'

We had a table for two by the window, with a clear view over the harbour. We'd finished eating and Ryan had gone to pay the bill. Through the window, the moon hung like an oversized pearl, white and luminous, in a pink and turquoise sky. The perfect backdrop to a romantic evening.

That was what scared me. How exactly did Ryan expect the perfect romantic evening to end? For that matter, how did I want it to end?

'Ready?' he asked.

'I think I might need to walk off dinner before we go back to our room,' I said.

'OK.' He held my hand and we strolled down towards the pier.

Despite the late hour, there were still boats returning from daytrips. A line of chalkboards tied to a railing advertised sightseeing trips to the other islands. One of the signs caught my eye.

> *Available for private hire.*
> *Visit the uninhabited isles.*
> *See seals, basking sharks and hundreds of birds.*
> *Ask for a quote.*

'Shall we?' I said, pointing to the sign.

And that was when I saw her. At first I thought I was seeing things, because she was dressed very differently. The suit was gone, replaced by a pair of shorts and a body-hugging T-shirt. She looked like a tourist. Her hair, which had been slicked back into a bun when I saw her last, now hung loosely down her back. But the way she walked, head straight, face unsmiling, limbs quick and efficient, gave her away. She wasn't looking for a pleasure cruise; she was on a mission.

'Ryan,' I whispered, steering him away from the harbour. 'Back up.'

His hand tensed in mine, but he said nothing. Once we turned the corner, he stopped.

'What is it?'

'Lauren.'

Ryan swore.

'How did she track us here?' I said. 'We used cash to pay for everything and we haven't used our real names.'

Ryan peered around the corner. 'What does she look like?'

'Tall, long brown hair.'

'I see her.'

'How did she find us?'

Ryan turned back to me. 'We don't know that she has found us.' He leant around the corner again. 'What's she up to? Why is she talking to the skipper of a boat?'

'Maybe she wants to take us to one of the uninhabited islands and kill us there. Maybe she already knows where we're staying and she's just sorting out where to finish us off.' I struggled to keep the panic out of my voice.

'There has to be another reason,' said Ryan. 'We've been careful.'

Suddenly my mind flashed back to Travis's flat. 'It's something to do with that ticket,' I said. 'It's what made me think of coming here.'

'Slow down,' said Ryan. 'What are you talking about?'

'When we went to Travis's flat, she found a return ticket to the Isles of Scilly on the *Scillonion*. She asked Miranda about it.'

'Travis had a ticket to the Isles of Scilly? Why would he have that?'

I shrugged. 'I don't know. He hadn't used the return portion. I guess he saved it in case he wanted to go back.'

'Maybe that's it,' said Ryan. 'She's following one of Travis's trails. Cleaning up any trace of him. This has nothing to do with us. It's just a coincidence because you thought of coming here from seeing the ticket, right?'

I thought about it. What an idiot. I'd led us into danger again. 'I guess I did.'

'Perhaps his time-ship is here somewhere. He could have ended his journey from the future on one of the uninhabited islands and hidden his ship there. He isn't able to come back and retrieve it, so his cleaner has.'

That made sense. My heartbeat began the journey back to normal.

Ryan looked around the corner again. 'She must be hiring a boat to take her to the islands tomorrow. She'll destroy the ship and then go back.'

'So we're safe.'

'We're safe. But I think we should follow her. See where she's staying.'

My stomach rolled over. 'Do we have to?'

'I'd sooner know where she is.'

'What if she sees us following her?'

'She won't.'

'Ryan –'

'Look, you head back to the guest house. I'll follow the cleaner. As soon as I know where she's staying, I'll come back. I won't sleep if I don't know where she is.'

The only thing worse than following Lauren was the thought of sitting alone in my room, worrying whether Ryan was OK.

'I don't want to be apart from you.'

'It will be easier to follow her if I'm alone. She knows you, but she doesn't know me from Adam.' He pushed the room key into my hand. 'I promise I'll come straight to the room as soon as I know where she is.' He took another look. 'She's coming this way. Go.'

I slipped the room key into my pocket and walked briskly up the road towards the guest house without looking back. This was not how I'd imagined our evening ending.

Back in our room, the smell of paint had faded and been replaced by the fresh laundry scent of the bedsheets. I closed the windows and the curtains and sat on the edge of the bed. Ryan seemed confident that Lauren being here was just a horrible coincidence. I needed to put her out of my mind.

I brushed my teeth and checked my breath and then dug through my overnight case for my pyjamas. They were a vest top and cropped bottoms with pink and white love hearts all over them. They were cute, girly, the opposite of sexy. If I'd had more notice about our little trip away, I would have bought myself something more sophisticated. Did Ryan expect to find me draped across the bed in a silk negligee? Or did he expect me to be tucked under the duvet in my girly pyjamas? And what if I undressed and went to bed and then Ryan came running to tell me that Lauren was after us and we needed to leave right now? I sighed. There was no way I was getting into bed until Ryan was back and I knew what was going on.

Silence. There was no television in the room to distract me. Not even a coffee-maker to hiss and bubble and make friendly noises. The double glazing kept out the sound of the sea, although it was just metres away. No one was walking along the thickly carpeted hallway outside my door. There was nothing but the rush of blood through my ears and the unnerving quiet.

I kept reminding myself this woman was a cleaner, and cleaners clean. And kill. Methodically. Efficiently. Probably quietly too. I swung around and looked at the door. Nothing. Just the sound of silence freaking me out.

I searched for something I could use as a weapon. Just in case. There were few furnishings in the room. I considered the wastepaper bin by the dresser, but when I picked it up it turned out to be made of thin metal. If I bashed someone over the head with it, all it would do was leave a dent in the bin. There was a New Testament in the bedside table, but it was a flimsy paperback.

I was about to give up when I noticed a set of fire irons in an alcove next to the boxed-in fireplace. It had a brush, shovel and poker. I lifted each one in turn. The poker was easily the heaviest of the three tools. Long and made from a heavy, black metal, it could probably do some serious damage if I hit someone on the head. I clutched it in my hands and stood by the door.

Right on cue there was a friendly *rap-tap-a-tap-tap*.

'Who is it?' I called.

'It's me,' said Ryan.

Feeling slightly stupid, I unlocked the door.

'Good thinking,' he said, eyeing the poker as he slipped inside. He locked the door behind him.

'So?'

He strode across the room and pulled the curtains open. Through the window, the daylight on the patio was nearly gone; the picnic table, the wall and the palm tree were blending into the shadows. He pulled the curtains shut again.

'You want the good news or the bad news?'

I felt a shiver scuttle up my back, like a spider. 'The bad news.'

'She's staying in this guest house.'

'You have got to be kidding me!'

Ryan sat on the edge of the bed. I stayed standing.

'The good news is that I'm certain the time-ship theory is correct.'

'Why do you think that? Did something happen?'

He ran his hands through his hair. 'After she left the harbour she walked up the street and went into the Co-op. I followed her in and bought a newspaper. She bought a lighter and some liquid paraffin. She'll use the paraffin to try and make it look like some kids set fire to something. It's a cover. She'll use the leftover gas in the fuel tank to destroy the ship. From there she came directly back to the guest house. I stayed several metres behind her, but when I walked in the front door she was deep in conversation with the receptionist. She was asking for a map of the most isolated islands. It all adds up.'

'Did she see you?'

'No.'

I hadn't realised I'd been holding my breath until I slowly released the air that had been trapped in my lungs. I sat beside him on the bed.

'I don't think we have anything to worry about,' he said.

'So, it's a coincidence.'

He put a hand on my leg. 'Yeah. But I don't like coincidences. I think we should leave the islands tomorrow.'

'The boat sails at four.'

'We'll keep a low profile until then.'

We stayed where we were for a minute or two, listening to the absolute quiet. It felt as though the room itself were trembling. My heartbeat. The booming silence. Knowing that an assassin shared our home for the night.

I turned and placed one palm over Ryan's heart. It beat a frantic rhythm against my skin.

'You're scared,' I said.

He placed his hand on top of mine. 'This has nothing to do with Lauren.'

He stood up, opened his overnight bag and took out his toothbrush and toothpaste. He opened the door to the bathroom and leant against the door frame. 'The door is locked and I'm going to leave this poker by the bed. Are you OK?'

I nodded.

My pyjamas were still stuffed in my overnight case. While Ryan brushed his teeth, I unfolded them and then refolded them and then unfolded them again. There was no way I could strip off here in the bedroom with all the lights on and Ryan just the other side of the bathroom door, almost finished brushing his teeth.

'Hey,' I said, as he came back in.

He smiled and glanced at the pyjamas in my hand. 'You gonna put those on?'

I nodded and rubbed the frayed strip of lace at the bottom of the vest top. 'They're kind of old.'

'They're cute.'

I stepped closer to the bathroom door. 'I'm just going to go in here and get undressed.'

Ryan shrugged one shoulder. 'OK.'

I took my pyjamas into the bathroom and locked the door behind me. Hurriedly, I stripped off my clothes and pulled on my pyjamas. The sliver of light under the bathroom door dimmed. Ryan was just behind that door. Waiting for me.

I took a deep breath, unlocked the door and pushed it open. The room was shadowy, the only light coming from the soft glow of the bedside lamp on one of the night tables. My gaze rested first on the bed. It was empty. Then I saw Ryan, standing by the patio doors, watching the last flush of the sunset redden the horizon. To my relief he was still dressed.

I joined him at the window, my blood pounding through every inch of my body.

'They look even cuter on you,' said Ryan, running a finger across the strap of my vest top.

I tried to smile, but my face was too tense to do it convincingly.

'OK,' he sighed. 'I guess we need to talk about the sleeping arrangements.'

I bit my bottom lip. 'What about them?'

'Which of us gets the bed and which of us gets to sleep here?' He pointed at the armchair by the fireplace.

'It's a big bed. I'm sure we'll both fit.'

'You don't mind sharing?'

I shook my head and clambered under the covers. Ryan took off his boots and jeans, but kept the rest of his clothes on.

'Aren't you going to get undressed?'

'I don't have anything to change into. And I thought I might freak you out if I stripped naked.'

I laughed. 'You got that right.' I leant across and switched off the bedside lamp, plunging the room into darkness.

'Goodnight then,' he said.

'Don't I get a goodnight kiss?'

He closed the wide space between us and found my face with his fingertips. I felt his warm, minty breath on my face and then he kissed me. My body was flooded with warmth and I kissed him back, all my inhibitions forgotten. For a few seconds, I was lost in the pleasure of the moment. And then, unwelcome and unbidden, an image of Lauren smoothing back her bun in Miranda's sitting room floated into my mind. I forced it out and tried to focus on the feel

46

of Ryan's skin, but my mind was bombarded with images and sensations. Lauren standing at the docks, her shiny brown hair swinging down her back. The dip and roll of the boat that had brought us to the islands. The moon glowing in the twilight. My once final resting place in the woodland.

Ryan stopped kissing me. 'What's wrong?'

'I'm sorry,' I said. 'I'm just a little tense. It's really hard for me to relax knowing that she's so close.'

'There's nothing to worry about,' he said. 'She's probably tucked up fast asleep in her bed. You want a back rub?'

I rolled away from him and he ran his fingers down the length of my back, making all the nerve endings tingle. He began kneading the muscles either side of my spine, starting in the small of my back and slowly working up towards my shoulders. My eyelids fluttered closed. Within minutes, I was lulled into sleepy forgetfulness. Just as I was tumbling over the dark abyss, about to leave the world behind, I felt Ryan roll away from me. The covers slipped over my body as he reached towards the door. I rolled over to face him just as he lay back down again.

In his right hand, he was gripping the poker.

CHAPTER 4

As soon as I set foot back on the mainland, I began to breathe more easily. Lauren's presence – however random – had transformed the islands from a subtropical paradise into a trap. The feeling of relief was short-lived.

'She knows where I live,' I said, as Ryan unlocked the car.

'You're not going home.'

The *Scillonion* hadn't sailed until late in the afternoon; it was now early evening. We would need to eat soon and find somewhere to sleep.

'So . . . are we going to the farmhouse?' I asked.

'Just to pick up some cash. We have to stay away from anywhere she could trace us to. We're not taking any chances.' He reversed out of the parking space and pulled on to the main road.

'Where will we stay?'

'Another B&B. Just till we're sure she's gone.'

The further we were from the dock, the better I felt. I leant back against the headrest and shut my eyes. I was tired. Maybe tonight I would sleep better.

'You OK?' Ryan asked.

I looked at him. His T-shirt stretched across his broad shoulders, the sun lighting the top of his head with golden streaks, the corner of his mouth twitching upwards in the beginning of a smile. How had I got so lucky?

'You know, when you were back in the future,' I began, not sure how to phrase this question without sounding insecure or jealous, 'I mean, you were there a long time.'

'Nine months.'

'Did you ever feel like giving up on coming back to 2012?'

'Never.'

'Did you ever wonder, though, if it might not be possible? If you might just have to let it go?'

He glanced at me. 'The thought never crossed my mind. I knew I'd find a way. Nine months felt like for ever, but I'd have kept on trying if it had been nine years or fifty-nine years. I wasn't going to let you die like that.'

'But when you were there, you must have had a life as well. You must have gone to school and had a social life and things like that.'

'School wasn't so great. I got kicked out.'

'How come?'

'Long story. I was on this elite program for pilots. It was intense. I was too distracted.'

'So what did you do?'

Ryan shrugged. 'I got a job in the shipyards with my friend, Pegasus.'

'What about your spare time? You must have gone out with friends.'

'I went out to a bar sometimes, but I spent most of my spare time trying to find a way back here. To you.'

He pulled off the main road and into the supermarket car park.

'So you didn't have a girlfriend then?'

He yanked the handbrake up and looked at me as though I'd lost my mind. 'Are you serious?'

'I was just wondering,' I said, unlocking my seatbelt.

He pulled the key out of the ignition and twirled the key ring round his finger. 'There hasn't been anyone else since I met you.'

'And before you met me?'

He shrugged. 'Well, yeah. There was this one girl before I met you.'

I wanted to ask him for details. Name, age, pictures. But I couldn't bring myself to. Not here in the bright light of a supermarket car park, while shopping trolleys rattled and clanged outside the car.

'You're not jealous, are you?' The shadow of a smile flitted across his face. 'You've no reason to be. She hasn't even been born yet.'

'I'm not jealous,' I said.

He opened the driver's side door. 'Come on.'

We walked across the car park in silence for a moment.

'So, this girl. Did you . . . you know . . .' The words stuck in my throat. I coughed.

'Are you asking me if I . . . ?' He smirked, but there was a noticeable flush across his cheek.

I nodded.

He stared at the ground as we walked. 'Yeah,' he said.

'And you didn't hook up with her again when you got back to your own time?'

We were at the trolley park by now, Ryan pulling a trolley out of its stubborn embrace with the one in front of it.

'Of course not. The only person I had any interest in hooking up with had been dead for over a century.'

He blushed even more deeply when he noticed the middle-aged woman, who'd clearly heard every word, waiting patiently behind us.

'That must have sounded weird,' he whispered as we pushed the trolley towards the store.

'Not to mention creepy.'

He paused just before the entrance. 'Is there anything else you want to ask me?'

I felt hot. I could feel my face burning. 'Why are we here?'

'Is that an existential question?'

'A practical one.'

'To buy food. If we're going to lie low until Lauren leaves, we're going to need supplies.'

We took a trolley and made our way up and down the aisles, grabbing food off the shelves and dodging the slow, got-all-the-time-in-the-world tourists.

'If I was going on holiday, I would never go self-catering,' said Ryan. 'How is it a holiday if you have to go supermarket shopping and cook your own meals?'

'Not everyone has a limitless supply of money, Ryan,' I said, smacking him lightly across the head with a baguette. 'Something you'd better get used to if you're going to be living on the wages of a flower picker.'

'Don't remind me,' he said. 'That's going to be so dull.

I'm going to need to sort out some fake ID and some qualifications as soon as I can.'

'And how do you think you're going to find somewhere to buy fake documents? The internet?'

''Course not. I've already found my source. This guy near Truro. I just need to go and make the arrangements.'

'Won't that be expensive?' I said, hesitating over a packet of chocolate Hobnobs. How much money did not much money mean? Was Ryan down to his last fifty quid, or down to his last fifty thousand? 'Should we get biscuits?'

'Sure,' he said, putting them in the trolley. 'I have more money back in the farmhouse.'

We pushed the trolley to the checkout. 'When are you planning to do this?'

'Soon,' he whispered. 'I need ID that can last a lifetime so it has to be good.'

My phone rang. My friend, Amy. I hadn't spoken to her in days.

'Hi, Amy,' I said.

Ryan began stacking the groceries on the conveyor belt.

'Where have you been hiding yourself?' she asked me.

'Just hanging out at home.'

'Sounds boring. Anyway, everyone's going to the beach tomorrow. Can you come?'

Obviously I couldn't. But the thought of doing something normal like hanging out at the beach with all my friends sounded so appealing.

'Not sure. I'll let you know,' I said.

'Call me back, OK?'

I hung up and helped Ryan bag the groceries.

'Who was that?' he asked.

'Amy. Inviting me to the beach tomorrow.'

'You can't do that.'

'I know.'

He put the bags into the shopping trolley. 'We just need a couple of days. Until we're sure she's gone.'

'How will we know she's gone?'

'She's a cleaner. She'll want to finish the job and get home. If she's interested in me, I'll know about it soon. If there's no sign of her for a couple of days, we can assume she's left.'

We loaded the groceries into the boot and then Ryan suggested I practise my driving. I agreed. I needed all the skills I could get.

'And if we get pulled over?' I asked.

'Drive well and we won't get pulled over.'

By the time we reached the turn-off for Penpol Cove, I was beginning to feel confident behind the wheel, dipping and releasing the clutch smoothly, remembering mirror, signal, manoeuvre. All I had to do now was drive down the narrow lane to the farmhouse, without meeting a tractor coming in the other direction. Reversing was not my forte.

I smelt it first. A bonfire. Wood and paper and dry grass. But there was a nasty undertone to it, like the smell of burning plastic.

'The villagers won't be happy,' I said, hitting the button to close the window. 'It's an unwritten rule that you don't light bonfires during the daytime in summer. It makes the washing smell like smoke.'

53

'Village life is so exciting,' said Ryan, laughing. 'Will this be in the local paper? *Local resident offends neighbours with untimely bonfire.*'

'Probably. Although it is evening, so I guess it's OK.' I turned to him, about to make a joke about the sorts of items that made local headlines, but the smile dropped from his face.

'Stop the car,' he said.

I hit the brake. 'What's wrong?'

'I think the smoke is coming from the farmhouse.'

'Really?' I squinted into the distance, but there were too many fields between us and the column of smoke rising into the sky.

'Back the car up, Eden.'

I moved into reverse and twisted round, looking out of the rear window. Slowly we backtracked up the lane. When I reached the mini-roundabout at the top, I started driving out of the village.

'Park the car,' said Ryan.

I pulled in to the kerb. 'What are we going to do?'

'We're going to find out if it is the farmhouse. But we're not going down the lane. There's a footpath through the fields, isn't there?'

We crossed a stile into a field of potatoes and skirted round the edge, heading towards the smoke.

'Tell me what you're thinking,' I said.

'I'm thinking Lauren just set fire to my time-ship.'

'She's on the Isles of Scilly.'

'She was. Is there another way to get to and from the islands, other than the boat?'

'There's a helicopter and a plane.'

He said nothing.

'It might just be someone having a bonfire,' I said.

'Maybe.'

Over the hedge, a combine harvester made its slow way through the field, dust and straw clouding the air around it. The next field was filled with cows. They all stopped chewing the ground and turned to look at us, their sleepy brown eyes widening with curiosity.

Ryan gripped my hand tightly as we walked across the field. The cows returned to their chewing.

By the time we reached the third stile, the smoke was thicker, toxic-smelling. We were just two fields from the back of the farmhouse. From here it was easy to see that the shed where Ryan had hidden his ship was on fire. Or had been. There were no flames, just smoke spiralling up from the smouldering remains of the shed.

He swore and fell into a crouch, pulling me down with him. My knees hit the dirt with a thud. He dropped my hand.

'Ryan,' I said.

He shook his head to stop me speaking and swore again, repeatedly, under his breath.

Now we knew. She was here for Ryan.

'Ryan,' I whispered. 'We need to leave.'

He looked up at me, his eyes wild with panic. 'All my money is in the farmhouse.'

'That doesn't matter now. We have to get out of here.'

He took his wallet out of his jeans pocket and pulled the notes out. 'I only have eighty pounds. It's not enough.'

I placed a hand on his arm; I could feel his whole body trembling. 'We have to get out of here,' I said. 'We'll worry about money later.'

We stayed low to the ground, half crouching, half running back towards the main road. When we reached the last stile, we stopped to catch our breath.

'I can use my debit card. I have some savings,' I said.

Ryan looked back over his shoulder. 'No. She's here for me. She'll be watching you too. That means she'll be watching your internet usage, your bank account, your phone calls. We can't use anything traceable.'

'I have some savings in my bedroom. I have my mum's wedding ring. We could get that.'

'We need to stay away from the farmhouse and your house.'

He looked around, his eyes searching. 'Give me your mobile.'

I handed it over. He threw it into a bin, along with his own phone.

'You can locate someone using their phone,' he said. 'We need to leave here. Fast.'

We ran to the car. Ryan jumped into the driver's seat and started the engine. He took the coast road, driving too fast, straddling the central line.

'Easy,' I said. 'We drive on the left.'

He pulled erratically to the left, grazing the side of the car against the hedge.

'Where are we going?' I asked.

'I don't know.'

We drove in silence, past fields of wheat and potatoes, past the wooden holiday chalets dotted on Perran Towans, past the golf course. A mile outside of Perran, the main town in the area, Ryan pulled off the road into a parking area that overlooked the sea. Below us, I could hear the waves booming against the base of the cliff.

'We can't be seen from the road,' said Ryan. 'We should be OK here for a bit.'

'And then what?'

'I need to get that money. I need to see that guy about my ID tomorrow and then I have to disappear.'

I stopped breathing. 'And what about me?'

He dropped his head in his hands. 'I'm sorry, Eden. She'll use you to get to me. You'll have to disappear too.'

I exhaled. 'Thank God.'

He looked at me. 'What?'

'I don't want you to leave without me. I don't want you to disappear and leave me with a cleaner.'

He unclicked my seatbelt and pulled me across the handbrake and into his arms. 'I'm not leaving without you,' he said.

'Where are we going to sleep?'

'These seats recline a bit. I've got a picnic blanket in the boot. It's not perfect, but it's only for one night.'

On the horizon, a thick band of sea mist was creeping slowly inland. Sea mist could appear – and disappear – very quickly in this part of the world. Soon it would smother the sun and the air would chill. Within a few minutes our car would be covered by a thick blanket of it; we wouldn't be able to see the edge of the cliff. We wouldn't be able to see anyone until they were right outside our window.

'I have a better idea,' I said.

'You do?'

'Head back to the Towans. Let's look for a vacant chalet.'

'It's the middle of summer.'

'It's worth a look.'

He pulled on to the road and headed back the way we'd come. We parked in the public car park and started walking across the sand dunes. The chalets were spread apart, each one surrounded by its own little patch of grass and sandy parking area. Families sat out on the decking, barbecuing chicken and drinking beer. The world was going on around us, innocently, peacefully, as we searched for cover, for escape.

It was easy to tell which chalets were occupied; even those with no car in the driveway and no people around had towels drying on the line and surfboards and buckets and spades stacked outside the front door.

'We should check out the more remote chalets,' I said. 'The ones closest to the beach always fill up fast.'

We climbed the dunes and headed away from the sea. It was quieter here; rabbits were beginning to emerge from their burrows and hop around, stopping to nibble at the thin grass.

'Wait,' said Ryan, putting out an arm to stop me. He was staring at a tatty, wooden chalet near the lifeguard hut. Blue paint was peeling from the clapboard and the front decking sloped to one side. 'I think that's the one,' he said.

We circled the chalet widely, hand in hand, as though we

were doing nothing more than taking a romantic walk on the dunes. There were no lights on inside the chalet, no tell-tale buckets or fishing nets drying outside.

'There's a back door,' I said.

'Perfect.'

I stood on the pathway acting as lookout while Ryan draped his thick jacket over one elbow and smashed the rear kitchen window. The glass exploded inside. My heart raced as I scanned the area while Ryan climbed through the window. Two minutes later he unlocked the back door.

'Be careful where you stand,' he said. Tiny shards of glass were scattered across the floor.

I went to check out the rest of the chalet, while he swept up the glass and patched up the broken window with a piece of cardboard from an old crisps box that was filled with beach toys.

It was obviously a privately owned chalet, rather than a rental. It was too shabby and much too full of personal items for the rental market. Which was a good thing, unless – by some unfortunate coincidence – the family that owned the place chose this night to head down to Cornwall for a break. There was a double bedroom at the front of the chalet and a twin bedroom at the back. Just one small bath-room. The kitchen and living room was all-in-one with windows to the front and rear.

'There's a bedroom at the back,' I told Ryan. 'It's the only room that doesn't face the front.'

'That's where we'll stay then,' he said. 'No one has any reason to pass by the back of the chalet.'

Ryan went to the car to fetch some clothes and the bags of supermarket groceries. I searched through the cupboards for towels and sheets. There were a couple of scratchy blankets, but no sheets or pillowcases. I checked the taps: water flowed. The electricity was off.

I glanced up through the window and saw Ryan heading back towards the chalet. A thin gauze of mist was in the air by now; the droplets shimmered in what was left of the sun. In his black jeans and jacket, Ryan reminded me of a fly caught in a spider's web.

'Everything OK?' I asked him.

'We're good.'

We made plates of sandwiches and chocolate biscuits and took them into the back bedroom to eat. The sun was lost behind the thickening fog and colour was gradually draining from the world outside. The bedroom was dim and shadowy; within an hour it would be dark.

'We should shut the curtains,' I said. I eased myself on to one of the beds and leant back against the wall.

Ryan took the opposite bed. 'If someone's outside, I'd sooner be able to see them.'

My stomach flipped and I put my plate of food on the floor.

'What am I going to tell Miranda?' I asked.

Miranda. Who was already grieving for her dead boyfriend.

'You're not going to tell her anything. We're going to leave some clothes and identification on the beach to make it look like we drowned.'

I squeezed my eyes tight, forcing back the tears. This was no time for crying.

'How are we going to pay for the ID?'

Ryan glanced out the window. 'I need to know where Lauren is. She can't spend every minute at the farmhouse. When she leaves, I go in and get my cash.'

'Where do you think she is?'

'My guess is that she's staying at my house. Using it as a base. But she'll be checking out your house. She'll look up your friends. Any places we've been known to use.'

'And when she realises we're gone, we'll be safe? She'll go back to her time?'

Ryan looked up and met my eyes. 'We'll never be safe. They know I travelled back in time. Unauthorised. They'll always be looking for me.'

'That's what I don't get. You said that small streams don't change the future. I'm only a small stream. And you too, right? So why don't they leave us alone? How much does you being here really matter?'

Ryan sighed. 'I thought I'd managed to leave without a trace. I stole a ship that was due to be scrapped. I hid my portal. But I'm guessing this is big news back in my time. My father is a powerful man. Think about it: the son of one of the Guardians steals a time-ship and travels back to the past. It's going to be a big deal. My father's opponents won't let this go.'

'We can hide. We can beat them.'

Ryan smiled thinly. 'I'm so sorry that I'm putting you through all this. I never wanted this for you.'

'I don't care.'

'You'll never see Miranda again. Or any of your friends. A new identity means giving up everyone you know. Everyone you love.'

'Not everyone,' I said. 'It means giving up everyone else for the person I love most. It's no more than you did for me.'

We lay down, fully clothed, on one of the twin beds, our bodies pushed against each other, the two thin blankets draped over us. Ryan's hand reached for mine and held on tightly.

'It's going to be OK,' he said.

'I know.'

He kissed my forehead and then shut his eyes, his hand still curled into mine. We lay like that for a while, neither of us saying anything, while the fog rolled inwards, swirling and folding itself around the chalet until it was lost within the darkness. Ryan fell asleep first. His breathing grew steadier, then his grip loosened around my hand. I don't remember falling asleep, but I must have, because I remember waking up.

A bright beam of light shone directly on my face. I opened my eyes. The light came from behind me, throwing sharp shadows on to the walls and the floor. Dread filled the pit of my stomach as I pushed myself up on to my elbows and turned to look behind me.

A full moon, shining like a searchlight in the clear, night sky, had captured me in its beam.

CHAPTER 5

Although the sun was shining and the air was warm, Ryan and I had our hoodies pulled up, hiding our hair, our faces disguised behind sunglasses. He raised an eyebrow at my strip of unflattering passport photos, lightening the mood for a second.

'You look like a hardened criminal,' he said.

'You don't look so hot yourself,' I said, pointing at his.

He pulled out his wallet and counted the rest of his money into my palm. Seventy-five pounds. 'Go to the phone shop and buy two cheap pay-as-you-go phones. Then take the bus back to the Towans and wait for me in the chalet. I'm going to drive to Truro and arrange for the ID.'

'Won't he want money now?'

'He'll get the money when he gives me the documents.'

He headed off in the direction of the car. I hurried into Perran Digital, picked up the two cheapest phones I could find, and hurried out again. There was still half an hour until the next bus. I walked down to the seafront furtively, sticking to the shadows, my hood up and my head low. Perran was a small town. I knew too many people.

Down by the harbour, I sat by the boats, away from the clean, warm sand that the locals and tourists preferred. The harbour beach was jam-packed. I saw my friends, Megan and Connor, at the other end of the beach. They were holding hands and paddling in the shallows. Amy and Matt and a few other kids from school were lying on a beach blanket under the wall, which was more sheltered. The tide was coming in. When it was high they would probably go jumping off the harbour wall. They always did.

I took my new phone out of its box and inserted the SIM card. The battery was fully charged, so I started adding the names and numbers of all my friends. I knew that it was stupid. I couldn't call them in case Lauren was monitoring their incoming calls. But it made me feel safe – connected – to have their phone numbers programmed into my phone. There was another ten minutes till the next bus. I shoved the empty box into the bin, kicked off my flip-flops and wandered down to the sea. I walked along the water's edge, leaving footprints in the damp sand. Halfway across the beach, I stopped and just watched.

I'd known them practically my whole life.

I would never see them again.

They would all go on to college together, celebrate their eighteenth birthdays, choose their universities and careers. How long would it be before they forgot me?

I would never forget them.

The bus rattled its way along the seafront road. I said a silent goodbye and turned back the way I'd come. My footprints had already been washed away by the incoming tide.

The bus was almost empty. The only people that ever used this service were the tourists staying at the chalets on the

Towans and the kids too young to drive. It was that time of day when most people had already headed out where they were going, too soon for anyone to be headed home.

I stared through the window at the sea as we passed by. Where would we go? I didn't really care so long as Ryan and I were together. But what if something happened to him? What if the cleaner caught him breaking into the farmhouse and took him back with her? What if something happened and I was left here all alone? Again.

We had to get out of here. Soon. We needed to put as many miles between us and Lauren as we could.

The bus pulled into the stop outside Perran Towans. I stayed aboard. I didn't want Ryan going to the farmhouse to collect the rest of his money. I had a better idea.

When the bus dropped me off outside the village stores in Penpol Cove, I pulled my hood up and put my sunglasses back on. I headed for the fields in front of my house and climbed the stile into a freshly ploughed field, the furrows in straight lines like a row of small waves. I walked along the perimeter of the field until I was just across from my house. Scrunching myself down, I peered over the hedge. The street was empty. I decided to give myself twenty minutes. If there was no sign of life from within the house in that time, I would risk it.

Minutes passed. Gulls tossed and screeched on the wind. Clouds raced across the sky. A boy dribbled a football along the street until his mother called for him to come home for lunch. Then nothing. My legs shook with the awkward effort of crouching behind the hedge. Surely a cleaner sent back to catch Ryan would have more important things to do than hang out at my house in case I came home. I scanned the parked cars on the street. There were six of them. Four I could see clearly. Two were partly hidden from view.

I stood up and shook the cramp out of my legs. She wasn't here. I made my way back through the field, across the stile and on to my street. Trying to seem like someone taking a casual stroll I walked up the road, flicking my eyes from left to right, making sure the parked cars were empty. They were.

For a moment I considered marching right up to my front door and unlocking it with my key. But a small part of me still felt uneasy. I kept on going right to the end of my street and then turned the corner, doubling back on myself along the rear alleyway. It was narrow. Both my street and the one behind it had back gardens that opened on to the alley. It was big enough for wheelie bins and not much else. There was no one there but me and the ginger cat who liked to come and visit us from time to time.

When I got to my back gate, I paused. The garden was small with nowhere to hide. Just a picnic table, a washing line and a few scraggly shrubs. I unlatched the gate and pushed it open with my toe. It swung inwards with a creak.

I would only need two minutes to get what I needed. One hundred and twenty seconds. In and out. Surely the odds were on my side.

I swallowed my fear and slowly put one foot in front of the other. There was no sound. I'd always enjoyed the quietness of Penpol Cove before; now, it just felt creepy. I pulled my house keys out of my jeans pocket and slipped the back door key into the lock. I turned it and pushed the door open.

I stepped inside. The kitchen looked just as it always did. The table still had a half-finished bottle of red wine next to the salt and pepper shakers. Miranda's mug was sitting in the sink. The address and phone number of the house she was staying at in Bath were stuck to the side of the fridge with a magnet. The house was silent. All I could hear was the hum of the fridge and the all too familiar pounding of my heart.

I left the back door open and tiptoed into the hall. The door to the sitting room was ajar. I glanced inside. Nothing. Exhaling deeply, I climbed the stairs.

It was an old house. Every other stair squeaked or groaned and some of the floorboards on the landing were loose. I wished I could remember which stairs and boards were bad, but I'd never been the sort of girl who liked to sneak out of the house at night. Upstairs were three rooms: my room, Miranda's and the bathroom. I was pretty sure that Lauren wouldn't be hanging out in the bathroom, but I pushed open each door in turn to check. Nothing.

My cash savings were in a jam jar on the top of my book-shelf, hidden behind a copy of *Great Expectations*. I pulled out the jar and emptied the cash on to my bed. One hundred and four pounds. Not a lot, but enough for petrol to get us out of Cornwall. Enough to buy food for a few days.

My mother's engagement ring was in my jewellery box. It was a slender band with a large diamond, which I had attached to a thin gold chain. Miranda had had it valued just a few months ago when renewing the house insurance. The jeweller had said it was worth three thousand pounds. The ring was all I had left of my mother, except for a handful of photographs. I put the necklace around my neck and picked up the framed photo of me and my parents which stood on the bedside table. It was the photo I said goodnight to every night before turning off the light. I was about to slide the photo out of the frame, when I remembered I couldn't. Ryan had said we would make it look like we had drowned. So no one would look for us. If I took that photo, Miranda would know I'd run away. Instead, I rummaged through the shoebox of photos I kept under my bed until I found another photo of my parents, as well as one of me and my friends on the evening of the Year Eleven Ball.

I heard a noise from downstairs. Light footsteps. Like someone trying to move stealthily. I stood perfectly still, holding my breath. The footsteps were coming up the stairs. Quickly. I spun around, looking for something to use to defend myself. The atlas. Just as I reached for it, the door opened a fraction and the ginger cat padded inside. He glanced at me, before jumping on to my bed and curling up on my pillow.

Stupid cat. Of course – I'd left the back door open.

'Sorry, Katkin,' I said, picking him up. 'You can't stay here today.'

I left my room, Katkin in my arms. He purred loudly, not yet understanding that I was about to kick him out. I didn't bother with keeping quiet any more. I just wanted out, back on the bus, back to the chalet.

I ran down the stairs, through the hall and into the kitchen.

I was not alone.

Sitting on one of the kitchen chairs, a gun resting on the table in front of her, was Lauren.

I stopped in my tracks. Katkin struggled and jumped out of my arms.

'Hello, Eden,' she said.

I opened my mouth to speak, but nothing came out except a strangled, 'What?'

'Sit down.' She nodded at the chair opposite her, a nod that managed to acknowledge her gun as well as the seat.

I glanced at the open door. If I ran, she'd have time to pump several shots in me before I crossed the threshold. But what if I screamed? Called attention to her. She wouldn't like that.

'I suggest you do as I say. Any other choice will not lead to a good outcome.'

I hesitated.

She picked up the gun.

I sat down.

'I'm going to make this simple for you,' she said, putting the gun back on the table. 'You have a choice. You can lead me to Orion Westland . . .'

'Never. I'll never do that.'

'Or I will kill everyone who has ever mattered to you.' She reached behind her and pulled the slip of paper with Miranda's contact details from the fridge. 'Starting with your aunt. And then your friend, Connor. And I will continue killing your friends until you lead me to Orion.'

I stared at her. 'What are you going to do with him?'

'Take him back where he belongs. 2123. I won't harm him.'

'You won't harm him? What about me?'

'You will have to come with us. To 2123. You know too much to be allowed to remain in this time.'

'And if I don't?'

'Then I will have to kill you.'

I rubbed my head. Could I trust her? She was a cleaner.

'It's a simple choice,' said Lauren. 'You and Orion come to the future with me and you get to be together. That's what you want, isn't it?'

I looked at her.

'Or you refuse to help me and everyone you care about will be killed.' She stood up. 'What's it going to be?'

He was in the kitchen, cutting a slice of bread, when I walked in.

'Hey,' he said, smiling.

'Ryan,' I said. 'I'm sorry.'

He looked confused for a millisecond. Then, when the knife clattered to the counter and he raised his hands above his head, I knew she'd come in as well.

'Why?' he asked Lauren. 'Why do I matter? Why can't you just let me run? I won't affect the timeline. You know that. You're from the future.'

'There's a bounty on your head, Westland. Three million credits. Can you match that?'

He swore and looked away.

'I'm sorry,' I said again.

'It's not your fault. This is what she does.'

'Actually, you were very hard to track,' said Lauren. 'My research told me that you would spend your first couple of weeks in the Perran area. After that you would disappear.'

'That's why you came so soon.'

'That's right.'

'What about Eden?'

'She's coming with us. She knows too much.'

Ryan lowered his hands. 'You know I won't run. You have Eden. But please, can I leave some of our stuff on the beach? So it looks like we drowned. Just to give some closure to Eden's family and friends.'

'Go ahead.'

Ryan took our beach towels, hoodies and my backpack and left to plant them on the beach. I watched him through the window.

'Who put a price on Ryan's head?' I asked.

'Ryan's father is a Guardian of Time. You don't get that powerful without making a few enemies along the way.'

I watched him walk away, along the small sandy path that led down to the beach. He disappeared behind a chalet and then he was gone.

Two boys, dressed in wetsuits, boards under their arms, ran past the chalet towards the beach. Seagulls swooped from the clifftops and then hovered, almost stationary, in the uplift. A palm tree bent in the sudden gust of wind.

I heard a car driving along the road. A small plane travelling overhead.

Would I ever hear such things, see such things again?

High clouds raced across the sky. Out at sea, white foam sprayed from the breakers. 2012 clouds. 2012 waves. My sky. My beach.

My home.

Two hours later we arrived at an isolated farmhouse on a remote part of the moor. Like Ryan, Lauren had hidden her ship in a barn. It was black and almost circular, with legs that held it off the ground, like a four-legged spider.

'Get in,' she said.

'Aren't you going to wait till dark?' said Ryan. 'We always travel at night.'

Lauren gestured around her. 'Who's going to see us here?'

I walked my last few steps across the springy moorland grass, breathed my last few breaths in 2012. I didn't want to leave my time. This was where I belonged. Something glinted from amid the purple heather and I stopped. It glinted again, a copper eye blinking up at me. Crouching, I parted the heather. It was a penny. Tarnished and weather-beaten, but still bright enough to catch the sun. I slipped it into my pocket for good luck. 'Goodbye,' I whispered to the world around me. My blood thickened and slowed, and a leaden dread filled me as I mounted the metal steps that led up to the hatch.

The inside was tiny. Just a cramped cockpit with a huge and complex-looking instrument panel and one row of seats behind it.

Ryan went first.

'Watch your feet,' he said.

Lying across the footwell was a body bag containing Travis. As I climbed into my seat, I was careful to avoid stepping on it.

Lauren sat in the cockpit. She tapped the console in front of her and the whole ship began to vibrate. A circle began to appear through the cockpit window. It began as a pinprick and gradually expanded until it was about three metres across. I could still see the moorland through it, though it was slightly opaque, like looking through cataracts.

'Stabilised,' said Lauren, checking her instruments. 'Are you both ready?'

For a few seconds it felt as though we were moving backwards. The moor retreated into the distance. Whether this was an optical illusion or we really were travelling backwards, I couldn't tell. The moorland began to distort until everything was curved. And then we were moving forwards into the circle, which – it became clear – was a tunnel.

No one said a word. Lauren appeared to be concentrating very hard on keeping the ship in the middle of the tunnel.

'Ninety seconds,' she said, reading the instrument panel in front of her.

I glanced sidelong at Ryan. He smiled and reached for my hand.

The edge of the tunnel was now completely black, while the centre was brightly illuminated. It reminded me of stories people told about near-death experiences – about travelling towards the light.

'Sixty seconds,' said Lauren.

It felt like the ship itself was holding its breath. I remembered Ryan telling me that portals through space-time were unstable and could collapse in on themselves and that travelling through portals this close to each other was like playing Russian roulette.

'Thirty seconds,' said Lauren.

Ryan crushed my hand with his. Suddenly the tunnel we were travelling through began to narrow and curve. I could see the blackness of deep space, the farmhouse shed we'd left behind and a bright green field all at the same time, as though looking at a marble. A light on the dashboard began to flash and an alarm began to sound. My nausea started to grow and I slammed a hand across my mouth.

'The portal's collapsing!' Ryan shouted.

'Hold on!' said Lauren as she frantically tapped away at the screen on the dashboard. 'We're going to have to make a slight adjustment.'

The ship rolled over. The sphere unravelled and we were travelling through a tunnel again. The shed, space, the green lawn were all gone.

'What's the destination?' asked Ryan.

'August,' Lauren said, hitting buttons on the dash. 'Or close to August. I'm going to land at the Institute.'

'We're going to make it,' said Ryan, squeezing my hand.

'Ten,' said Lauren.

The bright light at the end of the tunnel faded.

'Five.'

Colour returned to the edges of my vision and the curved tunnel we'd been travelling through opened out. Ahead of us was a large green field with curved white buildings in the distance. The tunnel collapsed into a pin-prick and we had arrived.

'Where is this?' I asked.

'SATI headquarters,' said Lauren. 'Space and Time Institute. Not our original destination, but with the portal collapsing I had to make adjustments.' She turned around to face us. 'You two had better say your goodbyes. Orion will be arrested the second we open these doors. You have ten seconds.'

'Where will they take you?' I said.

'They'll put me in a cell for a few days,' said Ryan. 'I'll be OK. Try to find my friend, Pegasus. He'll take care of you.'

'Pegasus,' I said. 'OK.'

He pulled me into a tight hug. 'Everything'll be fine.'

There was a sigh as the doors unlocked. We clambered out of the ship. Waiting for us on the grass was a man in a charcoal grey uniform, flanked by four heavily armed guards.

'Mission complete,' said Lauren. 'We have repatriated the remains of Travis Deckard and brought you Orion Westland. The girl is here both as a witness and a precaution.'

'You will need to be debriefed,' said the man in uniform. He nodded to the guards. 'Take these two to Central Holding.

CHAPTER 6

Lakeborough, Summer 2123

The room was small. As wide as my outstretched arms and not much longer than the metal bed – stained mattress, no blankets or sheets – that provided the only seating. Behind the bed was a toilet, a half-used roll of toilet paper and a small bottle of antibacterial hand gel.

When we had first arrived at Central Holding for processing – fingerprints taken, retinas and faces scanned, personal belongings removed and logged – I had hoped we would end up in the same cell while they decided what to do with us. A small part of me even hoped they would just let us go. But of course that didn't happen. Ryan was going to have to stand trial and I was going to be questioned. We were put in separate cells.

I looked through the barred window set into the door, but could see nothing except for a long white corridor and a large analogue clock on the wall opposite. A single guard, dressed in a khaki uniform, stood outside my cell. A large gun was strapped across his body and a bunch of keys hung from a loop on his belt. I banged hard on the window. The guard turned, looked at me briefly, then turned away. I banged the window again.

'Where am I?' I yelled. 'What country? What year?'

He didn't turn around again.

How could it be that just a few hours ago I was in my bedroom in Penpol Cove and now I was over one hundred years in the future, standing in a prison cell?

I was about to bang on the door again when I was overcome with a sudden tidal wave of weariness. It poured over me, gradual at first, then rapidly, until I had no choice but to sit on the filthy mattress and rest my head in my hands. A part of my brain warned me that I should be plotting my next move, my testimony, something. But my eyelids fluttered shut and my mind was pulled deeper and deeper towards sleep until I was gone.

It felt like I had slept for several hours when the hard clank of metal scraping metal woke me. I sat up to see the guard unlocking my cell. A tall man in a charcoal uniform came in and stood before me, his arms crossed in front of him.

I pushed myself up, embarrassed to have been caught sleeping.

'So,' said the uniformed man, running his eyes the length of my body and finally resting on my face. 'You're what this is all about.'

'I'm not sure what you mean, sir?' I said, rubbing my sleep-bleary eyes.

'You're the reason my son broke the Temporal Laws, stole a ship and ruined his family's reputation.'

'You're Mr Westland?'

'Admiral Westland.'

He looked me over again and I was reminded of the fact that I'd spent last night sleeping in my clothes, I hadn't had a shower for two days and my hair was a tangled mess. Not the sort of first impression I'd hoped to make with Ryan's family.

Admiral Westland shook his head and looked away. 'What was he thinking?'

I swallowed. 'I guess there's no accounting for taste.'

He looked up sharply. 'That's not what I . . .' he began. 'Never mind.'

'Have you seen him? Is he OK?'

'He's in a lot of trouble.' He sighed. 'And all for nothing.'

I stood up. 'It wasn't for nothing. He saved my life. That might mean nothing to you, but it's pretty damn important to me.'

Admiral Westland raised an eyebrow in a way that reminded me of his son. 'What do you mean?'

'I was dead.'

The admiral sat on the edge of the bunk. 'Tell me everything.'

I wasn't sure how much I should say. 'Ryan and his team were sent back to stop something from happening,' I said, choosing to be vague with the details.

'Miss Anfield,' he said, interrupting me, 'I am one of the five Guardians of Time. Every time mission has a Guardian to oversee it. I was the Guardian for the mission known as "The Eden Mission". I put together the team – including my son – who travelled to the past to work on it. I know what the mission set out to do. You don't have to be concerned about what you say.'

'They didn't stop it happening,' I said. 'Connor was about to discover something he shouldn't.'

'A planet,' said the admiral. 'I know about the planet.'

'I stopped Connor discovering it. And then, after Ryan left, the mission's cleaner killed me. When Ryan found out, he came back to save my life.'

A distant smile crossed his face. 'That changes everything. It wasn't merely an impulsive love trip. It wasn't just a selfish whim.'

I shook my head. 'It wasn't selfish at all. He gave up everything he has here in his own time – and everyone – to travel back and save me.'

Admiral Westland touched my arm. 'I need you to say all this in your statement. Make sure they understand why Orion did what he did. There is an old protocol that we might be able to use in Orion's defence.'

I nodded.

'Another Guardian is waiting to debrief you. Come along with me.'

'Do I need a lawyer?' I asked.

'No. You're not in any trouble. He will just want to ask you a few questions.'

Admiral Westland escorted me a short distance to a conference room. A tall man with grey hair and a full grey beard met us at the door.

'Thank you, Admiral Westland,' he said. 'I'll take it from here.'

Westland nodded at me, turned and strode back down the corridor.

An oblong table sat in the centre of the conference room, with about twenty chairs arranged around it. Lauren was sitting in one of the chairs, her back ramrod straight, her hair and make-up polished and professional. She caught my eye but didn't smile.

'I hope you haven't experienced too much discomfort?' the man asked. 'The Institute was never designed to hold prisoners, but the prison in New Marseilles is full. Our holding cells are very basic, I'm afraid.'

I shrugged, more uncomfortable now than I'd been in my cell. There were no windows in the room, but a low hum suggested some sort of climate control. I shivered, wishing I had my hoodie to pull over my T-shirt.

'Take a seat. I won't be keeping you long.' He poured a cup of coffee from a selection of drinks on the sideboard and placed it in front of me on the table. 'Have some coffee. You're probably very tired.'

I blew on the steamy drink and took a sip. It was much stronger, more bitter, than any coffee I'd tasted before.

'My name is Admiral Wolfe,' the man said.

It was an oddly appropriate name. His greying beard and hair surrounded a pair of green eyes flecked with yellow. Everything about the man – his build, his uniform, the way he moved – suggested power.

'You've already met Lauren Thomas,' said Wolfe. 'Though you will have known her as Lauren Deckard.'

I glanced at Lauren. She was a cleaner, a professional assassin. What sort of person chose to make a living that way?

'I am going to need you to make a statement,' Wolfe continued. 'When you have done that, you will be free to go.'

'OK,' I said. I wondered where I would go.

Admiral Wolfe tapped a thin membrane – some sort of ultra-thin, flexible computer screen on the desk in front of him. 'Begin recording,' he said. 'Mission 2123/2012 Fugitive Recovery. Date: 31st July 2123. Eden Anfield making her statement in the presence of Admiral Titan Wolfe and Agent Lauren Thomas.' He smiled at me warmly. 'Now, Eden, begin with the first time you met Orion Westland.'

'He was at my school,' I said. 'A new kid. Obviously he was undercover, but I didn't know that. Part of his mission required him to get to know my best friend.'

'Carry on,' said Wolfe.

'So he became a part of my circle of friends. But I could tell he was different.'

'How?'

'He didn't know things that everybody knows,' I said. 'Names of famous people and things like that.'

Wolfe turned to Lauren. 'Who was the researcher for that mission?'

'Cassiopeia Wade.'

'Continue,' Wolfe said to me.

'I didn't know he had travelled through time of course. I thought lots of other things at first. But then I came across a book that was written and published in the future.'

The air in the room grew colder. Wolfe looked at Lauren.

'This suggests some very sloppy work. Criminally so.' He turned back to me. 'Did you meet Cassiopeia Wade or Benjamin Hansen?'

'I knew them as Ryan's father and sister.'

'Where did you find this book?'

I hesitated. I didn't want to say anything that might make things worse for Ryan. Or Cassie and Ben – the other agents from the original mission – for that matter. I was going to have to bend the truth.

'I broke into their house. I was looking for answers.'

Wolfe nodded. 'And what did you do when you discovered the truth?'

'When I confronted Ryan, he denied everything. But I pieced together their mission and decided to help him. The main part of his mission was to prevent something from happening. He wasn't able to stop it happening. But I was. And then they left.'

Wolfe frowned. 'They just left? They didn't consider it necessary to bring you with them?'

I shook my head.

'And then Orion came back?' said Admiral Wolfe. 'Because he was in love with you?'

'No,' I said. 'He came back to save my life. After they left, the mission cleaner killed me. Ryan thought that was unfair since I was the one who completed the mission. So he came back to save me.'

I stopped talking and played with the frayed edge of my T-shirt, while Admiral Wolfe conferred with Lauren in low tones. I hoped I had said the right things.

'Is there anything else you would like to add to your statement?' he asked me.

My palms were clammy. I rubbed the sweat on to my jeans. 'Only that Ryan didn't travel back for selfish reasons. He travelled back to save me, to make things right. He shouldn't be punished for that.'

Admiral Wolfe stood up. 'You're free to go, but don't leave the city until after Orion's trial. You will be called as a witness.'

'Can I see him?' I asked.

'I'm afraid that's not possible,' said the admiral. 'The only visitor that young man can see today is his lawyer.'

Lauren stood up. 'I'll show you the way out.'

'Take her to the front desk for a resettlement pack,' said the admiral.

I followed Lauren along a series of long white corridors, each one lined with identical white doors, all shut, like a hospital without visitors. Sunlight poured through tall windows, blinding me with brightness. I squinted at the floor and hurried after Lauren who was striding ahead of me.

'A word of advice,' said Lauren as we entered the reception. 'Let me tell them you're eighteen. Unless you want to end up in a state care home for the next two years.'

Three women sat behind the long reception desk, each dragging icons across a transparent membrane computer and talking into a headset. One of them looked up at us.

'This is Eden Anfield,' said Lauren. 'She's eighteen. Out of time. She needs a resettlement pack.'

The woman spoke quietly into her headset, smiled and

passed me a card. It was the size of a credit card, but thinner and made of a soft flexible material.

'This flexi-card will cover six weeks at the Lakeview Hotel and enough credit to buy food and clothing for the same period,' she said. She reached beneath the counter and passed me a small resealable plastic bag containing my only possessions: my mobile phone; the gold chain with my mother's wedding ring; the penny I'd found on the moor; two photographs; and my wallet. 'I believe these are also yours.'

'Good luck,' said Lauren. She turned and walked back the way we had come.

A small transparent screen blocked the front door. As I approached, a red light quickly pulsed against my eyes.

'Eden Anfield,' said a melodic, disembodied voice. 'Cleared to leave the building.'

I walked through the front door and out into the brilliant sunshine.

That was when the full reality of my situation hit me. I knew no one. I didn't even know where I was. I had nothing but the clothes on my back and the so-called relocation package on the flexi-card thing I'd been given. The only person I knew was Ryan, and he was locked up inside.

I looked around me. The Institute was at the top of a hill. In front of me was a car park and a security gate leading to a wide avenue. I sucked in a deep breath and began walking.

I was halfway across the car park when I saw him: Ben, the agent who had led Ryan's original mission to 2012.

He was loading some files into the boot of his car. I stopped and stared. Back in 2012 he'd pretended to be Ryan's father, a science writer who liked to live in secluded locations where he wouldn't be disturbed. He'd stayed home most of the time, dressed in jeans and a shirt, a day's worth of stubble on his cheeks. Now he was dressed in a smart charcoal uniform similar to Admiral Westland's. His face was clean-shaven, his hair was short on the sides and slicked back on top.

Back in 2012, he'd always been kind to me.

'Ben?' I said.

He slammed the boot of his car shut and turned.

'It's me,' I said.

He blinked. 'Eden?'

I nodded and walked towards him.

'What the hell?' he said.

'Ryan came back for me. The cleaner killed me so Ryan came back.'

Ben just stared, his mouth open.

'But the Guardians found out and sent a cleaner after him.'

'I know. It's been all over the news: Admiral Westland's son has gone rogue and stolen a time-ship. The Institute refused to comment. They prefer to keep their affairs to themselves.' He shook his head. 'But here you are.'

'Ryan's locked up inside. There's going to be a trial.'

Ben glanced at his watch. 'I want to talk, Eden. But I'm running late for my flight. Can I give you a ride somewhere?'

'I'm going to be staying at the Lakeview Hotel. Can you drive me there?'

Ben nodded. 'Jump in.'

'This looks disappointingly normal,' I said, running my eyes over his car. 'I was hoping for hover cars or a jet pack.'

Ben gave me a look.

'I'm kidding,' I said, although I had expected the future to look more different than it had so far.

'Don't be fooled,' he said. 'It's the little differences that throw you the most. They're more unexpected. The big differences are easier to see.'

'Where are we, anyway?'

'Lakeborough, New Hampshire. Part of the Federation of North America. Lakeborough didn't exist back in your time; it was just a collection of small resort towns. Now it's home to the President's summer residence and the Space and Time Institute. It's a small city. You'll be able to see downtown in a moment.'

He started the car using a retinal scanner built into the dashboard and the engine gently hummed to life. We rolled through the gate and on to a wide, tree-lined avenue. I turned in my seat and looked behind me. The Space and Time Institute sat on the crest of the hill, all white granite and glass, like a diamond solitaire.

The peaceful avenue that led from the Institute merged on to a busier road. We drove round a corner and the city came into view, spread below us all down the side of the hill and across the flat land to a large lake.

'What month is it?'

'It's the end of July 2123.'

I did a quick calculation. It was one month, and one hundred and eleven years in the future.

'So tell me what happened,' said Ben.

I gave him the short version, about the cleaner coming back for Ryan and capturing us. I didn't mention the part about me returning to my house and leading the cleaner to Ryan.

'How long had Ryan been back in 2012 before the cleaner arrived?' asked Ben.

'Three days.'

'That's crazy! To portal in and out so close to when we portalled out.'

'I know it's dangerous. Our portal started collapsing on the way back here. We had to change course. I think we were supposed to have arrived in March.'

Ben shook his head.

'What do you think will happen to Ryan?' I asked.

'Unregulated time travel is one of the most serious crimes against time. He's going to need a good lawyer.'

'Admiral Westland said something about an old protocol that might help.'

'I don't know much about the law, but I do know that there isn't much public support for time travel in general. Ryan's going to have a fight on his hands.'

The car slowed down and pulled up outside a white concrete building with metallic reflective windows.

'This is the Lakeview Hotel,' said Ben. 'The Institute uses it for agents all the time. It's discreet. Food's quite nice.'

'Thanks,' I said, pulling the flexi-card from my pocket. 'How does this work?'

'It's like a credit card, but it's pre-paid,' he explained. 'You just hand it over when you need to pay.'

'Anything else I should know?'

He pulled a small device, about the size of a mobile phone, out of his jacket pocket. 'This is a port-com. Portable communicator. It's like a more sophisticated flexi-card. You use it to phone people, access the internet, and to pay for things once you have a bank account. You can't function without one. If I give you just one piece of advice, it's to get yourself a port-com as soon as possible.'

I nodded. 'Thanks, Ben.'

He passed me a business card. 'Call me any time. I've taken a new job. Moved on from time travel. I'm now captain of the Inter-Planetary Spaceport, a space station between Earth and the moon. I'm not close by, but if you have any questions or you need help with anything, just call.'

The doorman of the hotel was eyeing me warily. 'Can I help you, ma'am?'

I looked behind me. No one. I was the ma'am.

'I'd like to check in.'

He looked around me and frowned. 'Does madam have any luggage?'

'I'm travelling light.'

He ran his eyes over me in a way that made me feel very uncomfortable. And then I realised that I was dressed all wrong. I was wearing jeans and a T-shirt, but everyone else – other than those dressed in business suits – was dressed in a long tunic with leggings, like a body-con salwar kameez.

I followed the doorman into the lobby of the Lakeview Hotel. Its cool marble floors, potted plants and prints reassuringly reminded me of my own time. The doorman deposited me at the reception desk and left.

'I need a room,' I said.

'Single, double, deluxe or a suite?' the receptionist asked in a bored voice.

'Single.'

'Your card?'

I handed over the flexi-card and watched as he scanned it over a larger membrane. My picture and name materialised on the membrane, along with information regarding my credit. His expression brightened immediately.

'Delighted to have you as our guest, Miss Anfield,' he said, beaming at me. 'I've allocated you a room on the fourth floor. There are beautiful views of the lake from there.' He handed me back my flexi-card. 'If you need anything, don't hesitate to ask.'

I thanked him and took the lift to the fourth floor. My room was too big to be a single. It had a king-size bed, a large bathroom and separate sitting area with two couches and a large membrane on the wall. I wondered if he had charged me extra for this.

I shut the door. This was it: my home for the next six weeks. And then what? The future lay ahead of me, unlived and unknown, a small stream in the great ocean of time.

I had no clothes to unpack, no book to read, no friends to call. I switched on my new phone and waited for it to power up. Would old technology still work? Would my phone automatically download a software upgrade and continue to function? A tiny part of me held on to a small hope that a time-travelling phone from 2012 would be able to make calls to 2012. The bar at the top of the screen indicated that the battery was full – this little sliver of technology from my own time surviving in this wide new world – but there was no service. I scrolled through my list of favourite contacts – Amy, Connor, Megan, Miranda, Ryan.

Apart from Ryan, they were all dead now.

I pressed the call button next to Connor's name. I stared and stared at the words.

Call failed.

Of course it had. My brand new mobile phone was now nothing more than an expensive digital clock. They were all gone. Every one of my friends had lived their lives already. They'd gone to university, chosen careers, fallen in love, had children and grandchildren, grown old or sick and died. I would never see them again.

I tried to find a remote control for the screen – which I assumed to be a television – but there was nothing in the room. There were no buttons on the edge of the screen, nor was there room for them. The screen itself was transparent, like a thin sheet of Perspex hanging on the wall.

'Television turn on,' I said to the empty room, feeling foolish.

Nothing happened.

My phone said four in the afternoon. But that was a different day in a different month in a different century altogether. Overcome with weariness, I sat on the edge of the bed. I was tired, alone, dirty, had no change of clothes, no food, no friends and I couldn't even work out how to turn on the TV. The only person I knew in the whole wide world was Ryan, but he was locked up in a cell waiting for his trial and I had no idea how to help him. Numbly, I flopped back on the bed and shut my eyes tight, longing for sleep to pull me under.

CHAPTER 7

I stepped outside. The city was monochrome in the pre-dawn light. Tiny raindrops, shimmering in the white streetlights, hit the grey pavement and formed long silver rivers in the gutters. I shivered in my T-shirt and jeans but I didn't care. I'd woken with resolve. After a long sleep and a hot shower, I felt refreshed and determined. I would find a place to get breakfast, buy myself some clothes and go back to the Space and Time Institute to find out more about Ryan's trial.

I looked up and down the street, trying to guess which direction would lead me to food. The doorman was different to the one who had seen me arrive. He looked at me strangely. 'Costume party?' he asked.

I nodded. 'Where's a good place to get breakfast?'

He pointed down the street to my right. 'Keep walking straight ahead and you'll come to the lake. Make a right and you'll come to a diner called the Peacock Feather. Open twenty-four hours. They serve the best potato cakes in the whole of the Federation.'

I walked swiftly down the empty street, my flip-flops slapping against the wet ground. This was clearly the hotel district, a few blocks of wide tree-lined streets with hotels and expensive-looking restaurants. Doormen stood under broad black umbrellas as I hurried by. As I drew closer to the lake, the buildings looked older and I passed a sign that read Old Wolfeboro.

The sharp raindrops stung my bare skin and I picked up my pace. Now there were a few people on the street, wet and bedraggled like me, huddling under umbrellas or in shop doorways. A car whooshed by, sending up a spray of rainwater as it passed. No one paid me the slightest attention.

By the time I reached the end of the road, down by the lake, I realised I had reached the pulsing heart of Lakeborough's nightlife. On the lake itself, party boats lit up like Christmas ornaments were heading towards the dock. Along the shoreline, bars and clubs were emptying out on to the wet streets. Between the street and the lake was a boardwalk; a bronze statue dominated the space. A man – five times the size of a real man – stood trium-phantly, his hands holding up a distorted clock that reminded me of a painting by Salvador Dali we'd studied in art class. It looked almost like it was melting or warped, and the numbers were in the wrong places. I read the plaque: *Nathaniel Westland, creator of four-dimensional travel, was born in Lakeborough in 2020.* I was in Ryan's hometown. Just knowing that lightened my mood.

I saw the Peacock Feather easily. It was large and loud, a giant feather pushing through its roof. I headed inside and took a table by the window. It was a diner just like I remembered them from Hollywood films, with bright lighting, shiny vinyl seats and endless coffee. But that was where the similarities ended. Once the waiter – a tall, olive-skinned boy with fleshy arms – had filled my mug with bitter black coffee, I opened the menu and was both startled and disgusted. I'd expected burgers and fries. Or omelettes. Perhaps pancakes. Fried, greasy-spoon, carb-laden stodge. Comfort food. My stomach rumbled and I calculated that it had been about thirty hours since I last ate. No wonder I was hungry. But the first few offerings on the menu did nothing to whet my appetite. Kebabs made from in vitro veal. Cricket salad. Spirulina guacamole. Not exactly what I was expecting. Where were the potato cakes? A flush of nausea threatened, but I pushed it aside. I would find something to eat. I would find suitable clothes. And I would help Ryan. He'd done the same in my time.

'You want the Saturday night special?' asked my waitress, a bored-sounding girl dressed in green robes that flowed to her bare feet.

'Yes,' I said. 'Is it vegetarian?'

She shrugged indifferently. 'If you want it to be.'

'Yes,' I said. 'And more coffee.'

The waitress took my menu and glided away.

The front door swung open and a group of girls came in, dressed in short beaded dresses that looked like they belonged in the 1920s. They grabbed a booth in the middle of the café. I realised I had found the only place where my clothes were not deemed worthy of comment.

My food arrived – grilled portabella mushrooms with a

strange, suspiciously fishy tasting pesto, potato cakes, scrambled eggs, grilled tomatoes and thick, dark coffee. I ate slowly, and watched the people around me at the same time. Reassuringly, people didn't seem so different in the twenty-second century. The girls still giggled too much around the boys; the guys still laughed too loudly. There was the same kind of flirting that went on back home. I smiled to myself. Perhaps it wouldn't be so hard to fit in.

I finished my food and drank cup after cup of coffee, until the world outside my window transformed. The grey light of daybreak became the saturated colour of daytime. The fresh morning breeze blew the rainclouds away, leaving nothing but a drip, drip, drip from the rooftops and the tepid promise of sunshine. And the weary party-goers of yesterday were joined by the bleary early morning workers of today.

I went to the till to pay. I handed over my flexi-card and watched the waitress scan it across the large thin membrane I took to be the till.

'Would you like to add a tip?' she asked me.

'Fifteen per cent?' I said.

She shrugged in a manner that suggested it was neither too little nor particularly generous. 'You're kind of young to be working for the Institute, aren't you?' she said.

'I don't work for them.'

'So how come you have a standard-issue Institute flexi-card?'

I shrugged. 'It's part of a resettlement package they gave me.'

Her eyes brightened. 'You're a time traveller? Cool. When are you from?'

I wished I hadn't said anything. 'I'm not supposed to say.'

She narrowed her eyes at me. 'You're that girl, aren't you? The one Orion Westland went to save. I heard it on the late night news. He's been caught or something. Something about saving a girl.'

I shook my head. 'That's not me.'

I watched as my image and details came up on her screen. She charged the bill to my account and handed me back my card. 'Just tell me one thing. Is this your first meal in 2123?'

I nodded.

'Incredible! Eden Anfield's first twenty-second century meal is the vegetarian Saturday night special at the Peacock Feather!' She picked up her port-com and aimed it in my direction. 'Just say what you thought of your breakfast.'

'Err . . . just what I needed,' I said, slightly bewildered.

'Perfect,' said the waitress, putting the port-com back on the counter.

Outside, the first thing I noticed was my face on a giant billboard on one of the main buildings on the seafront. Then I heard my voice. *Just what I needed.*

I pushed past the tired, wasted partygoers who were – thankfully – too far gone to realise that the larger-than-life girl on the billboard was me and headed back up the avenue towards the Lakeview Hotel.

Two blocks later, I slowed down. The streets were beginning to get busy, and shops were opening. I turned left off the main street on to a road lined with bookstores, boutiques and estate agents. I carried on until I reached a department store called Whites. The holographic models in the shop window were wearing what looked to me like everyday clothing for this century.

I needed clean clothes. I went inside.

Thirty minutes later I left the store with three bags of clothes, underwear, make-up and shoes. Out on the street something was going on. Reporters, photographers and camera operators crowded round the entrance to Whites, pushing and shoving one another. I blinked in the bright morning sunshine and tried to get my bearings. Was it left or right to get back to the main street and the Lakeview Hotel?

'Eden!' someone shouted.

I turned towards the voice, wondering who on earth it could be. A light flashed in my face.

'Miss Anfield.'

I turned towards the other voice.

'What do you call those clothes? Are you from the wild west?'

'Eden!'

All around me, cameras flashed and questions bombarded me. I pushed through the crowd on to the street and turned right. The crowd swarmed around me.

'Where's Orion?'

'People are saying you are the twenty-second century Romeo and Juliet. Are you?'

'How do you like the future?'

I tried to block out their questions and the running commentary they were making as they followed me. Apparently my clothes were quirky, cool, radical, rare. The personal shopper at Whites had reported that I seemed to like blue. I had eaten breakfast at the Peacock Feather on my own. I was eighteen. I was seventeen. I had copper-coloured hair.

'Have you met the president?'

'Will you be testifying at the trial?'

'Is it true you're only sixteen?'

At the end of the T-junction I stopped and looked up and down the intersecting road.

'Do you know where you are?'

'Are you lost?'

'How would you like to be on the big screen?'

'Do you miss him?'

'Are you expecting his child?'

I said nothing, although I longed to shout at them to leave me alone. I did not want to hear my own voice broadcasting from one of those huge billboards. And then I recognised the Lakeview Hotel, up the hill, just a block away. I turned towards it, but the crowd had moved in front of me now, barring my way. I stepped to the side but I was still blocked. I turned around; the crowd had penned me in from all sides. Panic spiked. They had me trapped.

'Come now, don't be shy. How about a smile?'

The top of the Lakeview Hotel towered above the other buildings on the street, so close and yet so out of reach. I felt a flush of time lag weariness. I couldn't pass out here in the middle of the road. Just as I thought I was going to have to kick and punch my way out, the crowd melted away from me towards a black limousine that had pulled up to the kerb. I was about to make a dash for it when two burly men in charcoal uniforms appeared at my side.

'Miss Anfield,' said the older of the two. 'The admiral would like to escort you to your hotel.'

I clambered into the back of the limo. Admiral Westland was sitting on the back seat, his briefcase on his lap.

'I'm on my way to the office,' he said. 'But I noticed you were having a bit of trouble.'

The two uniformed men climbed back in and took their seats, one in the front of the car, one in the rear.

Westland grimaced. 'The Lakeview is usually very discreet; I don't understand how your identity has been revealed. Once the trial is over, I'm sure they'll leave you alone.'

The limo rolled smoothly into the stream of traffic.

'When can I see Ryan?'

'Most of his time is taken up with his lawyer. I'll let you know when you can see him.'

'How is he?'

Westland sighed heavily. 'He's OK. I've found an excellent lawyer. Very experienced. He'll want to interview you before the trial.'

'When will that be?'

'These cases are turned around pretty quickly. There are very few witnesses at a time trial, for obvious reasons. I imagine the trial will be in a week or ten days at most. In the meantime, you should start thinking about what you want to do, Eden. I know you've been given a resettlement package, but it won't last for ever. You'll need to find a job and a place to live. Get on with your life.'

'I can't get on with my life until I know what's happening with Ryan.'

'Listen to me. You need to prepare yourself for the possibility that the court will find him guilty.'

'They can't do that!'

He shook his head with an unhappy smile. 'Yes they can. He may have travelled through time for the right reasons, but the fact remains that his mission was not authorised. If the court finds my son guilty, he'll be facing a prison sentence.'

The limo drew to a stop by the Lakeview and one of the uniformed men got out and held the door for me.

'As soon as there's any news, I'll call you,' said Admiral Westland. 'In the meantime, you need to start building a life of your own.'

I couldn't build a life of my own; in the twenty-second century, Ryan was my life. My heart felt leaden. I was out of place and out of time.

CHAPTER 8

For the next three days the vans, reporters and photographers camped outside the Lakeview Hotel. At first, they called my room repeatedly, but then I told reception to block all my calls unless they were from Admiral Westland or the Institute. I stayed in my room, ordered room service and waited for the phone to ring. Admiral Westland had said he would let me know as soon as there was news. Surely he knew something by now? I couldn't stop thinking about Ryan. What did his lawyer think? What were his chances of being found innocent? Was he scared? Was he missing me? And what would happen if he was found guilty? What would become of me?

The only people I spoke to in all that time were the cleaner from housekeeping and the room service delivery person. I got a woman from housekeeping to show me how to turn on the TV – I had to scan my flexi-card in front of it to activate power and payment – and spent hours watching movies and the news. Ryan was the main story. Half the commentators, it seemed, felt Ryan would be found guilty; the other half believed he must have had a legitimate mission objective to travel back to 2012. It was clear that none of them had any real information. The only other news story? Me.

On the fourth day, the phone rang.

'Admiral?' I said.

The screen faded up from clear and a boy's face projected into my room. He looked about seventeen or eighteen, with skin the colour of wheat, and dark hair that gleamed like black coffee.

'No one's ever called me that before.' His eyes were brimming with amusement.

'I think you have the wrong number.'

'You're Eden, aren't you?'

'Are you a journalist?'

'Do I look like a journalist?'

'I have no idea. You all look like a bunch of hippies dressed for a beach party if you ask me.'

His eyes crinkled with amusement. 'I'm not completely sure what you're saying, but I think you just insulted me.'

I shrugged. 'How did you get through? I told them not to connect anyone unless they were from the Institute. What do you want?'

'Sorry about that. I'm calling from Admiral Westland's office. I'm a friend of Orion. I was wondering if you wanted to get the hell out of that hotel room you've been holed up in since you got here.'

'What makes you think I'm holed up in my hotel room?'

'There are about a hundred cameras and journos outside the front of the hotel, updating your status every half-hour. The doormen have confirmed that you're inside and haven't left the building in four days. So I'm guessing you could use a change of scenery.'

'How do I get out of the building without being seen?'

'Leave that to me. Can you call reception and ask them to let me up? I'll be there in ten minutes.'

'What was your name again?'

'Peg. Pegasus Ryder.'

A quick check in the mirror confirmed that I looked like I hadn't left my room in four days. I was unwashed, grey-skinned, still in my pyjamas. I had a quick shower, ran a comb through my tangled hair and pulled on one of my new out-fits, a long green dress with a high neck and no sleeves. The material was soft and light, perfect for the warm climate.

Right on cue, my phone rang and the face of the recep-tionist appeared on my screen. I stood in front of the screen and listened for the quiet click that confirmed my face had been scanned and the call connected.

'You have a visitor. A Mr Pegasus Ryder.'

'Send him up.'

I paced nervously, waiting for his knock on my door, wondering if he'd seen me on the receptionist's screen. I knew I shouldn't care, but I really didn't want Ryan's friend to form a poor first impression of me.

He thumped the door with what sounded like the side of his fist.

'Hi,' I said, opening the door.

He was tall and thin, dressed in a long sleeveless shirt and loose trousers, a smudge of black eyeliner under his eyes. One arm was completely covered in tattoos, the other completely bare.

'Come in,' I said.

'Nice dress,' he said.

I shrugged. 'I have no idea how to dress for this century.'

He had a satchel-shaped bag slung across his body. He took it off and pulled out a short blonde wig.

'It's my friend's,' he said. 'It'll help you get out of the hotel without being noticed.'

He helped me bunch my hair up into a hairnet and then pulled the tight blonde wig over the top. I looked in the mirror. I was transformed. Long green dress and short blonde bob was a million miles away from long red hair and jeans.

'You'll blend in for a few minutes at least,' he said. 'Long enough to get past those vultures at the door. You ready?'

I nodded, but my stomach tightened. I didn't want to be anywhere near that crowd of reporters. Peg linked an arm through mine and steered me towards the lift. His skin against mine felt strangely intimate. And yet he made me feel safe at the same time.

'Don't even look at them when we leave the building,' he said. 'Just stay close to me and act like we're a couple. They'll be looking for a girl on her own.'

We walked briskly, arm in arm, through the hotel lobby. As we approached the front entrance, Peg passed me a pair of sunglasses.

'Wear these,' he said quietly.

The glasses were large and wrapped around the top half of my face like ski goggles.

The doorman opened the door for us and we walked through, into the blinding summer sunshine. There was a flicker of interest from the journalists and photographers, but they soon turned away.

'My car is round the back,' said Peg.

The car was a small two-seater. He leant towards the retinal scanner built into the dashboard and said, 'Manual.'

'Where are we going?' I asked, as he pulled out into the traffic.

'Out of the city. Do you like mountains?'

'I don't know. But I don't really care where we go so long as there're no reporters there.'

'No reporters, I promise. Just a few hikers and – if we're lucky – the odd bear.'

'I don't think I care for that kind of luck.'

He drove quickly, frequently changing lanes to get past slower vehicles. I watched him out of the corner of my eye, curious about this strange boy who was Ryan's friend. The tattooed arm was the one closest to me, inked in every colour imaginable from his shoulder to his wrist, like a sleeve. There was a golden phoenix rising from the ashes on his wrist, a red dragon curling round his bicep, a mermaid rising from a wave over his shoulder. Every bit of space between the mythical creatures was filled with wild waves and raging flames. His face was all chiselled, sharp angles, and I'd probably have thought he was pretty cute if my heart wasn't already spoken for.

We left the downtown area behind, passed giant strip malls and supermarkets the size of aeroplane hangars. The roads were wider and straighter than at home, lined with both tall, leafy trees and massive electronic billboards.

When we approached the outskirts of the city, Peg slowed to a crawl. 'That's my high school,' he said, pointing at a low white building with tinted windows. 'It was Orion's too.'

I looked out of the window. The school was built from white stone; it sat amid neat green lawns and perfectly shaped maple trees. Lakeborough Space and Time Academy. A flag fluttered from the top of a pole – there were stars and stripes, but in the middle were two thick white circles: one with a red maple leaf and the other with a polar bear.

'It's not a regular school,' explained Peg. 'It's for Space and Time cadets.'

'So you want to work at the Institute?'

'My dream job would be as a pilot on the Inter-Planetary Spaceport. It's a long shot, though.'

'How come?'

'Very competitive. I'm on a good program, but I can't afford the best training.'

'How old are you?'

'Eighteen. I have three more years before I qualify.' He glanced at me. 'How old are you?'

'A hundred and twenty-seven.'

Peg smiled. 'So you won't be enrolling in the Academy then. Too bad. With all your experience, I bet you'd make a great time agent.'

'I don't really have much experience.'

'You've come face to face with a cleaner.'

'Two, actually.'

'And travelled more than a hundred years through time. You have more experience than all of the cadets in our class put together. More than some of the instructors.'

I laughed. 'Perhaps I'll apply for a teaching position then.'

A few minutes past the school, the road grew wider, the houses were bigger, each sitting in a beautifully landscaped garden.

'Ry's family live in a house down by Hidden Valley Pond,' Peg said, pointing towards my window.

'This looks like a wealthy neighbourhood.'

'His dad's an admiral.'

'What about you, Peg? Are you a rich kid as well?'

He smiled. 'Not exactly. My mother died when I was a baby and my dad's a miner. He's living out on Titan now with his new wife.'

'When you say Titan . . .'

'Moon of Saturn. The Titan colonies have been around for twenty-five years.'

'But Titan doesn't have an atmosphere?'

'There are domes on Titan. Huge domes, each one the size of a big city, with an artificial atmosphere.'

'Why would anyone want to live in a place like that?'

'Are you kidding? The chance to explore a new world? Imagine looking into the sky and there's Saturn.'

I thought then of the planet Eden, a living breathing world with pink cliffs and blue skies. A world with an atmosphere just like Earth's. Not a dead moon.

'And the money of course,' Peg continued. 'Miners on Titan make a fortune. Most do ten years, then come home, buy a big house and retire.'

I shook my head. 'I feel like I've ended up in a science fiction film. Are there any other planets or moons that have been colonised?'

'Only the moon.'

'That's so strange.'

'They say when you jump to the future the adjustment takes longer than travel to the past. They also say finding places that remind you of your own time helps. I hope you'll like this place in the mountains. I doubt it's changed one bit in the last hundred years. But to answer your question: I'm not rich. I have a full scholarship to Lakeborough Academy to pay for my tuition and flight time.'

We passed a sign that read *Charge, Food, Lodging* and Peg took the exit road.

'We'll need water,' he said.

He pulled into what looked like a petrol station, though the drivers appeared to be plugging their cars into some sort of silver battery charger rather than filling their tanks. Peg ran into the shop to buy a couple of bottles of water and then we were back on the highway again.

The road began to climb. I touched a button to wind down my window. The sharp scent of pine poured into the car.

'What do your parents do, Eden?'

'They're dead.'

He tore his eyes from the road and gave me an apologetic

look. 'Of course they are. Everyone you know is dead. Except Ryan.'

'They died when I was six. A long time ago. My mother's younger sister Miranda brought me up. She's a legal secretary. I guess I should say she *was*.'

It was the first time I'd thought about Miranda since leaving my own time. My throat closed up. I forced myself to swallow.

'It must be hard,' he said quietly, 'leaving everyone behind.'

'Ryan's dad told me to start building a new life, but it's not easy when you don't know anybody and things are so different it takes you two days to work out how to turn on the TV.'

'What's a tee vee?'

I sighed to myself. 'Technology has changed so much you don't even know what I'm talking about. It's a screen that you watch films on. It doesn't matter.'

The road wound higher and higher until we were up in the mountains, encircled by them, and the horizon was lost behind thick green trees and low cloud. There were no mountains where I came from, just miles of coastline and broad horizons where sky and sea met in a blur of blue. If Cornwall was blues and greys, this place was greens. Peg pulled off the main road and drove along a bumpy track. I breathed in the smell of fresh, living wood.

'This is it,' said Peg, parking the car on a dusty verge.

Outside the car, the sun poured down its thick, sticky heat.

'The trees will shade us,' he said, throwing me a bottle of water. He stuck his own bottle into his belt.

We walked to a poorly marked trail that snaked its way up the side of the mountain, hairpin bend to hairpin bend, each turn offering a view out over endless forested hills. Despite the shade from the leaves, I was hot and clammy and I emptied my water bottle in no time. Just when I was about to suggest we head back to the car, I heard a noise. A roar, like a busy road.

'Nearly there,' he said.

I didn't realise we had a destination.

We followed the trail around a corner of white rock and there it was. A wide, shallow pool with a raging, white waterfall cascading into it. I looked up. Above was another pool with a larger waterfall. The water thundered and rushed.

'The falls are bigger in the spring,' said Peg. 'But the water is warmer at this time of year.'

I pulled my sandals off and waded in. The water was colder than anything I'd ever felt. For a moment it took my breath away.

'Good, huh?' he said, oblivious to my complete and total body shock.

He was up to his thighs. His trousers had been discarded on the rocks, and he was wearing just his swimming shorts and a vest top. There was no way I was stripping down to my underwear. My dress was long, but light and loose. I was pretty sure I could swim in it. As I shuffled deeper into the water, he dived under the mossy green surface of the pool, emerging several metres away, under the spray.

'Come on!' he yelled at me. 'It doesn't get much better than this.'

His smile was so big and enthusiastic that, although my toes felt like they were going to turn to ice and fall off, I waded deeper, trying to ignore the ache in my flesh, the jolt of pain in my heart, the tightness in my lungs. And then, before I could talk myself out of it, I dived under the smooth green surface myself. The water was different to the scratchy salt water I was used to. This water was like silk; it was oily and slippery and coated my skin. When I surfaced, I gasped for warm air. Peg was treading water beneath the spray. I swam to him and when I was under the falls I leant back and opened my mouth a crack, feeling the icy water splatter on my tongue. This was the best feeling I'd had since arriving in the twenty-second century.

'You want to climb up to the upper pool?' Peg called out.

'Yes!' I yelled above the roar of the falls.

He pushed himself on to the rocks at the base of the falls and I followed. The rocks here were wet and slippery and I crunched my toes up tight to give myself traction. I followed Peg to the side of the waterfall and he pointed out the way up the rocks. It was only about fifteen metres, but I'd always been scared of heights.

'It's easy,' he told me. 'Much easier than it looks. Just follow my moves.'

He began the climb. I followed close behind, careful to match my handholds and footholds to his, making sure I never looked down. Every time a wave of nausea threatened to overcome me, I reminded myself that Ryan was locked up and facing trial. What I was doing was nothing compared with what he was facing.

When I finally hauled myself over the ledge and on to the sunny, rocky plateau by the upper pool, I was glad I'd made the effort. The waterfall here was even higher than the one below and tiny sequins of golden mist sprayed the air. Peg gestured to a flat, rocky area to the side of the falls. I joined him.

'What do you think?' he asked.

'It's gorgeous,' I said.

He smiled to himself and pulled his wet vest top over his head, laying it out on a sunny rock to dry. I was still in my green dress. Underneath I was wearing nothing but my underwear.

'You should take off your dress,' he said as if reading my mind.

'I only have underwear underneath.'

He shrugged. 'I only have these shorts.'

'That's different.'

But I knew he was right. Although the sun was powerful, the heavy wet material clung to my skin, chilling me to my bones. I peeled off the dress and laid it out on the hot rocks. Peg was lying near the top of the waterfall, his eyes shut. Feeling exposed in my matching blue bra and knickers, I lay on a flat rock nearby and shut my eyes.

'So what's a "tee vee"?' he asked after a while.

'Television,' I said. 'You watch movies and documentaries and the news on it.'

'So it's a com-screen?'

'What's a com-screen?'

'You know the big screen on the wall in your room? That's a com-screen. You can use it to call people and find out information about anything and watch movies.'

'Right. So it's a TV and a phone and the internet all-in-one.'

'If you say so.'

'The twenty-second century isn't so different from the twenty-first century. Just enough to make me feel stupid.'

'I'll be your guide to the twenty-second century. Any questions, just ask.'

'I have a million questions.'

'Shoot.'

'So is America still the most powerful nation in the world? Or let me guess – is it China?'

'America is still the most powerful country in the world. However, not the America you're thinking of.'

I waited for him to continue.

'The United States of America no longer exists. Most of what was once the United States, together with Canada and Alaska all now comprise the Federation of North America.'

'Really? Canada and America together?'

'Around the middle of the last century, climate change really hit America. A lot of farmland became too dry to farm. At the same time, Canada became much more suitable for farming. And then when the Arctic ice melted, everyone wanted to claim territory in the Arctic Ocean. By joining forces with Canada, America was able to do that, as well as putting in a claim for Greenland.'

'What happened to China?' I asked.

'China was the most powerful nation until about 2048. But climate change forced them to focus on feeding their population.'

'Anything else I should know?'

'Depends what interests you. Politics? Economics? The law?'

'Tell me about the Guardians of Time. I know a little, but not much.'

'There are five of them. In many ways, they have more power than the president, parliament and the supreme court together. They approve missions to the past and future and try all cases that come to the Time Court. Every two years one of the Guardians is elected president of the Space and Time Institute. The president sets the agenda for the next two years. Right now is election time. If Admiral Wolfe wins the presidency, there will be no time travel. He's dead set against it. If Westland wins, time travel will still be allowed.'

'And they're the people who will decide what happens to Ryan?'

'One of them will judge his case.'

'Which one?'

'I think they all get their quota of cases to try. Obviously Admiral Westland won't be allowed to judge the case because it concerns his son.'

I let that information sink in. It was a long way from my world. 'How long have you and Ryan known each other?' I asked, after a while.

'Since we were twelve. Middle school. We had the same art class. He did portraits. I did mythical creatures.' He held his arm out to me. 'These are all mine.'

I resisted the urge to reach out and run my fingers over his tattoos. 'They're good.'

'We both loved drawing but we loved flying even more. We applied to Lakeborough Academy at the same time.'

'Did he always want to be a pilot?'

'He wanted to be a time agent. Just like his dad. It's why he volunteered for the mission to your time.'

'What about you? What do you want?'

'I want adventure. Look at Orion. He's travelled back to 2012 twice over. He's helped save the planet from some unknown catastrophe. I know he's locked up right now, but soon he'll be free again. And you. You've saved the Earth and travelled forward in time. You've both lived. I want to live like that. I don't want to follow my dad into some dull nine-to-five job and worry about meeting my mortgage payments every month.' He sat up. 'Speaking of adventure, how do you feel about doing something adventurous right now?'

I laughed a short, nervous laugh. 'I'm not brave at all.'

'It only lasts about two seconds, it will get your adrenalin pumping and it's completely safe. I promise.'

I sat up. The sun was harsh. Already my underwear was bone dry. I pulled off my blonde wig and shook out my hair. 'What is it?'

'We jump from the top of the waterfall into the pool below.'

Of all the things Peg could have suggested, he'd managed to pick my biggest fear.

'I nearly drowned. Twice.'

Did he know that? Had Ryan told him?

'I promise you won't get hurt. It's much easier than climbing back down over the rocks.'

I didn't want to be afraid. I wanted so much to be brave and strong and good at things. I had jumped through time. Jumping from a waterfall should be so much easier.

Peg took my dress and wig and dropped them on to the dry rocks below. He held out a hand. 'If you want, we can jump together.'

I shook my head. 'No.'

He drew his hand back. 'Not a big deal. We can climb down.'

'No, I meant I don't want to hold your hand. I'll do this myself.'

He cocked his head to the side. 'Are you sure?'

'Are you sure it's deep enough?'

'It's over thirty metres deep.'

Swallowing the terror that was making its way up my throat, I inched my way to the edge of the waterfall.

'You first,' said Peg. 'I don't want to jump and then have to climb back up and get you.'

I didn't look down. I knew that if I did, the dizziness would paralyse me. I shut my eyes and counted backwards.

Three.

Images of the rocks by the harbour wall flashed through my mind.

Two.

Of Travis swimming after me and pushing me under. I didn't want to do this. I didn't want to die.

One.

I jumped. I fell through the air, my arms both shooting up above me, reaching for the sky. Someone shrieked and I realised it was me. And then, abruptly, a bitter coldness exploded over my skin from my toes to my scalp. I kicked my legs, swam towards the bright sunshine and gasped the warm air.

Peg whooped as he jumped, tumbling forwards, his hands hitting the water first in a graceful dive.

When he re-emerged, he shook his head like a dog. 'What do you think?' he shouted.

'It was good,' I said.

A complete understatement. My body was trembling from the buzz of it. The sick thrill of stepping off the edge, the rush of free-falling, the stream of adrenalin gushing through my veins. I'd never felt so energised, so scared and exhilarated at the same time. But most of all: I'd never felt so brave.

'That was impressive,' said Peg. He'd reached the edge of the pool and was clambering out. 'I've been here many times but I've never known anyone take their first jump so quickly.'

I shrugged and tried not to smile. 'If I'd thought about it, I'd never have done it,' I said, bending down to pick up my clothes. 'Come on.'

I led the way back down the mountain path in my

underwear, letting the warm air and dappled sunlight dry my skin.

The journalists outside the Lakeview Hotel were showing no signs of giving up and going home.

'You are the only news story right now,' said Peg quietly as he pulled into a parking space on the opposite side of the street. 'You and Ryan.'

'Can you help me with the wig?' I asked.

I bundled my hair into a bun and held it in place while Peg pulled the wig over it.

'Almost perfect,' he said, as he moved a wayward strand of wig hair into place.

'Thanks for rescuing me today,' I said. 'I think I'd have gone mad if I'd stayed in my room any longer.'

He passed me the sunglasses. 'You'll need these.'

I slipped the glasses on to my face and checked out my reflection in the rear-view mirror. I looked so unlike myself. 'Thank your friend for the wig. When will she need it back?'

'There's no rush. Belle has loads of wigs.' He hesitated, as though reaching a decision about something. 'I'm going out with a few friends tomorrow tonight. It would be great if you'd come along. Everyone would love to meet you.'

'Thanks. What should I wear?'

'It's just a bar. Wear anything you like. There's no dress code.'

'I don't know what casual looks like in the twenty-second century.'

'This dress is perfect. Anything like this would be fine.'

He told me he would pick me up at eight, from my room. I heard him start his car as I crossed the road, but he didn't pull away until I had thrust my way through the reporters and into the lobby.

CHAPTER 9

It was while I was flicking through my new wardrobe of clothes, looking for something suitable to wear to the pub, that I found Miranda. The com-screen was on, tuned into a lightweight political chat show.

'Admiral Wolfe believes that Admiral Westland knew that his youngest son planned to return to 2012,' one of the commentators was saying.

'If this was true, what does it mean for the Board of Guardians?'

'If Westland has helped his son break the Temporal Laws, he will be stripped of his title and put on trial for conspiracy. That would lead to an immediate election and almost guarantee that Admiral Wolfe will win the presidency.'

'What can we expect from Wolfe if he's elected president of the Board?'

'For starters, time missions to the past will come to an end. Wolfe has made no secret of the fact that he doesn't think there is ever a good enough reason to approve a time mission to the past.'

'That's bad news for Westland Travel.'

'Absolutely. Admiral Westland's fortune comes from building ships capable of travelling through four dimensions.

If time travel is eradicated, there will be no demand for his ships.'

'Is there any chance that Westland and his son are innocent?'

'Of course. Westland claims his son only broke the Temporal Laws in order to save the life of a girl who had helped the mission and been unjustly eliminated by the mission cleaner.'

'What sort of sentence is Orion facing if he's found guilty?'

'That will come down to the judge. Sentencing guidelines are very broad – he could be punished with as little as a six-month curfew program, or he could be looking at some serious time on the far side of the moon.'

I touched a button to turn off the TV show and accidentally brought up a search engine. There was still almost an hour until Pegasus was due, so I decided to look up Miranda. I'd avoided it – pushing all thoughts of her into the deep, dark corners of my mind – because our separation was still so fresh. Less than a week had passed since I left my own time. But from where I was now, she had lived her life and died.

I had no idea if Facebook still existed, but Ryan had said we all leave a digital footprint – it was how he'd found out what happened to me – so I decided to give it a go. I wasted almost twenty minutes looking for somewhere to type her name. Just before I was about to give up, I stumbled across the voice commands.

'Search for Miranda Honeychurch,' I said, then squeezed

my eyes closed and made a silent wish that she'd had a good life. I didn't think I could bear to discover that my sudden departure had ruined things.

There were thousands of results. But the result second from the top of the fourth screen was her. Her photograph was just as I remembered her from 2012, with an icon that said *Complete Profile*. I touched the icon.

A three-dimensional hologram of Miranda leapt out of the com-screen. It was life-sized. She was dressed in a red dress I recognised. She had bought it just a few months before I left the twenty-first century. Tears sprang to my eyes as I looked at her smiling face.

There were four folders on the screen: biography, photographs, blog and messages. I touched biography.

The hologram shrank back into the screen and a fresh page opened on-screen. It was brief.

Miranda Williams (née Honeychurch) was born in 1980, the younger of two daughters, to Ben Honeychurch, a teacher and Mary Honeychurch, a shop assistant. A bright child, she excelled in school and went on to study Law at Exeter University. Her legal career was brought to an abrupt halt, however, when her elder sister Beatrice died tragically in an automobile accident orphaning Miranda's niece, Eden. Miranda raised Eden for ten years. Tragedy struck again when, at sixteen, Eden disappeared without a trace. Miranda completed her legal studies as a mature student and went on to become a partner at Williams and Penhallow, where she married Thomas Williams, a senior partner. They were married in 2016 and had two children, Travis (b. 2017) and Eden (b. 2019). Miranda died from pneumonia following a hip operation in 2075, aged ninety-five.

Author: Eden Williams 2075

I made a quick calculation. Eden Williams had been fifty-six when her mother died at the ripe old age of ninety-five. She might even be alive herself. I made another calculation. She would be a hundred and four. Not likely then. But the knowledge that Miranda had had a career and a husband and two children made my heart sing.

I scrolled through the photographs, poring over pictures of her as an old lady, family photos with Thomas and her children. In later shots she was surrounded by little children again, grandchildren presumably. I must have relatives somewhere. I wondered if any of them had worked out that I was related to them. After the trial, I would look them up. Settle into the twenty-second century, as Westland had suggested.

I skipped over the blog and touched the folder that said messages. The page opened to a list of subfolders, each with a name: Eden, Travis, and other names I didn't recognise. I was about to close the page when one of the folders caught my eye. *Eden Anfield*. My heart thumping against my ribs, I touched the screen. A window popped open.

Password required. Clue: the name of our feline visitor.

'Katkin,' I said to the screen.

The folder opened, revealing a short message.

Dear Eden,

Many years have passed since the day I came home and found you gone. Not a day goes by without me thinking of you. But I believe I know what happened to you and I hope that I'm right. They told me you had drowned in the sea off Perran Towans. I never believed it. In my heart I knew you were still alive somewhere. For many years this was nothing more than a belief. But when Nathaniel Westland invented a way to travel through time, I worked it out. Westland was the name of the boy you were with. He was from the future. You followed him home. It's the only thing that makes sense.

I've had a rich and full life. Although I lost you and Travis, my life has been blessed with a loving husband, two delightful children and five grandchildren.

Ever since Nathaniel Westland invented time travel, I've hoped and prayed I will see you again. Now I am sick and I know I don't have very long left. It is my greatest hope that one day you will find this message and visit me or my children or grandchildren.

Whatever happens, I hope it's been worth it for you.

With love, for ever,

Miranda x

Tears were streaming down my cheeks. I wished so much that I could travel back and wrap my arms around her. I wanted to tell her everything. To say goodbye properly.

The screen went blank and then the face of the hotel receptionist blinked on my screen. Incoming call. I wiped my face on the back of my sleeve and pressed *accept call*.

'You have a visitor, Miss Anfield,' said the receptionist. 'Mr Pegasus Ryder.'

'Let him up please.'

I had become so immersed in reading that I had completely lost track of the time. I grabbed a blue dress out of the wardrobe and quickly shimmied into it. There was just time to apply a flick of eyeliner before he knocked.

'Nice dress,' he said, as I opened the door.

'You too,' I said, pointing at his sarong. 'Is that what guys wear in the twenty-second century?'

'It's not a dress,' he said, smiling uncertainly. 'It's pretty standard for a night out drinking.'

'Did Ryan dress like that?'

Peg nodded. 'Is there something wrong with what I'm wearing?'

'No. It's just not what I'm used to.'

He cocked his head to one side. 'Are you OK? You look kind of . . . upset?'

I wiped away a tear. I would not allow myself to cry in front of Peg.

'Hey, what's the matter?' he asked.

I scanned on the com-screen and pulled up Miranda's profile. He skimmed through her entries.

'Who is she?'

'My aunt. The woman who brought me up after my parents died.'

'I don't understand,' he said. 'She had a good life. She

figured out where you went. That reads like a pretty good ending to me.'

'It's a long time ago from where you're standing. But it's just days for me.'

Peg nodded silently. 'I can't really imagine what it's like to go through what you're going through.'

'I'm just so lonely,' I said, sitting on the edge of the bed. 'Everyone I know is dead. Or locked up.'

'I know it's not much, but you know me. I'm not dead. Or locked up. Not yet, anyway.'

I looked at him and tried to smile.

'And tonight you're gonna meet a few of Ry's closest friends.'

He helped me with the wig and once again we left the hotel incognito. We drove downtown to a car park close to the water. Although it was early evening, the air was still hot and stuffy.

As we walked across the car park, Peg put an arm around my shoulder. It was a friendly, non-threatening gesture, but I felt my body stiffen. 'Let me pay for everything tonight,' he said. 'If you use your flexi-card, everyone will know who you are.'

The car park opened on to a narrow alleyway with bags of rubbish piled up beside overflowing bins, and posters stapled to telegraph poles and doorways.

'Short cut,' said Peg. 'It will save us five minutes.'

We stopped for a moment by a machine at the end of the alley, so that Peg could top up the credits on his port-com. He slid the port-com into the machine and tapped a code on to the screen. Although the alley was deserted, it was just the sort of place I always avoided, the sort of place you were warned about as a child.

'Is Lakeborough a safe city?' I asked.

'It's one of the wealthiest cities in the Federation,' he said. 'Crime is low. But like any city, there are parts best avoided.'

The credit machine beeped and pushed the port-com back out through its mouth.

'Let's go,' said Peg, thrusting the port-com into his pocket.

With every step that brought me closer to the door of the inn, my heart squeezed harder. I was going to meet Ryan's friends. I knew nothing about them. Apart from Peg, he'd never told me anything about them. They would all be older than me. What if they didn't like me? What if one of them was Ryan's ex, the girl he'd dated before me?

'Hey, Albert,' said Peg to the bouncer at the door.

The bouncer nodded at him.

'They'll all be out the back,' said Peg.

Once inside, Peg dropped my arm. In single file we squeezed through the crowded bar. Music – an eerie, hypnotic combination of heavy drums and violins – blared from two huge speakers over by a raised stage. At the back of the bar was a sliding glass door that opened on to a large deck that extended over the lake. All sorts of boats, from small sailing boats to large ferries, floated across the water. Peg looked around, spotting his friends at a table right by the water's edge.

'Hey, everyone,' he said when we reached the table. 'This is Eden.'

There were three of them: two girls and a boy. The boy and one of the girls were pale-skinned and strawberry blonde. They were obviously brother and sister; later, I found out they were twins. The other girl was olive-skinned with long dark hair. All three of them stared up at me. And then the boy, who had a long thin cigar hanging out of his mouth, stood up to shake my hand.

'Antoine,' he said. 'Delighted to meet you.'

The fair girl stood then and held a pale hand out for me to shake. 'Isabelle,' she said. 'My friends call me Belle.'

The other girl was stunning. She had high, pronounced cheekbones and large, green eyes that reminded me of a cat.

'Hello, Eden,' she said, remaining seated. 'I'm Lyra.'

'It's a pleasure to meet you all,' I said stiffly. 'Thanks for letting me join you tonight.'

'You can all stop staring at her now,' said Peg.

He pulled out a chair for me and took the one right next to it.

'Is beer OK?' asked Antoine. 'I ordered a bucket of them. Dad said that was the popular drink back in your day?'

'Beer is great,' I said.

Antoine passed me a bottle from a bucket in the centre of the table. I gulped it quickly, glad for something cold. When I looked up, they were all still staring at me.

'I thought you had red hair,' said Lyra.

Automatically, I reached up and touched the soft fake hair on my head. 'It's a wig,' I said.

'We had to disguise her to get away from all those journos outside her hotel,' Peg explained.

'How's Orion?' asked Antoine. 'I can't believe he didn't get bail.'

'I don't really know how he is,' I said. 'I haven't been able to see him since we landed.'

'Have they set a date for the trial?' he asked.

'According to his father, it should be in the next few days.'

There was a pause.

'How did he get caught?' asked Lyra. 'When he said goodbye, he seemed pretty confident he knew how to cover his tracks.'

'I'm not sure how the cleaner found us,' I said, reddening.

'Are the stories true then?' Lyra asked, arching her eyebrows. 'Are you and Ry a modern day Romeo and Juliet?'

'Stop interrogating the girl,' said Antoine, nudging Lyra.

'It's so romantic,' said Belle. 'The two of you travelling through time to be together.'

'Perhaps,' said Lyra, with a half smile.

'So what's life like back in the twenty-first century?' Antoine asked, a little too loudly. 'What do people do on a Saturday night? Do they sit around the pianoforte and sing songs?'

I laughed. 'They go out drinking and dancing and to parties. Saturday night where I'm from looks a lot like this.'

'Really?' said Antoine. 'I thought you all wore corsets and had chaperones.'

Belle smacked Antoine's arm playfully. 'That's the nineteenth century, dumbbell.'

'I'm disappointed. I imagined that people from your time were different from us.'

For a second I considered telling them about Connor and me playing endless games of chess and Scrabble, but the thought made me so nostalgic that I decided against it.

'What do you think of Lakeborough?' asked Antoine.

'It seems cool. I haven't seen much yet. Although it was beautiful up in the mountains yesterday.'

'Which mountains?' asked Lyra.

I shrugged. 'I don't know what they're called. Peg took me there.'

'I took her to Twin Falls,' said Peg.

'Really, Pegasus?' said Lyra. 'You took Orion's girlfriend to Twin Falls.'

Peg drained his beer and slammed the bottle on the table. 'Yes. I wanted to take her out of the city, away from the reporters. And Twin Falls is one of Orion's favourite places.'

'Sure,' said Lyra with a smirk. 'That's why you took her there.'

'I love the way you always assume the basest motives in everyone,' said Peg. He stood up abruptly, tipping his chair back towards the floor. He pushed it up with the toe of his shoe. 'Looks like we're getting low on drinks. Beers again?'

He didn't wait for an answer.

'I'll give him a hand,' said Belle, standing up. 'I'm not letting him pay for beer.'

A shadow fell across my face as someone approached the table from behind me. He leant over and plucked the last bottle of beer from the bucket.

'Beer, huh? So, what's the occasion?'

I turned and saw a tall boy with light blonde hair. He untwisted the top with his hand, tilted his head back and poured half the bottle into his mouth.

'Hey, Clarence,' said Antoine.

Clarence nodded at Antoine. 'You gonna dance with me tonight, Lyra?'

'I don't dance any more.'

'I would hold you.' He turned to me. 'I don't believe we've met.' He passed the beer to his left hand and held out his right hand to shake.

I accepted. He shook my hand vigorously and then sat in Peg's chair. He leant close. 'Clarence Wolfe. And you are?'

I hesitated. Was he a friend? He seemed to know the others, though Lyra hadn't been especially warm to him. 'Eden Anfield.'

He smiled. 'Do I detect an accent?'

'British.'

'Are you vacationing in Lakeborough?'

'Something like that.'

His eyes lit up. 'You're *that* Eden. I didn't recognise you. Your hair is different.'

'It's a wig,' said Lyra in a bored voice. 'Now you've had a look at her, why don't you go bother someone else?'

Clarence stood up. 'Come on, Eden, it's time for you to learn how to dance twenty-second century style.'

'I don't think so,' I said. Back home I liked dancing, but the way people here were dancing was very different. 'It looks complicated.'

'I'm a great teacher.' He stood up and held out a hand to me. 'What do you say? Just one dance?'

Lyra rolled her eyes and Antoine looked away. Unsure whether I was about to commit a major faux pas or whether it would be rude to say no, I stood up and let Clarence lead me to the dance floor.

'Are you friends with them?' I asked.

'I'm in the same class as your friend, Antoine. Orion too before he left.'

'And Lyra?'

'We used to date. I think she still has a thing for me.'

'I kind of got the opposite impression. Anything else I should know?'

We were on the edge of the dance floor. I could feel the music vibrating through the wooden floor.

Clarence placed a hand on each of my shoulders. 'You are about to dance with the most eligible bachelor in the room.'

'Oh, really?' I said, raising my eyebrows.

'Really,' he said. 'Not only am I handsome and rich, but I'm also a fantastic dancer.'

'You're modest as well, huh?'

'I've never seen the point of false modesty.'

'Is that everything?'

'Don't believe everything you hear.'

Clarence pulled me towards him and then placed one of his hands around my waist. 'Just copy my moves,' he said. 'It's easy.'

I tried to find the rhythm of the music, but the beat was

odd. I looked around me at the other dancers, but everyone was wrapped up in their own moves; no one took any notice of me. Thank God for the wig.

'How am I doing?' I asked.

'Not bad for a beginner.'

I followed Antoine's lead and, for a few minutes, I forgot about Ryan and the reporters and being in the wrong time. I forgot about everything but the heat and the rhythm and the deep thrum of the bass that made the dance floor gently vibrate.

After three songs, I could feel my scalp sweating and itching under my wig.

'I think I'm ready for another beer,' I said. 'Or a glass of water.'

Clarence escorted me back to the table. The others were chatting and laughing and all of the tension from earlier had gone. I took a cold, sweating beer bottle from the bucket and held it to my forehead.

'How about it, Lyra?' asked Clarence. 'Will you dance with me?'

Lyra narrowed her eyes. 'I don't think so.'

No one spoke for a second. Lyra and Clarence just held each other's gaze, and I was reminded that these people had a shared history that I was not a part of.

'Well,' said Clarence after a few seconds. 'It's been a pleasure to meet you, Eden.' He shook my hand again and left.

Antoine took a long, slender case from his jacket pocket and opened it. Inside were several more of the thin cigars he'd been smoking when we arrived. He offered them around the table. Lyra took one and leant in close to Antoine as he flicked open his lighter and held the flame to the tip. I watched, wondering if they were together.

'You gonna dance with me now?' Peg asked.

I leant close and whispered in his ear. 'I just danced with Lakeborough's most eligible bachelor. That's a hard act to follow.'

'I think I'll cope,' said Peg, taking my hand.

We walked on to the dance floor just as the music changed to a slow number. Peg held my waist and shoulder loosely, not too close, and we swayed gently to the music.

'Clarence isn't wrong when he describes himself as Lakeborough's most eligible bachelor,' said Peg. 'There are a lot of girls in this room who'd like to dance with him tonight.'

'But not Lyra?'

'Clarence and Lyra have a complicated relationship.'

'Are you going to elaborate on that?'

Peg shook his head. 'Not tonight.'

'What about you?' I said. 'Are you single?'

'Between work and school, I don't have time for a relationship.'

'Got your eye on anyone?'

He laughed, but there was something about his look that suggested I'd embarrassed him. 'No one.'

We left the bar just after midnight. As we shoved our way through the throngs, Lyra held on tight to Peg and he put his arm around her. It wasn't until we were outside and we were able to walk more easily that I noticed Lyra had a pronounced limp.

'The night is young,' said Antoine. 'And there's a party boat just about to sail. How about it?'

'You guys go,' I said. 'I'm pretty tired. I'm going to head home.'

'I'm beat too. I'll walk you,' said Peg.

'How chivalrous of you,' said Lyra. Her wide smile didn't reach her eyes.

'I'll see you tomorrow, Lyra,' said Peg.

She kissed his cheek, but her eyes were on me. 'Behave yourself.'

'Hey, Eden,' said Belle. 'Are you coming to New York with us on Sunday?'

I shook my head; it was the first I'd heard about a trip to New York.

'Come. It'll be fun.'

'I should probably stay in the hotel in case there's any news about the trial.'

'Nothing will happen over the weekend,' said Belle. 'And Monday is a public holiday. Come to New York with us.'

'I don't know.'

'I'll talk her into it,' said Peg.

'If we don't get a move on, that ship is going to sail without us,' said Antoine. 'See you both tomorrow.'

Peg put an arm around my shoulders and we turned away from the others. The next thing I knew I was blinded by a bright light. And then we were surrounded. Lights flashed in my face and reporters thrust microphones under my chin. I turned back to see if Antoine and the others could see what was going on, but my view was blocked by yet more photographers, their oversize cameras blocking my view.

'Lovely wig, baby,' said one of the reporters. 'Where did you buy it?'

'Who's your escort?' asked another.

'Can you give us a smile?'

'Have you seen Orion?'

'Are you enjoying the twenty-second century?'

'Will you be testifying at Orion's trial?'

'Is it true that you're pregnant?'

I froze to the spot. We were surrounded.

'No comment,' said Peg.

'Who are you? Her bodyguard?' jeered one of the younger male reporters.

'This is not the time or place for an interview,' said Peg calmly. 'We'd both appreciate it if you'd let us go home.'

'Where is home?' asked a female reporter.

'Are you staying with her at the Lakeview Hotel?'

'Excuse me,' said Peg to the male reporter in front of us.

We stepped forward, but the man didn't step aside. I was beginning to panic. Cameras continued to flash in my face. Fear began to coil around me.

'Would you mind stepping aside to let us pass?' said Peg.

'Just answer a couple of questions,' said the man. He pushed his microphone in front of Peg's face.

Peg swiped at the microphone, sending it spinning to one side.

'Hey!' shouted the reporter.

Peg swung for him. One second the man was hurling abuse at Peg, the next he was lying on the ground, sprawled across his microphone.

'Let's go!' said Peg. He grabbed my hand and we ran.

I glanced back. Some of them were running after us.

'Don't look back!' yelled Peg.

We raced around the corner and along another street. Peg had a tight hold of my hand and was dragging me behind him. He turned abruptly up a narrow alley. The alley divided into two. We took the left lane and slowed to a walk. There were takeaways and bars, tattoo parlours, girls heavily made-up and lounging against door frames. Peg walked up to one of the girls, a heavily tattooed girl in a black corset and not much else.

'Hey, Millie. Is there a game on?'

She nodded. 'Who's your friend, Peg?'

'She's my cousin.'

'Course she is.'

Peg and I slipped through the doorway and into a small, dark room at the back of the house. There were five round tables, six people crowded around each, all playing cards. A makeshift bar was set up against one wall.

The girl behind the bar, who, like the one out front, was wearing little more than her tattoos, winked at Peg. 'Your usual?'

'Yeah. And a beer for my cousin, Jennie.'

'Hi, cousin Jennie,' said the girl, pushing a bottle of beer across the bar to me. She turned back to Peg. 'You joining a table? We have stud, Texas Hold 'Em and blackjack.'

'Not tonight. Jennie and I just fancied a nightcap before heading home.'

'Suit yourself.'

I followed Peg through a door and into another dimly lit room, this one with couches and candles spread around. The room was empty apart from a couple sitting on a couch in the darkest corner of the room, their hands on each other's bodies. Peg chose a couch as far from the other couple as possible and sat down.

'So, do you come here often?' I asked as I sat next to him.

He smirked. 'Are you trying to pick me up? Because, you should know, that line's really old.'

I shoved him with my elbow. 'Thanks for the tip.'

Peg took a sip of his beer. 'I thought this would be a good place to hide for a while until those parasites outside get bored and go home.'

'I'm glad you brought me here. I want to see the real twenty-second century, not just the tourist spots.' I looked around and caught the eye of the girl on the other couch. She smiled at me.

'You wanna join us?' she asked.

I shook my head and looked away quickly. 'Did – does – Ryan ever come here?'

'Sure. He's been here a few times.'

My chest constricted. There was so much about Ryan's life in the twenty-second century I didn't know.

Peg looked at me. 'We didn't come here for the girls. We came for the cards.'

'Oh.'

'You didn't think . . . ?'

'I didn't know what to think.'

'Great.' Peg laughed to himself. 'I've clearly made a good impression so far.'

I tried to shrug off my embarrassment. 'I thought things might be different now. In this time.'

'We only ever came here to play cards. We needed money to buy parts for the ship Ryan used to get back to you, and playing poker against a table of drunk old men was a good way to do it.' Peg turned to face me, and held his bottle up in the air. 'Cheers. Here's to evading those scumbags.'

I clinked my bottle against his. 'How do you think they worked out it was me?'

Peg shrugged. 'Dunno. I hoped the wig would be enough. But your face has been all over the com-screens for the last week, so I suppose we shouldn't have been surprised.'

'What's the story with Lyra? She didn't seem to like me very much.'

'Lyra was born sarcastic and she's been ten times worse since she injured her leg.'

'What happened?'

'She was in a car accident. Her leg got crushed.'

'Clarence said he used to date her. Do you think it both-ered her that I danced with him?'

Peg took a long swig from his bottle. 'They went on a couple of dates. That's all. The only thing that bothers Lyra is not being the centre of attention. And right now, you're the centre of attention.'

'I don't want to be. I wish everyone would leave me alone. Maybe I should just hold a press conference and be done with it.'

'Maybe you should.'

'I'm just scared I'll say the wrong thing and make things worse for Ryan.' I sighed. 'What if the court finds him guilty? I don't know what I'll do if that happens.'

Peg put his hand on my arm. 'Let's hope that doesn't happen. But we'll cross that bridge when we come to it.'

I liked the way he said *we*. I had finally found a friend – an ally – in this new world.

'Do you think the trial will be fair?'

'I guess. Ryan's father – Admiral Westland – is one of the best people I know, but he won't be allowed to judge the case. Admiral Shastri and Admiral Hwa are generally in favour of space-time exploration. If either of them is the judge, I think he'll get a fair trial. Admiral Philp is a wild card. And Admiral Wolfe opposes most space-time exploration. He is likely to be the harshest judge of Orion.'

'Let's hope Ryan doesn't get Wolfe then,' I said.

'The thing is, Eden, I think Admiral Wolfe is behind Orion's capture. I think it's personal.'

I looked at him. 'What do you mean?'

'It's no secret that Westland and Wolfe hate each other. Wolfe has these mining colonies on the moon. He uses prisoners to work in the mines. Westland wants to put a stop to that, claims it is cruel and unusual punishment.'

'What's that got to do with Ryan?'

'Not sure. But if anyone was in a position to travel back through time without being detected, it was Orion. The ship he took had been marked for scrap. I work in the ship-yard, so I altered the records to make it look like it had been sold for parts. He calculated his portal so that the energy signatures would be lost among other portals. It would be hard to find Ry if you weren't looking for him.'

I stifled a yawn.

'It's just a hunch,' he said. 'Let's get you home.'

'They'll probably be there, at the hotel entrance,' I said.

Peg put his bottle on the table. 'Why don't you stay at my place tonight?'

'I don't want to impose,' I said, shaking my head.

'You wouldn't be imposing. In fact, you'd be doing me a favour; my place is much closer than the hotel.'

'Are you sure?'

Peg stood up and held out a hand. 'Come on.'

Peg's flat was only a two-minute walk away from the gam-bling den where we'd hidden. It was above a noodle bar on another back alley. The noodle bar was still open; steam hissed and fat sizzled and I began to feel hungry.

'Are those noodles any good?' I asked.

'If you like greasy.'

'I like greasy just fine.'

Peg ordered us each vegetable dim sum with noodles and miso broth that came in plastic trays with chopsticks. I inhaled the smell of onions and grease and my stomach

rumbled. The food at the Lakeview came in small, perfectly healthy portions. I needed this, especially after the
three bottles of beer I'd drunk tonight.

'How come you have your own place?' I asked as Peg
unlocked the front door.

'My dad and his new wife moved to Titan right at the
beginning of summer. I had the choice of moving there
with them or staying here. I chose to stay.'

I followed him up the stairs and inside. It was surprisingly large for a flat in a back alley. The living room
stretched across the full width of the building, with views
out over the lake. There were two couches, a large com-
screen and a bookshelf. Against one wall was a display case
filled with certificates, medals and trophies. I wandered
over to take a look. Every one had Peg's name on it. *Maths
champion 2119. Debating Society winner 2120. Navigation 1st
Place 2122.*

'These are all yours?' I said.

He shrugged and ran one hand through his dark hair.
'This is my dad's place. He insisted on displaying them all.'

'You must be really smart.'

He shrugged again and went to make up the bed in the
spare room. I wandered over to the window and looked out
across the lake. A dozen pleasure boats were sailing across
the darkening water, their lights ablaze. I wished I was on
one of them, drinking and dancing with no worries in the
world other than what classes I would take when school
resumed at the end of the summer.

'The bed's made up, whenever you want it,' he said,

scanning on the com-screen and flopping on a couch. There were two couches in the living room, both angled towards the com-screen. I took the other one and opened my box of noodles.

The screen opened to the news. The first thing I saw was a large image of me in my blonde wig, Peg's arm around my shoulders.

'I'm sorry. I'll switch channels,' he said.

'No, don't. I want to know what they're saying.'

'First night out on the town in the twenty-second century,' the reporter was saying. I recognised her from our ambush outside the club. 'Sporting a cute blonde wig and blue dress, Eden was seen drinking and dancing with pals at the super-cool Watering Hole.'

The reporter thrust a microphone under a young woman's chin. 'She looked like she was having a really good time,' said the girl. 'She danced with two different men that I saw, maybe more.'

'According to our sources, Eden still hasn't returned to the hotel where she is staying, which begs the question: just where is she spending the night?' said the reporter. 'Back to the studio.'

The newsreader had a serious expression. 'In other news, protesters spent a third day demonstrating outside Wolfe Energy Headquarters in New Marseilles.' The screen showed a crowd of several hundred people holding signs that said *Rehabilitation not Exploitation* and *Close the Lunar Prison Now!*

One of the protesters began speaking to the camera.

'The average lifespan of a prisoner on the lunar colony is five years. They work seven days a week in horrendous conditions. There's no opportunity for these prisoners to be rehabilitated. The lunar colony has nothing to do with justice, and everything to do with cheap labour for Wolfe Energy.'

'You sure you want to watch this?' said Peg.

'Is this Admiral Wolfe's company they're talking about?' I asked, twisting a mound of slippery noodles between my chopsticks.

'Yup.'

'On the news this afternoon, one of the legal commentators said Ryan might get sent to the moon.'

Peg looked at me. 'That won't happen.'

'Why do you say that?'

'To start with, his dad will hire a shit-hot lawyer. But if things do go wrong, we'll find a way to help him. I'm not letting Orion get sent to the moon.'

I tried to smile. But words were cheap. I just wanted the trial to be over and Ryan safely back in my arms.

CHAPTER 10

The phone call came on Saturday morning, just after Peg dropped me back at the hotel. When the screen clicked on, I expected to see Peg telling me he'd forgotten something, but it was Admiral Westland. I quickly smoothed over my hair as the call connected and tried not to think about the news coverage he must have seen: Peg punching a photographer or me arriving back at the hotel this morning after our night out.

'Hello, Eden,' he said, his voice tired and strained.

It had been less than a week since I'd last spoken to him, but he looked like he'd aged ten years. His brown hair seemed greyer and his cheeks seemed hollow, with two deep vertical lines running from his mouth to his jaw.

'Do you have news?' I asked.

'The trial is set for Tuesday. An official announcement is about to be made. I wanted you to hear it first.'

'Tuesday,' I said.

Three days and Ryan could be free.

'Orion's lawyer would like to meet you this morning. He will talk you through what will happen in the court and discuss your testimony.'

'Where do I need to go?'

'My driver is waiting for you outside. He will bring you to my apartment at the Institute.'

The admiral disconnected the call.

I checked my reflection in the mirror. As I thought – bags under my bloodshot eyes and hair matted and tangled from hours spent tucked inside a wig. Admiral Westland was going to think I was a slob. What I really wanted was time to shower and do my hair and try on a few of my new outfits to see which made the right impression. But Westland's car was waiting for me and what really mattered was speaking to Ryan's lawyer and getting my testimony right.

I found a dress with a high neckline, tied my hair back into a ponytail and dabbed some concealer under my eyes. It would have to do.

When we reached the Institute, the driver pulled round to a side entrance and stopped by the front door. I reached for the handle to let myself out, but there wasn't one. The driver, who was dressed in a black suit and white gloves, opened his door and came back to open mine for me. His face was flushed and beads of sweat glistened on his upper lip.

'Ma'am,' he said. 'I will collect you after lunch.'

I nodded and walked up to the front door.

Admiral Westland was waiting for me just inside the lobby. He nodded at the doorman. 'Come inside,' he said to me. 'Saul White, Ryan's lawyer, is waiting in my study. He'll just want to hear your story, so there won't be any surprises on Tuesday.'

We took the lift up to the next floor. It opened on to a wide hallway, lined with framed photos. I stopped when I saw a photo of Ryan in a school uniform, grinning at the camera. He looked about thirteen. There was another one of him holding a trophy. One of him and two other boys, all dressed in identical school uniform.

'My sons,' said Admiral Westland.

I followed Westland along the hallway to the last door on the left. Inside was a bright, book-lined room with a long conference table in the middle. Sitting at one end of the table – like the head of a family at a dinner party – was a man in a grey suit. He stood up as I walked in.

'A pleasure to meet you, Eden,' he said, pumping my hand up and down enthusiastically. 'I'm Saul White, Orion's defence attorney. Sit down.'

I sat down in one of the chairs near him. A crystal decanter and four crystal glasses on a silver tray were placed in the middle of the table. Above, an old-fashioned ceiling fan sliced through the warm air, whirring like a slow helicopter.

'Mr White, do you think the court will find Ryan innocent?' I asked, my insides twisting.

'Please, call me Saul,' he said. 'I believe we have a very strong case. There is an old protocol – dating back to the earliest years of time travel – that states that in an exceptional circumstance a clean-up will not occur. The protocol says that a participant must have had an "unusual and vital contribution to a mission". My job is to prove to the court that you played an unusual and vital contribution.'

'Can we do that?'

He smiled warmly. 'I certainly hope so. Tell me your story.'

Two hours later, after telling Saul the story about my best friend Connor discovering a planet that was the catalyst for Earth's destruction, about Ryan's mission to prevent that discovery, and my part in keeping Connor away from the telescope he was destined to use that fateful night, Mrs Westland came into the study to ask if we were ready for lunch.

Saul had taken copious notes, coached me in how to answer his questions and talked me through Time Court protocol. My head was aching with information and my throat dry from talking.

The dining room was large, with an entire wall of glass so clear that at first I thought there was nothing between us and the world outside. Beyond the glass a silver lake glimmered, its edges blackened from the shadows cast by the deep forest that reached to the horizon.

'It's beautiful,' I said, staring through the glass.

'The apartment comes with the job,' said Admiral Westland. 'We don't usually spend a lot of time here; we have a home just out of town. But this week, we've stayed here a lot. Closer to Orion.'

That explained the feel of the place. It was too clean and tidy. Beautiful, expensive-looking furniture, but all styled like a show home photographed in one of those dream home magazines Miranda sometimes read. Apart from the family photos, there wasn't much personal stuff lying around.

Mrs Westland came into the room with two men who I guessed were in their early twenties. Immediately I recognised them from Ryan's photos.

'Sit anywhere,' she said.

The table was set for six. I took one of the end places.

'Let me introduce everyone before we eat,' said Mrs Westland. 'These are my sons. This is Jem.' She gestured towards the taller of the boys. 'And this is Jove.' The two boys shook hands with me and Saul. They both had the same brown eyes and hair as Ryan, although Jem was taller and Jove was stockier.

'This is Saul White, Orion's lawyer,' Mrs Westland continued. 'And this is Eden Anfield, the girl . . .' She seemed to run out of words.

I could feel everyone looking at me.

'The girl from 2012,' said Saul. 'The girl who is Orion's best chance of a not-guilty verdict.'

'Yes,' said Mrs Westland. 'The girl from 2012.'

Two women came in then, with platters of food. There was a silver tureen of cold green soup, a plate of rice cakes, pieces of meat in spiral shapes that reminded me of worms, squares of toast no bigger than postage stamps, platters of berries and a bowl of salad. One of the women began serving the green soup.

'So does Ry have a good case?' asked Jem, the older of the two brothers.

Saul reached for the rice cakes. 'We will be arguing that

Orion invoked the Clemency Protocol. It's an old proto-col, from way back when time travel was first invented. It's only ever been used in a time trial once before.'

'What is it?' asked Jem. 'I've never come across it in my studies.'

'It allows clemency for a civilian who would otherwise need to be cleaned up,' said Saul. 'It can only be used when that civilian has made an important contribution to a time mission.'

'Eden made an important contribution?' asked Jove. I caught him looking at me sceptically.

'She certainly did,' said Saul. 'She succeeded where your brother and the other time agents failed. She is the only reason their mission was a success.'

'So it's an open and shut case?' said Jove.

Saul sighed. 'Nothing is ever as simple as that. However, I believe we have a strong chance of success. It will be very difficult for the Court to deny that Eden made an unusual and vital contribution.'

Jem frowned. 'So where's the element of doubt?'

Saul took a sip of water. 'Law is open to interpretation. It is my judgement that Eden's rescue falls clearly within the remit of the Clemency Protocol. However, if the court believed that Orion travelled back to 2012 for reasons other than clemency, they could disregard the protocol.'

'You mean, if Ry travelled back because he was in love with her or something,' said Jove, throwing a quick glance in my direction.

'Correct.'

'Was he in love with you?' asked Mrs Westland.

My spoon slipped out of my fingers. It clanged against the side of my soup bowl. 'He came back to save my life.'

She held my gaze a second longer before turning away.

'The prosecution will try to argue that Orion went back for love rather than duty,' said Saul. 'Which reminds me – make sure you're dressed in a suit, Eden. Tie your hair back. It's important to make the right impression.'

'I'll have a suit sent to you,' said Admiral Westland. 'It will save you having to deal with reporters following you around the stores.'

'How's Ry coping?' asked Jem.

Admiral Westland's face tightened. 'He's putting on a brave face.'

'It's the media speculation,' said Mrs Westland. 'I've told Ry not to watch the news, but he insists on watching it. All this talk about the lunar colony. Of course he's scared.'

'They won't send him there,' said Jove. 'That place is reserved for terrorists and murderers. He's not exactly in the same category.'

'That's what I keep telling him,' said Mrs Westland. 'He's just a boy. He should never have accepted that mission in the first place. He hadn't completed his training. He was too immature. Too impulsive.' Her eyes brushed across me. 'He has too strong a sense of duty.'

'All things I will be saying at the trial,' said Saul.

'Can I see him?' I asked.

'That won't be possible,' said Mrs Westland. 'Ry is only allowed one thirty-minute visit a day, apart from time with his lawyer. Jem and Jove have both flown in from Greenland today to see him.'

I nodded. 'Oh.'

'I think we can spare ten minutes of our time,' said Jem. 'If Ry finds out we stopped him seeing Eden today, he'll kill us.'

Ryan was dressed in a green long-sleeved T-shirt and grey trousers, each marked with the Institute logo, the elongated clock with the distorted numbers. The clothes were too baggy on him; they hung off his body, making him seem thin and underfed.

He stood up from the table and pushed his hair from his eyes. 'Eden.'

I crossed the space between us in seconds and wrapped my arms around his waist, pulling him tightly towards me. He smelt different and the same all at once. Different soap maybe, different clothes, but the same clean boy smell of his skin.

'No physical contact,' said the guard.

For a moment we ignored him. Ryan bent his head down and let his lips brush lightly against mine.

'I said no contact,' said the guard. 'Unless you're looking for a full body search, Westland.'

I dropped my arms to my sides, but we remained standing in front of one another, as close as it was possible to be without touching. My skin prickled with the desire to close the gap between us, to feel skin against skin.

'Opposite sides of the table,' said the guard. 'Sit down. Hands where I can see them.'

We did as he said, our hands side by side on the table, just a hair's breadth apart.

'I've missed you,' he said.

'I tried to see you before, but they wouldn't let me,' I said.

'I'm hardly allowed any visiting time. Most of my days have been taken up with my lawyer.'

'Saul seems great,' I said. 'He was telling me about the Clemency Protocol.'

He looked up, hope shining from his eyes. 'I'm feeling good about this, Eden. No one can argue that you weren't important. Hell, if you hadn't been there, Earth would be dying. I'd say that's a pretty vital role.'

'It's going to be fine. In three days you'll be out of here.'

He smiled. 'Yeah.'

'You should get your hair cut before the trial,' I said. I liked the way it looked, but it was kind of scruffy. Without anything to style it, his fringe fell into his eyes.

'Don't worry. My mom has arranged for a haircut and a smart suit and all that stuff.'

We just stared at each other for a moment, smiling.

'How are you coping?' he said. 'Have you been OK? I saw all those photographers following you on the news.'

'Ugh,' I said with a shrug. 'It's no big deal.'

'I see you found Pegasus.'

'Pegasus found me. He rescued me from my hotel room and took me up to the mountains.'

Ryan flicked his hair out of his eyes. 'I can't wait to be out of here so I can show you around myself.'

'Me too.'

'Have you met anyone else yet?'

'Peg took me out last night. I met some of your friends.'

'I saw you guys on the com-screen when you were leaving the bar. Are you OK? Did you get hurt?'

'Everything was fine. I'm fine.'

He lifted one of his hands from the table and chewed at the skin on the side of his thumb. 'You didn't go back to the hotel last night?'

'You've been watching too much TV.'

He didn't say anything.

'Peg offered me his spare room. It was easier than dealing with the reporters outside the hotel.'

'Right.' He pulled his other hand off the table and on to his lap.

'Hands where I can see them,' said the guard.

He put his hands back, but kept them on his side of the table.

'Ryan,' I said, reaching across, placing my hands as near his as I could reach. 'What's wrong?'

'Nothing,' he said, meeting my eyes with his. 'It's just so hard being locked up here while you guys are out there.' He slid his hands back across towards mine.

'Time's up,' said the guard.

CHAPTER 11

I had no idea what to wear to New York. I looked through my new wardrobe, at the dresses and tops and tight leggings I'd bought. In the end, I chose a long blue top, and a pair of white leggings. I added a white jacket to finish it off, applied some mascara and lipgloss and put my flexi-card into my new bag. Checking my reflection in the mirror, I could imagine myself walking down whatever the main shopping street was in New York. And if my outfit was not quite right? Well, who could expect me to know what the current city fashions were, considering I was from the previous century and a different continent?

Peg arrived just after breakfast. He lent me a baseball cap to help hide my hair and face, and we sneaked out the back entrance of the hotel. It probably wouldn't be long before someone tipped off the press that I was using that door, but for today, at least, I wouldn't be followed.

Antoine was driving. His car was much bigger than Peg's with seats for six people: two in the front and four in the back. Belle sat in the front with Antoine; Peg, Lyra and I sat in the back.

'You look very smart,' said Belle, once we pulled away from the hotel.

'I didn't know what to wear,' I said. They were all wearing long T-shirts and shorts. 'I guess I'm overdressed.'

'There's no dress code,' said Belle. 'You're fine.'

Antoine pulled on to a fast road with about ten lanes in each direction. He touched some icons on the dashboard that switched the car over to automatic and then left the car to drive itself. I felt slightly sick. Cars were racing along both sides of us, much too fast, with no one at the helm.

'Don't computers make mistakes in the twenty-second century?' I asked.

Antoine swivelled his chair around so that it faced the interior, his back towards the windscreen. 'Occasionally.'

'Don't you think you should face the front then, in case you need to drive manually?'

They all laughed.

'You can't drive manually on the expressway,' said Antoine. 'It's not an option. In any case, thousands of computers control the traffic on this road. If one glitches out, the others will compensate.'

Belle tapped the dashboard and the windows darkened. 'Now you can't see the traffic,' she said.

The interior of the car felt like a cave. All the seats faced each other. There was a small table that popped up from the floor. Antoine opened a mini-fridge and took out a bottle of champagne.

'Everyone want a glass of fizz?' he asked.

'Hold on a sec. Let me record this,' said Lyra. She dragged her port-com out of her bag and aimed it at Antoine. 'Just be natural.'

'Yeah, because it's so easy to act natural in a small space with a port-com under your nose,' said Belle. 'Why are you filming?'

'I'm doing an exposé on rich kids in Lakeborough. It's for my end of year project.'

Peg smirked. 'You *are* a rich kid from Lakeborough, Lyra.'

'Which gives me the perfect *in*,' she said. 'Look, the rest of the world is fascinated by us. They think we're over-privileged and spoilt. Let's show the world the truth.'

'But you *are* overprivileged and spoilt,' said Peg.

Lyra sighed and rolled her eyes. 'Who cares? I need a good story for my end of year assignment. It's the only way I'm going to get sponsored by a major news agency.'

Antoine shrugged and poured five glasses of champagne into crystal glasses. No one spoke a word.

'For God's sake, say something,' said Lyra.

'Maybe you should save the filming for New York,' said Belle. 'This is a bit too up close and personal.'

'You're all so inhibited,' said Lyra, pushing her port-com back in her bag.

They talked about school for a while and I just sat back and listened. Lyra was hoping to study journalism at university in a couple of months' time, but needed to be sponsored by a news agency if she was to get on the advanced program. Antoine and Peg were both cadets at the Lakeborough Space and Time Academy. Belle wanted to study theatre, but her parents were dead set against it.

'What about you, Eden?' asked Belle.

I shrugged. 'Back where I'm from, I'd have two more years of school before I had to choose. Now I'm in the twenty-second century, I'm not even sure what the options are.'

'You should come to the Academy,' said Antoine. 'With your experience, you'd fit right in.'

'That's what I told her,' said Peg. 'She'd be brilliant.'

Lyra widened her eyes. 'Did you single-handedly fly a time-ship through one hundred and eleven years of time, Eden? I didn't realise. You see, I thought you just strapped yourself in the back and let a professional fly the ship. I must be mistaken.'

'I just sat in the back,' I said slowly.

'Oh. So Antoine and Peg don't actually think you're a brilliantly experienced pilot, they just think you're hot and want you in their class.' She took a cigar out of her cigar case. 'That's really loyal of you, guys. With Orion locked up at the Institute and everything.'

'Shut up, Lyra,' said Peg.

'I so wish I'd recorded that,' she continued. 'It would have been a great introduction to the piece. Flattery is so vulgar.'

'You can't record me. I'm not a rich kid – remember?' said Peg.

Lyra lit her cigar. Thick, musky smoke quickly filled the interior of the car. 'You're not a rich kid, but you like to hang out with us and feed off the crumbs from our tables.'

'Wow,' said Peg. 'I never knew you held me in such high esteem. So why do you let me hang out with you?'

Lyra narrowed her eyes and blew a plume of smoke to

the ceiling. Belle turned towards the dashboard and tapped an icon that activated an extractor fan which instantly sucked all the pungent cigar smoke out of the car.

'You're pretty cute. You're useful to have around in case I ever feel like slumming it.'

I looked at Peg. He ran his hand through his hair. 'Whoa, that's harsh, even by your standards, Lyra.'

'I'm all about the truth.'

'Really? And yet you lied about your accident. You weren't all about the truth then, were you?'

'OK, children,' said Belle. 'Stop squabbling.' She turned to me. 'They love each other really.'

'Time for another drink,' said Antoine, bending down to take another bottle of champagne out of the fridge. He popped the cork and champagne bubbled and spilled over the lip of the bottle.

'Do you go to New York very often?' I asked Peg.

'No,' he said. 'But it's a holiday weekend. Everyone goes somewhere for the August holidays. I think you'll like New York.'

'I've always wanted to go,' I said, although that wasn't strictly true. Nothing against New York, but when I'd fantasised about travel, I'd usually pictured tropical islands with white sand beaches and perfect blue skies.

By the time we'd polished off the second bottle of champagne, the dashboard computer announced we had reached our destination. The car windows cleared and the engine switched off. We were in a vast outdoor car park. Overhead, the sun dazzled.

It wasn't until we were outside, away from the perfectly controlled climate of the car's interior, that I felt the full, muggy force of the sun, however. I'd never been anywhere truly hot before. What passed for hot in Cornwall was a slightly breezy day pushing 20°C. This was in a different league altogether. It was the sort of sticky heat that makes you feel as though your skin is covered with a coating of honey. I realised now why the others weren't dressed in anything smarter than T-shirts and shorts.

'I rented us a boat,' said Antoine. 'It's on pier nine. Comes with cold drinks, fishing gear and UV protection.'

'I do not want to hang out on a boat surrounded by dead fish,' said Belle. 'This is supposed to be fun for all of us. It's not a boys' day out.'

'I thought we were going to New York,' I said.

'We are,' said Peg. 'Come on.'

The captain of the boat saluted Antoine and winked. 'Bonjour, Monsieur.'

'Why are we taking a boat?' I asked.

Antoine held out a hand to steady me as I walked the short gangway. 'How else would we get to New York?' he said.

'By car? By train?'

'South Shore Seaport is as close as you can get,' said Antoine. 'The only way from here is by boat.'

'I don't understand. Has something happened to New York? Why can't we drive into the city?'

'It's underwater,' said Belle. 'Not all of it, but almost ten metres of it is. And sinking.'

'New York is sinking? Like Venice?'

Belle nodded. 'A lot like Venice. Most of the city has been abandoned, though certain districts are still inhabited.'

I didn't truly understand until the boat left the pier and sailed east, away from the town. There, out on the horizon, was a city of skyscrapers rising out of blue sea.

'Eden, what would you like to see?' asked Antoine.

I shrugged. I knew very little about New York in 2012; I knew even less about it now. 'What do you suggest?'

'We could visit the Statue of Liberty.'

'Is it underwater?'

He laughed. 'No. It's well above current sea level. We could do the whole tourist thing – stop off at Liberty Island, sail under the Brooklyn Bridge and then head back to Seaport. Or we could go scuba-diving. The whole of downtown is a marine park. Or we can sail the canals of midtown. There are some cool restaurants there.'

'Anything but the Statue of Liberty,' said Lyra. 'I went there on a school trip once and we had to line up for hours.'

In the end, we agreed to do a mixture of sightseeing and scuba-diving. We sailed slowly down the Hudson River and past the Statue of Liberty, but without stopping to do the tour. It was much too hot to sit on the small deck, so we stayed inside the cabin with its tinted windows and air-conditioning, drinking icy bottles of mineral water and snacking on sushi. Lyra periodically took out her port-com to film the view or our conversation.

Around midday, we headed for the marine park, so that Antoine and Peg could dive. They offered to take me along and teach me, but I got the impression they were just being polite.

'You sure you don't want to come too?' said Peg.

Both boys were already in their wetsuits; their masks, breathing apparatus and flippers were on the deck, ready to be used.

I shook my head. 'Not today.'

'Where do you want to start?' asked Antoine.

'The sphere?' said Peg.

'Sure. Then up to Wall Street.'

They pulled on their flippers and masks, strapped on their tanks and tumbled backwards off the boat into the sea.

The skipper sailed us a short distance away into the shade of a nearby building.

'I'll fix us some drinks,' said Belle, heading into the cabin.

That left just Lyra and me on the deck. I made sure I was in the shade and began slathering Factor 50 all over my exposed skin.

'What's the deal with you and Peg?' Lyra asked me suddenly.

I glanced over at her. She was sitting on a deckchair under the shade of a parasol, black sunglasses shielding her eyes from me.

'What do you mean?' I said.

'Just don't go thinking that Peg can be your backup boyfriend if things don't work out for Ry.'

'I don't need a back-up boyfriend,' I said.

'Good. Because he deserves better than that.'

This seemed a bit off coming from the girl who'd told

Peg earlier he was worth having around in case she felt like slumming it. 'We're just friends.'

'You stayed over at his place on Friday night.' She seemed to be staring at me, but I couldn't tell for sure because of her glasses.

'It was easier than going home and facing the reporters.'

'He lives in a shitty neighbourhood. You'd have been safer at the hotel.'

'I preferred to stay with Peg,' I said.

'These are the best,' said Belle, coming on to the deck. She passed me an amber-coloured drink in a tall glass with fruit floating in it and a piece of cucumber straddling the rim. 'It's just a light drink. You don't want *too* much alcohol in this weather or you'll dehydrate.'

'Thanks,' I said.

I sipped at my drink. It was too sweet. I put it down on the deck, disappointed.

'So?' said Belle. 'Do you have a date for the trial yet?'

'Tuesday,' I said. 'I saw Ryan yesterday. And his lawyer.'

'How is he?'

'He's OK. His lawyer seems to think he's almost certain to get a not-guilty verdict.'

'You must be so excited, Eden,' said Belle. 'In forty-eight hours, this could all be over.'

'I'm terrified, actually,' I said. 'I don't want to screw up in court.'

'There's nothing to screw up,' said Lyra. 'That's for the lawyers to worry about. All you get to do is answer their questions truthfully.'

'I just want to do everything I can to help him.'

Lyra sucked on the straw in her drink. 'The bookies are offering odds of three to one against Ry being acquitted.'

'Lyra,' said Belle.

'What? She needs to know the truth. Chances are Ry will be found guilty and locked up.'

'I don't believe that,' I said.

I was finishing my third drink when the boys arrived back. The captain lifted the anchor and began sailing into the city. Just as my stomach began a series of loud rumbles, we sailed into the canal system of midtown. The skyscrapers that towered either side of the canals cast deep shade on to the boat, so we sat out on the deck.

We moored up outside a building with a crown of terraced arches that glinted silver in the sunshine above us.

'This is the Chrysler Building,' said Belle. 'There's a great restaurant just above canal level. Everything is fresh and locally produced. And the view over the canals is amazing.'

The restaurant was called the Better Health Bar and it was buzzing. Before going to the table Antoine had reserved, we each stood in a full body scanner that measured our height, weight and vital statistics, before pricking our thumbs for a drop of blood.

'How exactly does this work?' I asked.

'You'll be served a meal that meets your nutritional needs,' said Belle. 'You eat to live right? This helps you live healthier. And it always tastes good.'

I stood in the scanner. It measured me in about three seconds.

'Any dietary restrictions?' asked the waiter, holding out a small square box, about the size of a coaster. He placed my thumb on the box. I felt a slight scratch and I was done.

'Vegetarian,' I said.

Once we were seated, Lyra took out her port-com and continued her documentary. 'Better Health Bars are the ultimate in laziness,' she said, filming a three hundred and sixty degree circle of the room. 'No longer do people need to think about what they eat and make a decision to be healthy. They let machines make their decisions for them. And this doesn't come cheap. A single meal at the Better Health Bar comes in at just over one hundred credits. That's a week's rent in most districts. However, for Lakeborough's teens, that's just pocket change.'

Antoine put up a hand in front of his face. 'I'm not agreeing to this, Lyra. I think you need to find yourself a new subject.'

Lyra put down her port-com and rolled her eyes. 'What else am I supposed to do? The slummy side of the city with Peg?'

Peg smirked. 'Please stop flirting with me, Lyra. It's getting embarrassing.'

When my meal showed up it was a large lentil and steamed kale salad, with freshly squeezed orange juice to drink.

'Typical dinner for the anaemic,' said Belle. 'That's why you're so pale.'

'I'm always pale. It's my colouring.'

She shrugged. 'And anaemic.'

'If I do stay in the twenty-second century, I think I'll open a pizza parlour,' I said.

'What do you mean *if* you stay in the twenty-second century?' said Peg. 'You don't exactly have a choice.'

'Sometimes this whole thing feels like a dream,' I said. 'I expect to wake up in my old bed in my old village, with the seagulls screeching overhead and the smell of the sea in the air.'

Peg stopped eating and stared at me. 'Do you wish you hadn't come?'

'Of course not,' I said, pushing my food around my plate. 'I want to be wherever Ryan is. But I wish we could've stayed in 2012. I don't know what I'll do if . . .' I couldn't finish the thought.

'So tell us what a pizza parlour is,' said Antoine.

I poked around at the salad on my plate while telling them all about different pizza bases and toppings.

'Wheat used to be cheap back in your day,' said Belle. 'It's much more expensive these days. We're lucky because Canada has perfect conditions for growing wheat, but for most of the world it's a luxury. If you opened a pizza restaurant now, it would be an upmarket sort of place.'

Just then, a large group came into the restaurant and the noise level quadrupled. They were all boys, dressed like Antoine and Peg in long shorts and shirts, but with massive conical hats that reminded me of the sort Chinese field workers used to wear. There were about ten of them. As soon as they were scanned in, they made their way to the table next to ours, laughing and joking and slapping one another across the shoulders.

'That's the group I really want to write about,' said Lyra.

'You know them?' I asked.

'Lakeborough crowd. Not just wealthy, but entitled and obnoxious.'

'That's your friend, isn't it?' I said, recognising the blonde boy from the Watering Hole.

Before she had a chance to respond, Clarence Wolfe came over to our table. He winked at me. 'We have to stop meeting like this. People will start to talk.'

'Hey, Clarence,' said Peg. He didn't smile. 'You guys down here for the weekend?'

He pulled off his straw hat and ran his hands through his blonde hair. 'Just for the day. We went diving in the marine park.' He turned back to me. 'So Eden, how would you like to come to the Guardians' Ball next weekend?'

I shrugged. 'I don't know anything about it.'

'These guys will fill you in, but it is the highlight of the social calendar. The grand Late Summer Ball at the Institute. Music, food, drink, entertainment. And it's invitation only.'

'I'm not really in the mood for partying,' I said.

'Why ever not?' said Clarence. 'You're young, beautiful, it's summertime.'

'And my boyfriend is locked up.'

'Aww, come on,' said Clarence. 'He'd want you to go. His family will be there. His dad's a Guardian.

'I'll think about it.'

Clarence shrugged. 'That means *no*, right? Let me ping you my number in case you change your mind.'

'I don't have a port-com.'

'I've got your number, Clarence,' said Belle. 'If Eden wants to be your date for the ball, I'll call you.'

Clarence kissed Belle's cheek, slapped Antoine and Peg across the shoulder and then made a big show of dancing his way back to his own table.

'God, I hate that guy,' said Lyra.

After dinner, we sailed the canals and bar-hopped from the Empire State Building back to the Rockefeller Centre and on to the Plaza Hotel. By the time we were back in the car at South Shore Seaport it was four in the morning. We popped into a twenty-four-hour diner and picked up some coffee and potato cakes for the journey home. Antoine drove the car manually on to the expressway before setting the automatic pilot and swivelling his seat to face the interior.

Peg and I were sitting next to each other, but Lyra was across from us, one hand cradling her cup of coffee, the other holding a cigar. Despite the fact it was dark, she was still wearing her sunglasses and I couldn't tell if she was staring at me, Peg or even sleeping.

I yawned. The others were talking about work schedules and internships and a trip to the mountains next weekend. They spoke about people I didn't know and places I'd never heard of, and although they kept trying to fill me in so I could keep up, it was obvious that I had no place in this conversation. Eventually, my eyes fluttered shut and the voices began to retreat. I surrendered to the gentle movement of the car and the deep, magnetic pull of sleep.

I woke to a crick in my neck and a bony shoulder under my cheek. Coming to, I realised my head had fallen on to Peg's shoulder. I straightened myself and checked my mouth to make sure I hadn't done anything embarrassing like dribble on him. The others were all still awake, but quieter than they had been earlier.

'We're nearly home,' said Peg.

'Sorry. I didn't realise I was leaning on you.'

'It's fine. You were tired.'

The windows of the car were clear and I could see the lights of downtown Lakeborough ahead of us. As we exited the expressway, Antoine swivelled his seat to face the windscreen and took over manual control of the car.

'You're first, Eden,' he said.

'Thanks for bringing me and everything,' I said.

'No problem. Peg, you'll be right after Eden.'

'What's your schedule, Pegasus?' Lyra asked.

'Sleeping all day today. Working all morning tomorrow.'

'Sleeping alone?' she asked.

'Unless you're offering.'

'In your dreams, little boy.'

Peg smiled and drained his coffee. 'Will I see you on Tuesday after work?'

'If you can fit me into your busy schedule.'

'Aww, come on, Lyra. Don't give me a hard time. You know I have to go to work and fit in my flying time.'

'Not to mention taking good care of Orion's girlfriend.'

'There's always time for you, Lyra.'

She stubbed her cigar out in her coffee cup. 'Are you sure? Maybe you should check your diary in case you have plans to show Orion's girlfriend your medal collection.'

'I think you're having a go at me again. But I'm much too tired to give a damn. Are you coming by on Tuesday or not?'

'I'll be there.'

Antoine pulled up by the kerb right outside the Lakeview. Just a half dozen reporters were stationed there.

'Still a few diehards, I'm afraid,' said Antoine.

'Good luck tomorrow, Eden,' said Belle. 'You'll be great. Just imagine the Guardians with their clothes off.'

I fought to suppress a nervous laugh. 'Why would I want to do that?'

'It's supposed to help with nerves. You know, under-neath their pompous uniforms they're just human beings like you and me. Humans who burp and fart and –'

'Come on, Belle,' said Antoine, lightly swatting his sister across the head. 'Before we all bring up our dinner.'

I opened the door and stepped on to the pavement.

'Eden,' said Peg, 'when is the verdict going to be announced?'

'Wednesday.'

'We'll all come to your hotel right after the verdict. Hopefully you'll have Orion with you. And if not . . .'

'If not,' I said.

Neither of us could bear to finish the other half of that sentence.

CHAPTER 12

The Space and Time Institute stood at the crest of the hill, as though keeping watch over the city that lay below it. As clouds passed in front of the sun and then cleared, light glinted from its tall windows, like the warning beam from a lighthouse.

A car, with a driver and security escort, had been sent to collect me. We drove through the front entrance and turned to the left, the opposite side of the building I had visited when I arrived. This was the infamous south wing, where the Time Court was situated.

I smoothed my skirt as the car pulled into the car park. Admiral Westland had sent me a suit, as promised. It was a deep charcoal grey and fitted me perfectly. The skirt fell below my knee and the jacket was long, down to my hips. Everything about it was perfect: the opposite of girlish and love-struck. Just wearing it made me feel like a different person – a more mature, confident version of myself. Dressed in this suit, I could see myself explaining carefully and calmly that Ryan had returned to 2012 to save my life and set the timeline straight. I would hide my feelings for Ryan from the courtroom. I would not be his love interest. I would not allow Ryan to lose his freedom because of me.

The car came to a stop and the security officer guided me to the front entrance of the Time Court. I should have expected the reporters and camera operators with their lights and microphones and cameras. I composed my face into a mask of blank calm and strode alongside the security officer, ignoring their questions and the flashing of cameras.

Although it was clearly less than a century old, the building's wood panelling and gilt-framed portraits of former Guardians gave it a feeling of ancient grandeur. My shoes clicked on the polished wooden floors as I made my way to the front desk.

'My name is Eden Anfield. I'm a witness in the trial of Orion Westland,' I told the receptionist.

'Stand in front of the retinal scanner,' he told me.

My eyes were scanned and I was escorted by a different security officer to a waiting room at the end of the hall.

There were enough seats for about twenty people, but the waiting room was empty. The security officer gave me a quick nod and walked away. I was much too jittery to sit down so I went to the window and looked out over the city down to the water. The blue of the lake and deep green of the trees were drenched in the bright light of summer. I imagined Ryan and me on a boat on the lake or swimming in the water. Was this where we would spend our life together? Or was this where I would spend my life alone?

'Miss Anfield. The court is ready for you.'

Already. I hadn't had time to calm myself yet. Turning around, I saw a court usher dressed in a funereal black suit standing in the doorway. I followed him down a long hallway towards the double doors that led to the courtroom. Two doormen, dressed in white suits, were positioned either side of the doors; above them was a large circular crest with the words *Ad Astra* engraved above it. When we were just halfway along the corridor, the doormen pulled the doors open and two men left the court. One was an usher, the other was, like me, a witness.

'Ben?' I said.

'Eden! How're you holding up?'

I shrugged. 'OK, I guess. How was it in there?'

'Ma'am,' said the usher. 'The court is waiting.'

'Will you be here for the verdict tomorrow?' Ben asked.

'Of course.'

'We'll talk then.'

'Ma'am,' said the usher.

The size of the doors did not prepare me for what was inside. The doors suggested a large space, something grand, but the courtroom was bigger and more imposing than I could have imagined. It was a circular room and everything inside was curved to its shape. Five long convex windows stretching from the high ceilings to the floor framed the city below. Twenty-four enormous clocks were spaced around the room, the name of a prominent city displayed underneath each. Above the door I entered by was a high gallery filled with empty seats.

In front of me were five stone and glass chairs – thrones almost – arranged in a semicircle. Four of them were empty; in the fifth sat Admiral Wolfe. My heart sank.

Immediately I scanned the room for Ryan. He was behind a small desk on the far side of the room with Saul White, his lawyer. Like me, Ryan was wearing a charcoal suit. The trousers were cut slim and the jacket was so long it looked like he was wearing tails. He was clean-shaven and his hair had been cut shorter than I'd ever seen on him. If this had been a wedding instead of a trial, I might have mistaken him for the groom.

He turned his head and locked eyes with me. My heart hammered against my chest. He looked gorgeous. And scared.

For a moment everything else vanished – the thrones, the lawyers, the clocks on the wall – and all I could see was Ryan, a look of hope and fear in his eyes. I wanted to run across the room, pull him into my arms and tell him everything was going to be OK.

Instead, I gave him a quick smile and tore my eyes away.

'Ma'am,' said the usher. 'This way.'

I followed the usher to the witness box and took my seat.

Now I was facing the five thrones. Admiral Wolfe, dressed in a flowing white gown, was calmly observing me. I took a deep breath and tried to ignore the uneasiness that was growing within me.

'Do not be afraid,' Wolfe told me. 'You simply need to tell the truth. The court lawyer will ask you a few questions and then Orion's representative may wish to ask you some questions as well. It will be quite informal.'

It didn't feel informal. At all.

'We have a simple truth to uncover,' Admiral Wolfe

continued. 'And that is whether Orion Westland defied the Board of Guardians and broke one of our most sacred laws so that he could travel back to 2012 and be with the girl he loved. Or whether he was enforcing the Clemency Protocol which spares the life of someone who makes an exceptional contribution to a time mission.'

The usher placed my hands on two flat screens. I'd expected a Bible.

'These screens will monitor your physical responses to the questions,' said the usher. 'Please keep your hands flat on the screens at all times. If you tell the truth, your monitor will remain in the green zone. The amber zone indicates confusion or uncertainty. The red zone will inform the court that your answer is not truthful.'

The court lawyer was dressed in a white suit with a clock symbol over one pocket. He approached the witness stand and smiled a practised smile.

'Please state your name and date of birth for the record,' he said.

'Eden Anfield. I was born on 6th September 1995.'

I glanced at my screens. Green zone.

He smiled again. 'There. That wasn't difficult, was it, Eden?'

I said nothing. Already I'd decided I hated this white-suited man with his patronising tone. His job was to trick me into saying something that would help him find Ryan guilty.

Admiral Wolfe stood. 'You say you were born in 1995?'

'Yes.'

'So you are a minor. Where is your legal guardian?'

'I don't have one. I'm a hundred and twenty-seven. I'm older than all of you.'

I smiled to myself; my truth monitor was green.

'All minors are appointed a legal guardian along with their resettlement package. Did no one speak to you about this?'

'I don't want a legal guardian. I want to be on my own.'

'You have twenty-four hours to find a legal guardian of your own, or the Institute will appoint you one.'

Wolfe took his seat and the lawyer approached me again.

'OK, Eden, let's begin by telling the court how you met Orion.'

I hated the way he used our first names, as though we were all friends.

'We had classes together at school. We sat next to each other in Art. He asked about my friend, Connor.'

'This is Connor Penrose, the subject of Orion's time mission?'

'Yes, although I didn't know that at the time of course.'

'Of course. So you introduced Orion to Connor?'

He continued with his questions about Ryan and Connor. He wanted to know how they met and what sort of role I had played. I explained that as I was friends with Connor – and Connor was the reason for the time mission – I had become friends with Ryan as well.

'At what point did you become more than friends?' asked the lawyer. His voice was quiet, solicitous, encouraging confidences.

I kept my eyes on him. 'We were never more than friends.'

'May I remind you that you are under oath,' he said, glancing at my truth monitor. I was in the amber zone. 'Let me rephrase the question. At what point did you develop romantic feelings for Orion?'

'Just before he left.'

'And how did those feelings manifest?'

I swallowed. Surely he wasn't asking me for intimate details. Personal details. 'I don't know what you mean.'

'When did you start having an intimate physical relationship with him?' he said.

To my irritation, I felt the warmth of a blush on my cheeks. Surely Ryan's lawyer should be shouting *objection* across the court by now?

'We didn't. I knew he was leaving.'

White Suit looked at my truth screen. I was safely in the green zone.

'But you were in love with him?'

I felt sick. This was none of his business. 'I cared for him,' I said, forcing myself not to look at Ryan. 'But I was not in love with him.'

I glanced at my screen. My physical responses had elevated into the red zone.

The lawyer smiled. 'Let the records show that the witness's truth monitor was in the red zone for that answer.' He turned back to me. 'Sometimes we don't realise the depth of our emotions for another person.'

I wanted to punch him. Evidently these truth monitors

were going to make it impossible to play down my true feelings.

'OK, Eden,' he continued. 'So you cared for each other. And Orion had trusted you enough to tell you about his mission.'

'No. He didn't tell me about his mission. I worked it out.'

I expected the lawyer to ask me how I'd worked it out, but he didn't. Of course he had already spoken to Cassie and Ben and probably Ryan as well. White Suit seemed interested in one thing only: my relationship with Ryan.

'Once you had worked out what Ryan's mission was, did the two of you spend a lot of time together? When he was off-duty, for instance?'

These were not the sort of questions I wanted. I needed to tell the court concrete stuff regarding my involvement in saving the planet. I needed the court to understand that I didn't deserve to die. That I had made an *exceptional contribution*. 'He needed to be friends with Connor so I invited Ryan around when I knew Connor was going to be there.'

'So Ryan spent time at your house?'

'Yes. But I did more than that. I helped . . .'

'Stick to the question, Eden. For the moment, I need to know about your relationship with Orion.' He paused and looked at me. 'I know it's difficult to talk about personal, intimate matters. But this is important. So, can we agree that you were very *fond* of Orion?'

'Yes.'

'And sometimes you spent time alone together?'

'Yes.'

'Did you ever hold hands with him?'

'Yes.'

'Kiss?'

I exhaled and watched my monitor moving into the amber zone. 'Yes.'

'Had things been different, you and Orion would probably have formed a deeper romantic attachment. But you ran out of time. Would you say that's a fair explanation?'

I shrugged. 'We can't possibly know what would have happened.'

White Suit smiled. 'You're right. Let's not speculate. Let's talk about your feelings again. At the time he left, you were *fond* of each other. You would have liked more time together.'

'I suppose so.'

'Yes or no?'

'Yes.'

White Suit smirked. 'That sort of fondness, in this time-scape, is commonly referred to as love. Thank you, Miss Anfield. No further questions, Your Honour.'

But he hadn't asked about my part in the mission, or how Travis had tried to kill me. He hadn't given me the chance to explain that Ryan had come back to save my life because I had made an *exceptional contribution* to the mission and didn't deserve a death sentence, not just because he loved me. He'd only asked about one small part of what happened; the part that helped him prove that Ryan was

179

guilty of stealing a time-ship and travelling back to 2012 because he wanted to be with his girlfriend.

Wolfe turned to Ryan's lawyer. 'Your witness.'

I took a deep breath. This was my chance to set the record straight. Saul White approached the witness box.

'You say that you and Orion were never more than friends during his original mission. Is that correct?'

'Yes.'

'Did you ever try to convince him to remain with you in 2012?'

'No.'

'Did you try to return to the twenty-second century with him?'

'No.'

'So you were reconciled to the fact that the two of you would never see each other again?'

'Yes.'

'Why do you think Orion stole a time-ship and travelled back to your time-scape?'

'Speculation!' said White Suit.

'Let the witness answer,' said Admiral Wolfe. 'I'm curious.'

I stared at my screen. 'Because he thought it was wrong for me to be killed by the mission cleaner. There was no need. I wasn't a threat to the timeline. The mission leader – Benjamin Hansen – didn't feel I was a threat. And the mission would have failed if it wasn't for me.'

My screen remained in the green zone.

'You don't think it was because he was in love with you?'

'No,' I said. My voice shook and my screens registered amber.

Ryan's lawyer noticed my amber response too. He frowned and then smiled broadly.

'So let's back up,' he said. 'You believe that Orion travelled back to 2012 because he knew that you had made an exceptional contribution to the mission and did not therefore deserve to be killed by the mission cleaner.'

'Yes,' I said, though it had been a statement, not a question.

Saul White nodded solemnly. 'Miss Anfield, why did the mission cleaner kill you?'

'Objection!' said White Suit. 'This is speculation.'

'We can't put the mission cleaner on the stand and ask him,' said Ryan's lawyer, 'because he's dead.'

'Objection sustained,' said Wolfe.

'Let me rephrase the question. Miss Anfield, why do you believe the mission cleaner killed you?'

I knew what he was asking me. This was my chance. 'He didn't understand the role I had played,' I said. 'Without me, the mission would have failed. Benjamin Hansen knew that and so did Orion. That's why Orion came back for me. I saved the future; I was not a threat.'

'No further questions, Your Honour.'

'Thank you, Miss Anfield,' said Wolfe. 'You can step down from the witness box.'

CHAPTER 13

Back in my hotel room, I hung my suit in the wardrobe and changed into something more comfortable, a pair of shorts and a T-shirt. I lay on the bed and scanned the com-screen till I found a news channel.

They were speculating about events inside the court-room. It was a closed trial, and none of the reporters had a clue what was actually going on. I saw myself arriving and leaving. The usual comments about star-crossed lovers were made. I saw Cassie arrive and leave, and Ben. A woman who was identified as Travis Deckard's widow was the only witness who spoke to the camera. She accused Ryan of murdering her husband so he could be with his girlfriend.

I needed to get out. I tucked my hair inside the baseball cap Peg had lent me and crept out the back door of the hotel. So far this was still safe. The hotel backed on to a lane filled with service trucks and the stench of overflowing dustbins. Holding my breath, I hurried to the end of the lane and made my way back to the main road. A quick glance over my shoulder told me the press was still hanging around outside the front of the hotel. I'd done it.

I strolled to the waterfront and watched the pleasure

boats for a few minutes. If I'd had cash instead of the stupid flexi-card that announced my identity to the world, I might have bought myself an ice cream and stayed there longer. I didn't want an ice cream enough to trade in my anonymity.

I left the waterfront and wandered slowly through the backstreets of Lakeborough. Whereas the main streets were wide and clean and felt like they could have been any city anywhere, the backstreets had a different feel altogether. There were fruit and vegetable markets along one lane, a flower market along another, hot food traders along a third. The lanes smelt of rotting vegetables and rose petals, of sharp blueberries and fried rice. My stomach rumbled and I realised I had completely forgotten to eat lunch. It was half past four by now. I probably would have started heading back to my hotel room to order some food, but I suddenly found myself outside the gambling den where Peg and I had hidden a few days ago. Peg's apartment was only a couple of minutes away. I had no idea whether or not he would be working, but decided to give him a try.

The greasy noodle bar underneath his apartment had a busy afternoon trade. Children, dressed in a smart blue school uniform, queued up to buy a small tub of sweet cricket noodles. Once again I wished I had cash instead of the flexi-card; there was no way I was willing to sacrifice the secrecy of Peg's apartment for a carton of greasy noodles.

The door to the apartment complex was open so I climbed the stairs and knocked loudly on Peg's front door.

He answered the door dressed in nothing but a pair of brown trousers and a loose vest. His feet were bare and his hair was mussed up in such a way he looked like he'd just got out of bed.

'Did I wake you? I'm sorry. I was just passing.'

Peg smiled. 'I wasn't sleeping. Come in.'

He held the door wide open for me. I crossed the threshold just as someone came wandering out of his bedroom dressed in nothing but a red satin bra and pants, a dress trailing across the floor in her hand, an unlit cigar in the other. Lyra.

My face burned. 'You have company. I didn't realise.'

'Lyra's just leaving,' said Peg. 'She has to get back to work.'

Lyra stared at me. She seemed unembarrassed by her near nakedness and perhaps if I'd had a body as lean and taut as hers, I wouldn't have rushed to cover it up either.

'She works around the corner,' he said. 'She comes here to do her physio during her break.'

'How was the trial, Eden? I saw you on the com-screen,' said Lyra. 'Did you prove that you're *exceptional* or whatever it is you're supposed to be?'

'I'm really not sure how it's going,' I said. 'I was only allowed in the courtroom for my questions.'

'What did they ask you?' she said, as she slipped her dress over her underwear.

'The prosecuting lawyer just focused on our relationship. He wasn't interested in hearing the whole story. It had nothing to do with discovering the truth. All he wanted to do was prove that Ryan went back to 2012 because he loved me.'

Lyra straightened her dress. 'That's a given surely. That's always been their angle.'

'Ryan's lawyer asked the right questions. I think he did a good job. But Wolfe is the judge.'

Lyra swore. 'That is bad news. Anyone else and he'd have a fighting chance.'

'It's not over yet.'

'Wolfe's been all over the news saying that the children of wealthy, influential families should be treated no different to anyone else. I think he made his mind up before the trial began.'

'He can't do that. He has to listen to the arguments,' I said.

She grabbed her bag from the floor. 'I'll see you tomorrow, Eden. After the verdict. Are we meeting at your hotel?'

'Yes, at the hotel.'

Peg walked her to the door. 'Come here as soon as you finish work and I'll drive us to the Lakeview.'

'OK,' she said, placing one hand on his shoulder. She glanced at me and I quickly looked away. 'See you later, Pegasus.'

The door slammed shut and I turned back to Peg.

'I'm so sorry I interrupted the two of you. I didn't realise –'

'You didn't interrupt us,' said Peg, walking towards me. 'We were finished before you got here. Lyra was leaving.'

'Right. So does she usually do her physio in her underwear?'

'She wears shorts and a T-shirt. She was just changing – it's not the way it looked.'

I held up my hands. 'It's none of my business.'

He rolled his eyes. 'Lyra is not interested in me.'

I smirked. 'She called you cute.'

'From what I remember, that was a backhanded compliment – something about slumming it?'

'She likes you.'

He turned away. 'I'm not interested in Lyra, Eden. For a start, she's Orion's ex-girlfriend. That would be weird.'

My heart raced. 'What?'

'They were together for over a year. That's a long time. I wouldn't be comfortable. But it's irrelevant, anyway, because I'm not interested and she's not interested.'

'Peg,' I said. 'Why didn't you tell me that Lyra used to date Ryan?'

He shrugged. 'I dunno. It never came up.'

'It never occurred to you that I might want to know that?'

'No.'

'Is that why she doesn't like me?'

Peg threw himself down on one of the couches. 'She doesn't dislike you. She's just not the warm and cuddly sort.'

My stomach tied itself in knots.

'What does it matter?' said Peg. 'It's old news. Ry broke up with her before he even accepted the mission to 2012.'

'That's something, I guess.'

Peg yawned and stretched. 'I'm starving. Shall I get some take-out from downstairs?'

★ ★ ★

It was getting dark outside. Peg was stretched out on the couch, one eye on a baseball game playing on the com-screen, the other on a maths problem he was working on for college. I was reading a fashion magazine that Lyra had left behind, despite the fact that fashion had never inter-ested me. I dropped the magazine on the floor and checked to see if Peg was still working.

'I can put something else on,' he said, when he caught me looking at him. 'I can find out the score later.'

I shook my head. 'I should probably leave, anyway. You've got work to do.'

Peg dropped his essay on the floor and sat up. 'I'll drive you. I need a break from the mathematics of portal creation – it makes my head hurt. I can drop by the shipyard on my way back.'

'What exactly is your job?' I asked.

Peg stood up and stretched. 'Why don't I show you?'

His car was parked a couple of streets away, wedged between a fire hydrant and large recycling container.

He checked his rear-view mirror and groaned. 'Belt up. We're going to need to lose that lot.'

I turned around just as a camera flashed. Stupidly, I'd left the baseball cap at Peg's.

'How did they find out where you live?' I asked.

'I guess it was only a matter of time.'

He whipped around the corner and took several quick turns, navigating the back streets of Lakeborough rapidly. Once he was sure that no one was on our tail, Peg headed for the highway out of town, the same highway that led to the Space and Time Institute. The large building glimmered under its lights, a white fortress against the dark sky.

Peg turned off the highway a couple of miles out of town and we drove along a single lane road that was surrounded by trees.

'I promise you, this is going to be the most spectacular thing you have ever seen or done in your life,' he said.

'You seem very confident.'

'If you're not blown away, you have no soul.'

A few minutes later we pulled up to a security checkpoint. Peg handed over a pass.

'Can I get a visitor's pass for my friend?' he asked. 'I'm gonna put in some flight time. She'll be in the viewing area.'

The woman glanced at me and passed over a lanyard with a bright red *Visitor* sign hanging from it. 'Wear this at all times,' she said.

He continued driving, slowly, our windows wound down. The road was narrow and we were surrounded by trees, their trunks gently creaking in the light breeze.

'This is where you work?'

'Yeah. I'm going to take you to the repair yard. I'm training to be an engineer. One of the perks is that I get some flight time. It helps to supplement the time I get at the Academy. The Elite students get most of the flight time there. This helps me to keep up.'

The road split and he took the left turn. We passed a sign that said *Repairs* and kept driving.

'This place is huge,' I said.

'Nearly there.'

A couple of minutes later he parked the car next to an ugly concrete office block. A large sign said *All visitors must report to reception and remain in the building at all times.*

'Let's go,' said Peg, locking the car.

He started walking across the yard, a torch in his left hand lighting the ground in front of him.

'Shouldn't I report to the reception?' I asked, pointing at the sign.

'Technically. But then you wouldn't get to see the ship I've been working on.' He grabbed my arm. 'Come on.'

'Won't we get seen?'

'No. This place is huge. All the important equipment is at the front near security. Out here, it's just old ships, waiting for repair or to be sold for parts.'

We jogged across the yard until we reached a gate in a metal fence. Peg swiped his ID card through the gate key reader. At once, it swung open.

'I can't afford to get in any trouble,' I said.

'Stop worrying. I'm allowed to be here. And no one knows that you're here.'

We entered another yard, Peg's torch beam illuminating several ships until he found the one he wanted. They were all about the size of a small bus. The one Peg selected was gunmetal grey, and shaped like a giant bug.

'This is a lovely little ship,' he said. 'Known in the trade as a space hopper, because she's only used for little hops to the Inter-Planetary Spaceport. She's still got lots of life left in her. I spent the last six weeks helping the engineer tweak her engines. Isn't she lovely?'

'I guess,' I said.

I couldn't even identify a car beyond its colour; did he really think I would get excited about a hunk of grey metal?

Peg pressed a button and a hatch opened up. A small metal stairway slowly lowered to the ground.

'After you,' he said.

I climbed up the clangy metal steps to the hatch. Inside was a small cockpit with two seats. Behind the cockpit were several rows of seats, facing forward like on a bus. It was much bigger than the time-ship.

'Where should I sit?'

'Right up front. You can be my co-pilot.'

Peg pulled himself through the hatch and sat next to me in the cockpit. He pressed a button and the stairs collapsed and tucked themselves inside the ship. Another button closed the hatch.

'You ready for the best ride of your life?'

'You're not really going to fly this thing are you?'

Peg smiled. 'You surely don't think I brought you here just to show you the ship I've been working on?'

'But won't people see? I mean, this is a spaceship. Won't it have fire and flames and lots of noise?'

Peg looked at me as though I was insane. 'Fire and flames? I hope not. If this thing sets alight, I've seriously messed up its engines.'

'But, on the TV, when rockets and spaceships lift off . . .'

'Ahh, the tee vee,' said Peg with a smile. 'It has a lot to answer for. There's no fire or flames or rockets involved in a twenty-second century spaceship.'

'You're sure we won't be seen?'

'Of course we'll be seen. I'm allowed to do this. I'm just not qualified to take passengers yet.'

'Where are we going?'

'Wait and see.'

'Is it safe?'

Peg didn't even bother to answer the last question. He pulled on a headset and began speaking to someone. He listed coordinates and tapped away at buttons on the console.

'OK,' he said, turning to me. 'We're cleared for a twenty-minute flight. Are you strapped in?'

I nodded and took some deep breaths.

He tapped away at some more buttons on the console, and moved a big, cross-shaped controller. I felt the ship vibrate in the same way the time-ship had. The world out-side was all darkness, but even so, I had the strangest sensation of moving backwards, which I knew was impossible as there was a big shed behind us. And then I felt we were moving forwards. A tiny beam appeared in front of us, like a pinprick of light at the end of a long dark tunnel. We moved rapidly towards it.

'Where are we going?' I asked.

'Not very far,' said Peg. 'Just far enough to give you a magnificent view.'

The pinprick of light at the end of the tunnel grew wider and larger until it filled the view in front of the cockpit window. Just as quickly as it grew, it shrank and then disap-peared into nothing.

'Where are we?' I asked. I couldn't keep the unsteadiness out of my voice. Peg was only eighteen. He was still studying engineering and just a little earlier he'd told me that portal mathematics made his head hurt.

'Close to home,' he said.

He jerked the controller to the left and the ship slowly rotated until a huge mass of blue and white came into view.

'That's not really, that can't really be . . .'

'Planet Earth,' said Peg. 'We're passing over Egypt right now. It's just about dawn down there. Right below us is the River Nile.'

I looked down through the ship's window. From this height, the shape of the continents was clear. I could make out the eastern end of the Mediterranean, the top part of the African continent.

'We're really in outer space?' I said, although the view through the window answered the question for me.

Peg smiled. 'Low Earth orbit,' he explained. 'You get the best views of the planet from here. Further out you get to see the whole planet and sometimes the moon, but you don't get the detail that you get from this orbit.'

A swirl of white cloud obscured the shape of the continents and I lost sense of where we were.

'How fast are we travelling?'

'Thirty-four thousand miles an hour.'

'What!'

'Don't worry. It's safe. You have to travel fast at this height or else gravity will pull you in. But it's actually perfect because you can circumnavigate the globe in forty-five minutes.'

'I thought you were exaggerating, Peg. But you're right. This is the most incredible thing I've ever done.'

'Well, it's not like travelling through time . . .'

'It's better. Much better.'

'I love it,' he said with a smile. 'It's better than the moon or Titan or any of the other planets. This planet's alive.'

I leant forward in my seat and tried to pick out features beneath me. The land below looked tan and dry, with swathes of white muslin swirling above it.

'Eden,' said Peg.

'Just a minute.'

If that was the Nile and we were heading east, then below must be Saudi Arabia? Iraq?

'Eden,' said Peg again.

The view from the window disappeared behind a fog.

'I can't see,' I said.

'I've been trying to tell you, you're fogging up the glass,' said Peg. 'Sit back.'

'Shall I wipe it off?'

'No, just wait.'

I sat back and watched the screen gradually clear. And then I remembered Eden.

'Do you think we'll ever find another living planet?' I asked.

Peg looked at me. 'Of course. The universe is unfathomably large. There must be millions of living planets out there.'

'So why haven't we found one yet? Don't you think that

by now we'd have found another planet with life, if one existed?'

'It's expensive to travel through space to investigate possible planets. And all our efforts so far have yielded nothing. People don't want to pay more taxes to fund dead-end exploration. But that doesn't stop me believing there's life out there.' Peg tapped my elbow. 'Look. There's India. Can you see it?'

I leant forward; the triangular shape of the subcontinent angling down into the Indian Ocean was unmistakable.

'It looks thinner than I expected,' I said.

'Its landmass is smaller than it was in your time. Sea levels have risen quite a bit.'

He moved the controller. 'I'm going to take us over the North Pole now. You'll get to see the dark side of our planet briefly before we go home.'

Home. That reminded me.

'Peg, I need to ask you something,' I blurted out.

It was now or never. The Institute had only given me until tomorrow to find a legal guardian myself; after that, they would choose someone for me.

'What is it?'

'I need to ask you a favour.'

He shrugged. 'OK.'

'It's a lot to ask, so I won't mind if you say no.'

'This sounds serious.'

'I'm kind of embarrassed to even ask, but . . .'

'Just ask.'

I swallowed. 'Well, the thing is, I'm sixteen.'

'I thought you were a hundred and twenty-seven?'

'The court wouldn't accept that. I'm supposed to have a legal guardian. The Institute said I could find my own guardian by tomorrow or they would appoint one and put me in a care home. It can be anyone, so long as they're over eighteen.'

Peg laughed. 'You want to move in with me?'

'Just for a while.'

'And you want me to be your dad?'

'No! Well, I suppose. Sort of. I would have to live with you and you would be responsible for my welfare until I'm eighteen. But as soon as Ryan is free, I can live with him.'

There was a sudden jolt to the ship and the view through the window wobbled. For a second or two we lost sight of the planet. Peg frowned and pulled the controller to one side until Earth was clearly in our sights again.

'Space junk,' said Peg. 'You can't afford to lose focus for a second. Sorry about that.'

'What's space junk?'

'Mostly bits of obsolete space stations,' he said. 'But you also have to watch out for dead satellites that haven't entered the atmosphere and burned up yet. And then there's the debris from shipwrecks. They're the worst.'

'Shipwrecks?'

Peg laughed. 'You're quite the stress freak, aren't you? We're in a stable orbit, with a sound ship and a very talented pilot. Relax and enjoy the view.'

He hadn't answered my question. My chest tightened. I

wrapped my arms around my middle and looked out of the window as we flew north.

'We're flying over the Himalayas now,' said Peg.

I leant forward again, but the mountains were obscured by thick cloud cover.

'Of course I'll be your fake dad,' said Peg.

'Are you serious?'

'Eden, it's not a big deal. I'd actually like a room-mate. I spend a lot of time alone.'

If he wasn't responsible for flying this spaceship, I would have hugged him. 'Thank you, Peg. I really didn't want to be sent to some stupid care home.'

'We're flying over the Arctic Ocean right now,' he said. 'Once we get close to Greenland, we'll have to head home. We don't want to be mistaken for a hostile.'

'What's going on in Greenland?'

'The Greenland War. The Federation, Scandinavia and Russia are still disputing territory there.'

'I thought Greenland was just a pile of snow and ice.'

'With valuable fuel deposits. Much cheaper to extract fuel from Greenland than mine it on the moon.'

My stomach rolled over. The mines on the moon were where Ryan could end up if the Time Court found him guilty. I didn't want to think about that.

'Do you come here often?' I asked, to change the subject.

'I've clocked up several hours.' He glanced at me. 'This is the first time I've brought someone with me, though.'

As we rolled over the globe, Earth grew darker. A band of deep yellow and orange hugged the surface of the planet.

Above that, a thin band of pink and blue. And then there was nothing but the unending blackness of space.

'Take a last look out the window,' said Peg. 'I'm going to land her in thirty seconds.'

There was the sensation of moving backwards for a few moments and then the speck of light appeared at the end of a dark tunnel. We hurtled towards it. Just as the white light filled the screen in front of us, it shrank to nothing and we were back in the dark shipyard.

CHAPTER 14

I sat next to Ben in the gallery. Although the court had been closed during the trial – and each witness appeared separately – the court was open to close family, witnesses and reporters for the verdict. Admiral Westland was in the front row with his wife and sons. Travis Deckard's widow was there with her two children. And I spotted Lauren, the cleaner from the most recent mission.

'This will only last for a few minutes,' Ben said to me in a low voice. 'The admiral will announce the verdict, and if he's found guilty, the sentence. That's it.'

There was a hush as Ryan and his lawyer entered the room. An usher directed Ryan to the front bench. I watched him scan the gallery until his eyes rested on me. He smiled; I smiled back, doing my best to convey good luck and all my positive energy his way. He scanned the gallery again, this time his eyes resting on his mother.

And then Wolfe came in. Everyone stood.

'Be seated,' said Wolfe.

He began by telling us all that it was a troubling case, that time trials are never easy because only a select few are privy to the full details of a time mission.

'However, there are several things that have caused me

grave concern,' he went on. 'Any time mission must be authorised by the Guardians. Only then can we be certain that all possible permutations have been duly considered. The theft of a time-ship and an unauthorised mission to the past – whether performed with good intentions or not – is a breach of our most sacred law.

'There is one exception to this rule. And that is if the Clemency Protocol applies. The Protocol may only be invoked in "exceptional circumstances" when a participant has made an "unusual and vital contribution to a mission". And that, ladies and gentlemen, is the point of debate.

'I have listened with great care to the testimonies of all those involved in both missions,' Wolfe went on. 'And I have reached my verdict.'

Ryan and his lawyer stood. Ben squeezed my arm.

'Mr Westland claims that he thought that it was morally right to save the life of the young woman who assisted his mission. To that end, he presented his concerns to a panel of the Guardians.' Wolfe checked his notes. 'Admiral Philp and Admiral Shastri were the Guardians who considered his case. They did not agree that it was necessary and correct for the mission outcome to be altered in any way. At that point, Mr Westland should have accepted their decision, unless he considered that he had a duty to act under the Clemency Protocol. Mr Westland did not convince me that was the case. I believe that he stole a time-ship and travelled without authorisation for personal reasons rather than altruistic reasons. As a consequence I find Orion Westland guilty as charged and an Enemy of Time.'

There was a gasp from the gallery.

'Furthermore, I do not believe Orion Westland was acting alone,' Wolfe continued. 'The difficulty in acquiring a time-ship, along with the expense of procuring enough fuel to make the journey, persuade me that he was assisted by another or others. I will be opening an inquiry into what amounts to a conspiracy against time forthwith.' He paused and ran his eyes across the members seated in the gallery. 'And now to sentencing.'

He paused again and I realised he was doing so in order to allow the photographers from the press the chance to get a good still image of him.

'The sentencing guidelines are wide,' said Wolfe. 'However, Orion Westland is a young man from a considerably advantaged background. He has had the benefit of a top-class education, including a privileged position on the Elite Program at the Lakeborough Space and Time Academy. I believe that he wilfully and knowingly chose to disregard the sacred Temporal Laws so that he could pursue a personal agenda with a girl he had become infatuated with.' He paused again and posed for the cameras. 'Due to the seriousness of this case, I believe it is important that we make an example of this young man. I will be sentencing Orion Westland to life imprisonment on the International Lunar Correctional Facility.'

For a moment, the room appeared to hold its breath. And then all hell broke loose. Ryan's mother shouted something, but I didn't understand what she was saying. One of his brothers yelled something. There was noise all around me. I said nothing. It felt as though my heart had stopped beating. Wolfe didn't think my life was worth saving. He was punishing Ryan by depriving him of his. This was all wrong. Ryan looked at his parents and then at me. His expression was blank.

Wolfe rapped his gavel on the bench. 'I have arranged prison transport for next Tuesday. The defendant will remain in custody until that time. Family and close friends should head to Waiting Room B if they wish to say their goodbyes.' He banged his gavel, stood up and exited the room.

Ben and I were alone in Waiting Room B. I went over to the window. It looked out over the visitors' lawn. Two children were laughing and chasing each other around a fountain. Adults sat on benches and picnic blankets, doling out food to their children. They had all the time in the world. Above them, a flock of tiny blue birds took flight from a treetop.

Ben was buying two coffees from the drinks machine. I sat in one of the armchairs. And then I realised that in just a few minutes I would be with Ryan for the last time. Nervously I ran my fingers through my hair, smoothing it, tucking a flyaway strand behind my ear.

'You look lovely,' said Ben. 'Don't worry.'

He put the hot drinks on the glass-top coffee table in the middle of the room. If it wasn't for the drinks machine in the corner, we might have been in a sitting room in a private house. Ryan's parents and brothers weren't there. I guessed they were waiting somewhere else, the admiral's office perhaps.

Ben was called first. For the hundredth time I wished I'd

bought a port-com. I could have called Peg. He'd want to say goodbye to Ryan. So would the others. It didn't seem fair that only those of us present at the verdict had the chance to say goobye.

When Ben came back he kissed my cheek. 'Careful what you say in there,' he whispered. 'They're listening to everything.'

'Thank you,' I whispered back.

The usher led me to the same meeting room I had seen Ryan in before. A single guard was standing outside.

'You have ten minutes,' said the usher.

The guard nodded and unlocked the door. Inside was a table with three chairs and a plastic jug of water in the middle. Ryan was sitting in one of the chairs, resting his head in his hands. Above, on the wall behind him, was a com-screen with a rolling newsreel. The sound was off.

As soon as I came through the door, he stood up. He was still wearing the suit he'd worn in the courtroom, but the jacket was slung over the back of a chair now. His eyes were red and his hair was too short, but when he smiled and his brown eyes crinkled, he looked like himself again. I ran across the room and hugged him tight, ignoring the bony ribs and sharp nodules of his spine. I reached up and touched his face. His cheekbones were prominent in a way they hadn't been before. How could someone get so thin so quickly? Either they weren't feeding him enough or he wasn't eating.

Ryan pulled away and held me at arm's length, a wild desperation in his eyes. 'God, you're beautiful,' he said.

'Ryan,' I began.

202

'We don't have long,' he interrupted. 'Let me speak first.'

We were standing face to face. His arms on mine. It took every ounce of my self-control not to kiss him. But I had to let him speak. These could be the last ten minutes we ever had together.

'No touching,' said the guard.

Ryan dropped my arms but held my eyes with his own. 'I wish this hadn't happened.'

'It's wrong.'

'Yes it is, but we don't have time to discuss that now. I want you to pass on some messages.'

'OK.'

'Are Peg and Lyra together yet?'

'No. I don't think that's going to happen.'

'She likes him. And I know he likes her. We've always liked the same girls.'

Even though they were history, the thought of them together twisted my stomach. 'Peg said it would be too weird because of you and Lyra.'

Ryan rolled his eyes. 'Could you remind Peg that I moved on some time ago. And I'm not exactly going to be around to make him feel uncomfortable. Tell him to get over himself and go out with her.'

'OK.'

'Peg's my best friend. He's a good guy. He'll take care of you.'

'He said I can stay with him.'

Ryan nodded. 'That's good. He hates living alone. I'm going to get my dad to transfer some credit to Peg's account.

And to yours. You should decide on a school or college course. Anything. You could go to the Academy if you want.'

'I don't care about going to school,' I said. 'None of that matters.'

Ryan shut his eyes, then pulled me in for another hug. I could tell by the rhythm of his breathing that he was on the edge of tears.

'No touching,' the guard said again.

We ignored him.

'Eden,' he sighed into my hair. 'I'm not going to be able to get out of this. Promise me you'll move on with your life.'

I said nothing.

Ryan took a step back from me. His eyelashes were wet. 'Please promise me that. When I'm up there, I don't want to be worrying about you. I want to know that you're happy and that you have friends.'

'I promise,' I whispered.

He leant towards me, his breath gentle against my skin. And then his lips met mine. I knew this kiss. This kiss meant goodbye. It was desperate and painful; it was filled with a lifetime of lost opportunities. I wrapped my arms around his back and under his shirt, feeling the soft heat of his skin under my fingers. The rest of the world disappeared.

'OK, people, your time is up,' said the guard.

Ryan and I pulled apart.

'I love you,' he said.

I wanted to tell him I loved him too, but instead I leant in to tell him one last thing. 'This is not goodbye,' I whispered.

CHAPTER 15

Ben had a car parked just outside. 'You want to get some lunch?' he asked.

I had no appetite, but I needed to talk to Ben.

We drove in silence into town. I was empty and numb. Every second was a second further away from Ryan. I wanted to hold on to everything about him: the feel of his arms around me, the smell of his skin, the shape of his eyes. The thought that I would never see him again was unbearable. I'd totally believed that the court would find Ryan not guilty. Saving my life was so obviously the right thing to do from where I was standing.

Ben chose a quiet restaurant at the edge of town. He ordered us both coffees and grilled cheese sandwiches.

'Tell me about the Lunar Facility,' I said.

'It's the worst place in the world.' He laughed bitterly. 'It's on the far side of the moon; the face we never see from here on Earth. People say that it was built on the far side so that the prisoners never get to see their home planet. They mine helium-3. It's our main fuel source these days.'

The sandwiches arrived then, grilled cheese oozing out of two thick slices of toasted white bread.

'I thought you'd like this place,' said Ben. 'It serves old-fashioned stodgy food, like they eat back in your time.'

The smell of the toast brought my appetite rushing back to me. I took a huge bite and savoured the tangy hot cheese. A com-screen on the wall was showing a report about the verdict. Admiral Wolfe was addressing the reporters outside the Institute. Although the com-screen was set to mute, subtitles told the story. *'The families of powerful, influential people should not expect preferential treatment,' says Admiral Titan Wolfe after the sentencing of trainee time agent Orion Westland. 'The Time Court must be tough on crime. And that means all criminals.'*

Ben poured cream into his cup and stirred it slowly. 'I know it must be really hard for you right now. But you need to think about what you're going to do next.'

I stopped chewing and looked up at him. 'The whole trial was a sham,' I said. 'Wolfe should never have been allowed to try the case. He'd decided the outcome before he even heard it.'

'It doesn't seem right,' Ben agreed.

'He'll have to appeal,' I said. 'He could argue that Wolfe was not an impartial judge.' I brushed the crumbs from my mouth. 'How soon will he be able to appeal?'

'Eden, you can't appeal against a decision made in the Time Court. It is the highest court in the world. Its decisions are final.'

My appetite went. I pushed the plate to one side. 'You mean . . .'

'The sentence will stand.'

The room tilted and swayed. I grabbed the edge of the table to steady myself.

'Drink some water,' said Ben, quickly pouring me a glass.

I took a small sip. The panic turned to nausea. 'What am I going to do?'

'There's nothing you can do.'

Ben changed the subject then. He asked about the Lakeview Hotel and whether I'd found a legal guardian. Was I looking for work or did I want to finish my schooling? Had I met Ryan's parents? What about his friends?

'Are the reporters following you everywhere?' he asked.

'I try to give them the slip. I have a baseball cap that helps.'

'You should move somewhere else where no one knows you. Start over. Or move to Penpol Cove.'

Nothing would make me sadder. The thought of going back to Penpol Cove over a hundred years after I'd left – when everyone I knew was dead and buried – was unthinkable.

'What about you? What's this new job of yours?'

'I'm not a time agent any more,' he said. 'I had to plan ahead. If Wolfe becomes president of the Institute, he's planning to ban all time travel. I don't want to be obsolete. I'm now in charge of the Inter-Planetary Spaceport. It's like a border patrol for all ships entering or leaving Earth's airspace.'

'So will Ryan's ship have to dock there on the way to the moon?'

'Yes. His ship will dock for a crew change and for

routine quarantine procedures. Typically a prison ship docks for twenty-four hours.'

'Will you get to see him?'

He nodded. 'I'll make sure I do. You have my contact details, Eden. If you wanted a job on the spaceport, I could fix you up with something. Food and accommodation come as part of the package. You can make good money, even as a cleaner or a waitress.'

I had no interest in making lots of money working on a spaceport as a cleaner. But I knew Ben was trying to help.

It was two in the afternoon. My limbs felt restless. Back in my time, I would have gone for a run, but here in Lakeborough it was too hot. I wandered aimlessly along the road that led out of town. Away from the cooling breeze of the lakeside, the air grew hotter and sticky; the tarmac seemed to be melting under my shoes. Sweat beaded on my skin and scalp. I passed the old library and a few semi-derelict clapboard houses that had probably once been rather grand homes, past the timber warehouses, past the sliproad to the highway, until I was on the old road that led to the suburbs and the mountains.

My head was spinning with worries. The mere thought of Ryan locked up for ever in a prison on the moon with no visitors and no hope of ever leaving was so distressing that every time my mind strayed in that direction, I pulled it back. And then there was me. I had enough credit to last a few more weeks. Moving in with Peg would help, but I was going to have to find some kind of job as soon as possible. I'd never had a job before, not even a part-time job, so I had no skills or experience to draw on. Was I going to stay here in Lakeborough? Did it really matter where I was if Ryan was on the moon? The only people I knew at all were Ryan's friends and Ben. Should I go to the spaceport where Ben was captain? That was closer to Ryan than here on Earth, but not close enough. I had no answers.

I hadn't counted on it being this hot. I had no sunscreen, no hat, no water to drink. I was about to turn around and head back into town when I recognised the Lakeborough Space and Time Academy building. That meant I was no more than a ten-minute stroll from the road that led to Ryan's family home. I decided to walk a little further, ignoring the dryness in my throat and the sweat that was trickling down my back.

The road leading down to Ryan's house was wide and tree-lined and I was able to stay in the shade all the way to the bottom of the hill. The air smelt like pine needles and hot tar. The houses were all different, each surrounded by a wide garden and a dense thicket of trees that allowed privacy between them. Instead of house names or numbers, each one had a sign announcing the name of the family who lived there. I followed the curve of the road past the Foxes and the Unterthiners, the Goldbergs, the Maudes and then finally the Westlands.

I don't know why I went there.

But there I was. Staring at this big wooden house with the white shutters and a complicated roofline of gable ends and turrets that suggested a house that was more than a simple arrangement of rectangular rooms. A million miles from my home.

Through the trees, I caught a glimpse of a dock, a small red sailing boat moored alongside it. There was so much I didn't know about Ryan. I didn't know he lived in a big house, that he went to an expensive school and had friends who went scuba-diving in New York City for the weekend. He had given all of this up to save me, and then given up his freedom as well. He'd given up too much.

The driveway was semicircular so that any car approaching the house could drive in on one side of the semicircle and out the other without turning around. There was a double garage with a basketball hoop attached to the wall between the two doors. I closed my eyes and tried to imagine Ryan and his brothers shooting hoops when they were kids.

There were no cars parked in the driveway and Admiral Westland had said that he and his family were staying at the Institute to be closer to Ryan, so I risked walking towards the house. The trees rustled either side of me and I could hear the faint slap of water against the dock. This was where Ryan had spent his childhood. Here.

I walked past the house towards the lake. Three boats were tied up against the dock – a small rowing boat, a sailing boat and a canoe. There were maybe ten other houses bordering the lake that I could see. In the distance was a sailing boat heading back to shore. I could see half a dozen kids whooping and diving off the dock of a neighbouring house.

'Hey!' a voice yelled from behind me.

I turned quickly. Jem was running down the steps from the upper level of a deck on the rear of the house.

'I'm sorry,' I said, embarrassed now at being here uninvited.

'Eden?' he said.

I nodded.

'Come on up.'

I made my way to the upper level of the deck, wondering how I would explain myself.

'What are you doing here?' he asked.

I shrugged. 'I started walking and just ended up here.'

'Come inside. You look hot. You want some ice water?'

'Thank you.'

He pressed an icon on the fridge and filled a glass with crushed ice and cold water. I took the glass which was cloudy with cold, and held it against my overheated head.

'Did you say goodbye?' asked Jem.

'I saw him,' I said. 'I didn't say goodbye. I couldn't do that.'

Jem nodded. 'I couldn't either.'

We stared at each other for a few moments and I almost considered asking him to help me rescue Ryan. But then he told me that he had a flight back to Greenland in a couple of hours and needed to finish packing his things.

'I should get back,' I said. 'I have friends waiting for me.'

'Do you want to see his room before you go?'

I nodded.

Jem led me into a wide hall. 'His room's at the end. I'll drive you back to the hotel just as soon as I'm done packing.'

'You don't have to do that,' I said. 'I can walk.'

'It's on my way.'

Jem went into his own room, leaving me at the threshold of Ryan's room. I pushed the door open.

There were all the things you expected to see in a bedroom: the bed, the chest of drawers, the built-in closet, the desk. There was a bedside table with a pile of books. The walls were painted blue; Ryan's sketches were tacked up all over the place. Some of them were of a planet with three suns and two moons. Others were of a small cove I recognised as Penpol Cove. And then there were sketches of me. My hair flowing down my back. My face. My eyes. Just my mouth. My hands holding a shell.

On his desk were notebooks and leafs of loose paper, covered in scribbles. There were mathematical equations I couldn't even begin to understand, photos and schematics of ships and time-ships. Dates and timelines. Printouts of fuel grades and prices.

I moved to the window. It had a perfect view over the dock and the lake. The kids next door were still jumping into the water, shrieking with laughter. A loon called plaintively from out on the lake. The sun was falling behind the treetops. Ryan was going to the moon, but down here life was carrying on.

Everyone was waiting for me in the lobby of the Lakeview. Peg stood up as soon as he saw me and pulled me close.

'I never really thought this could happen,' he said into my hair.

212

'It's like a bad dream,' I said. 'I can't quite believe that this is it.'

'Where have you been?' He drew back from me and took in my sunburnt, sweaty appearance. 'I came here as soon as I heard the verdict. We all did. We were so worried about you.'

'I needed some time to think.'

'Shall we go to your room, Eden?' asked Antoine, looking around.

People were starting to stare at us. Even the hotel staff – usually so discreet – were whispering amongst themselves. I nodded and we all made our way to the lift. No one said anything till we got to my room. Once inside, Antoine and Belle took one couch, Lyra and Peg the other. Lyra leant forward and put a bag on the table.

'What's that?' asked Peg.

'Food. I know we have bad news, but people still need to eat.'

She lifted her bad leg and slipped it over Peg's leg until it rested between his thighs. Absently, Peg began running his hand along her calf. I looked away. Today, of all days, I didn't have the stomach for it.

'Eden, put the com-screen on,' said Lyra. 'I heard something downstairs about Ryan's father.'

I scanned on the screen. It was still tuned to a news station.

A tickertape message at the bottom of the screen read *Breaking News*.

'Extraordinary turn of events,' the news reporter was saying.

The crew were standing outside the Institute, but not by the entrance to the Time Court; they were on the other side, where the residences were located.

'Admiral Westland was arrested less than two hours after the court delivered the guilty verdict on his son Orion. He was at his apartment with his wife and one of his sons. It has been alleged that Admiral Westland aided and abetted his son's time travel by acquiring a time-ship and the necessary fuel for that trip. Travel through time requires immense quantities of top-grade fuel; without the right credentials, it's almost impossible to get hold of. There had been no reports of break-ins at fuel depots and there is speculation that it was an inside job.

'Of course if Admiral Westland is found guilty, the presidency of the Institute will almost certainly go to Admiral Wolfe. Wolfe and Westland have been at loggerheads ever since Westland introduced a Bill to Parliament that would close the Lunar Facility. Westland's arrest . . .'

'Turn it off,' said Antoine. 'We don't need to hear this.'

'What was that about?' I asked. 'About them being at loggerheads.'

'Westland wants to close down the Lunar Facility,' said Antoine. 'He thinks it's inhumane. Problem is, it's owned by Wolfe. Wolfe basically gets free labour as the prisoners have to work in the mines. And Wolfe wants to ban time travel. The trouble with that is that Westland makes time-ships, so a ban on time travel would affect his business.'

'It's all stupid,' said Belle. 'Both families are already filthy rich.'

Lyra stretched noisily. 'Maybe I should go to the press and tell the truth,' she said.

'Why?' asked Peg. 'How will that help anything now?'

'The whole family has been through so much and now this. We all know Admiral Westland didn't help Orion get the fuel. We should go public with the whole story.'

'What is the whole story?' I asked.

'I stole the ship, Lyra,' said Peg, ignoring me. 'And helped with the cover-up. You want to see me on the moon with Ry?'

'Of course not. But Admiral Westland shouldn't have to take the blame either.'

'They won't be able to find any evidence against him because he didn't do it,' said Antoine.

I went over to the minibar and poured myself a glass of water from the jug. I was starting to get a headache. Peg joined me.

'You OK?' he asked quietly. He stood close to me, shoulder to shoulder.

'I'm dehydrated. I have a headache,' I said, focusing on the things that were simplest to fix.

'Anyone have any painkillers?' asked Peg.

'I do.' Belle dug through her handbag until she found a small bottle of blue pills. 'Two of these and a full glass of water will make you feel better.'

Nothing would make me feel better, but at least they would deal with the headache.

Lyra leant forward and unwrapped the bag of food in the middle of the table. 'I have bread rolls with shredded minis and berries.'

'Bread,' said Belle, lifting a roll. 'Good job, Lyra.'

'I know. The beauty editor got engaged today and brought them in for lunch. These are the leftovers.'

'You should try one, Eden,' said Belle as she split her roll into two. 'Bread's amazing.'

I lifted one of the rolls and turned it over; it looked just like an ordinary bread roll to me.

'Break it in half,' said Belle. 'And then fill it with some minis and berries. It's called a sandwich. It's real good.'

'What are minis?'

'Mini livestock. You know, ground-up insects and stuff. Lots of protein.'

I put the roll back on the table. 'Maybe later. I'm not hungry right now.'

'I'll get room service to bring us some drinks,' said Antoine. 'What's everyone want?'

I just wished everyone would leave so I could stop struggling to hold myself together and let the tears flow.

While the rest of them ate, I stood at the window and watched the pleasure boats out on the lake. Everything I'd done up to now seemed so stupid. I'd trusted that the Time Court would see the truth and Ryan would be freed. I'd spent eleven days in this time-scape hoping Ryan would be acquitted and had done nothing to plan for a disaster like this. I should have done more.

'You really ought to eat something,' said Peg, appearing by my side.

'I'm not hungry.'

'I know. But you still should eat something.'

I let him take my hand and lead me to the table. 'You want a plain roll or shall I make you a sandwich?'

'As it is,' I said, taking a bread roll. 'You know, back in the twenty-first century, bread is just peasant food. Everyone eats it. We toast it for breakfast and we eat sandwiches for lunch all the time, though we usually have peanut butter or cheese, rather than ground-up insects.'

'Oh, isn't that interesting?' said Lyra. There was a slight edge to her voice. 'And in the twenty-second century we don't hold hands with boys we're not dating.'

I looked down at my hand still holding Peg's and quickly let go.

Peg flopped down on the couch next to Lyra. 'You're just jealous,' he said. He picked up her bad leg and began massaging her calf again. 'You want me all to yourself.'

She pulled a face at him. 'Do I look *that* desperate?'

'I've missed bread so much,' I said. 'This looks great.' I took a big bite. The bread was soft and still warm. Under different circumstances I would have loved it, but right now it just stuck to the roof of my mouth and made me feel sick. I gulped at my glass of water to wash it down.

'Have you thought about a job, Eden?' asked Belle.

'Not really. I'll need to sort out something soon.'

'I could probably get you a job at the theatre if you don't mind working Front of House.'

I wasn't sure where to sit. Peg and Lyra were cuddled up close to one another on one couch and Belle and Antoine were spread out on the other.

'Thank you. I might take you up on that,' I said, opting

217

to remain standing. 'A friend of mine also offered me a waitressing job. On the Inter-Planetary Spaceport.'

They all looked at me.

'Why would you do that?' asked Antoine. 'All your friends live here.'

'I probably won't. It's just another option.'

'Are you serious?' asked Peg. 'You have a job offer on the spaceport? Really?'

'Umm, yeah.'

'Do you know someone there? Do you think you could put in a good word for me? It's my dream to work on the spaceport.'

'I know the captain. He was the leader on the 2012 mission.'

'You know Benjamin Hansen?' said Peg. 'I wrote a paper on him.'

'Calm down, fanboy,' said Lyra.

'Why don't you go back to school and finish your high school education?' said Belle. 'Lakeborough High is a very good school. You would have more choices if you got your diploma first.'

'Maybe.'

'The colleges in New Hampshire are good as well,' said Antoine. 'That's why none of us are moving away. Peg and I are at the Academy in town. Lyra and Belle are at the university here. Those would both be options for you.'

'You don't have to rush into a decision,' said Belle. 'Why don't I try and fix you up with a job at the theatre? The

sooner you get into a routine, the easier it will be to . . .'
Her words faded away into nothing.

They'd given up. Every one of them had simply accepted it was over for Ryan.

'We have to do something to help Ryan,' I said, trying – and failing – not to raise my voice.

'There's nothing we *can* do,' said Lyra.

'When Travis – the cleaner – killed me, Ryan stole a time-ship and travelled through time to save me. He didn't just give up and settle into a routine to make it easier to forget!'

'And didn't that plan work out well for the two of you?'

'I'm alive, aren't I?' I said, looking at Lyra. 'He didn't accept my fate – he worked to change it. He saved my life. I'm not going to let them send him to the moon for the rest of his.'

'Eden,' said Belle gently. 'If there was anything we could do, we would. But he's just been convicted by the highest court in the world. There's no appeal process. I don't see what we can do to help him.'

'We have to help him escape,' I said. 'Before they send him to the moon.'

Lyra rolled her eyes. 'With all due respect, Eden, you have no idea what you're talking about. This is the Space and Time Institute, not the public library.'

'Nothing is impossible. If Ryan can steal a time-ship and travel back a hundred and eleven years to save me, surely I can find a way to break him out of the Institute.'

There was a knock on the door. Peg opened it and let

room service bring the various drinks to the table. There was beer and wine, as well as mineral water and orange juice. Peg pushed what was left of the bread rolls and fillings to the edge of the table.

'He's going to be at the Institute until Tuesday,' I said, once room service had gone. 'And then he gets transported to the spaceport for twenty-four hours. Then it's the moon.'

'Even if we did plan something crazy, that doesn't give us much time,' said Belle.

'He's just been convicted of a crime in the Time Court,' said Antoine. 'His face is all over com-screens all over the world. Where would he go, even if you did manage to help him escape?'

'We'd find somewhere. That part is easy,' I said.

'It *wouldn't* be easy,' said Lyra. 'With retinal scanners and fingerprint locks and port-com security, he'd get picked up.'

'I'm not letting them send him to the moon.'

'You can forget the spaceport and the moon,' said Belle. 'You'd never even get close to them. And you can't just walk into the Institute with a gun and shoot your way to Orion's cell.'

'I know that,' I said. 'We'd need a plan.'

'There's no time for a plan,' said Antoine.

'I'm going to try and rescue him,' I said. 'With or without your help.'

The sandwiches and drinks were reduced to a few crumbs and a tray full of smeared, empty glasses. Belle and Antoine had spent the last ten minutes telling me about the trip they were planning to take to the mountains at the weekend. Peg had said nothing. He just sat on the couch, absently rubbing Lyra's leg and staring out of the window.

'What do you think?' asked Belle. 'It would do you good to get away from town.'

'Probably not,' I said.

'There's no way we can rescue him from the moon,' said Peg, lifting Lyra's leg and placing it on the couch. He stood up. 'It's a maximum security prison with no free air to breathe. If we're gonna have any chance of rescuing Ryan, it's gonna be the Institute or the spaceport.'

I felt the tiniest flicker of hope: Peg wanted to help.

'The Institute is the best option,' Peg continued. 'For obvious reasons.'

'Right,' I said. 'So we're going to rescue him from the Institute. And we have less than one week to do it. Where do we start?'

'We need a map of the interior,' said Peg, 'and a map of the grounds.'

'You can get a satellite image of the grounds,' said Antoine. 'The interior is a different matter.'

'Antoine, Belle. Your mother is a test-pilot for the Institute. Can't we use that as a way into the building?' asked Peg.

Belle shook her head. 'Mum has an office at the Institute, but she's never there. She spends most of her time at the Westland Space Centre.'

'But she does have an office at the Institute. That's good. I mean, we might be able to use that somehow.'

'I'm not sure how useful it would be,' said Belle. 'She

only goes to the Institute for meetings and briefings. Her office is just a desk and a few books.'

'Do you know your way round the inside of the Institute?'

'No. I know how to get from the administration entrance to her office, but that's it. Antoine and I have only been there a handful of times.'

'Eden, do you remember anything from when you arrived?' asked Peg.

'It's such a blur,' I said. 'The inside of that place is a labyrinth.'

'Damn,' said Peg. 'Antoine, is there any way you can get your mother to draw you a map?'

'Sure. I'll just tell her we need a map because we're planning a break-in,' said Antoine.

Peg sighed. 'I know that was a stupid suggestion.'

'I'll check through her computer,' said Antoine. 'It has a link-up with the Institute. Maybe I can find a map of the interior that way.'

'Antoine, you'll never be able to do that,' said Belle. 'The login and password security will be impossible to hack. Even for you.'

'I'll give it a try,' said Antoine. 'We can wait until she's working. Then I'll run into the office and tell Mom you've burned yourself or something. She'll run out to make sure you're OK without bothering to log off and I'll go through the Institute file database.' He smiled.

'So I have to injure myself, while you just have to lie.'

'Belle, who's good with computers – you or me?'

Belle rolled her eyes. 'Fine. But I'm not deliberately burning myself.'

'This entire conversation is stupid,' said Lyra. 'Even if you have a blueprint of the Institute and the grounds, how are you going to get him out of a locked cell? Or out of the building? Or off the grounds? It really is heart-warming that you all want to help Orion, but really?'

'I don't think it's such a crazy idea,' said Antoine. 'It's not a prison. It was never meant to be one. It has a few holding cells that are designed for short term stays. The main reason for security at the Institute is to protect VIPs from crazy gunmen and to protect information. It would be much harder if we were trying to bust him out of a real prison.'

'That's right,' said Peg. 'The Institute has public rooms and a residential wing. Lots of the building is designed for public access. I'm not saying it'll be easy, but there must be a way.'

'Is there any way we can get on to the grounds?' I asked. 'To look around?'

'Sure,' said Belle. 'There's a museum open to the public. If you visit the museum, you can also look around the grounds. They even have pedaloes for hire on their lake.'

'I can do that tomorrow,' I said.

'I'll come with you,' said Peg.

Lyra pushed herself to a standing position. 'Eden, could you help me get some ice?'

I grabbed the ice bucket from the table and held the door open for Lyra as she limped through it. She said nothing as we made our way along the corridor to the ice machine by the lift. I placed the ice bucket under the spout and she pressed the button for extra frozen.

'Pegasus really likes you,' she said.

The machine clanked and shook as a torrent of white ice tumbled into the bucket.

'I like him too.'

'He likes you too much.'

The ice torrent stopped. I cradled the bucket.

'He's trying to impress you,' she continued.

'I don't know what you're talking about.' I started walking back to my room. Lyra grabbed my arm and a couple of ice cubes spilled on to the floor.

'I've seen the way he looks at you.'

'You're imagining things, Lyra. Ryan is his best friend. He wants to help him. That's all.'

'He's always been reckless, but this is crazy. You can't let him try to break Orion out of the Institute. It won't work.'

I ignored her and pulled free from her grip.

'He's expendable to you,' she said. 'You just see him as a means to an end. But if he gets caught, he'll get the moon too. It's not just a life sentence, Eden. The mines. They work them all day in heat like you can't imagine. And the temperature at night is so cold, people die of hypothermia in their beds. It's not a life sentence, it's a death sentence. No one has ever lasted more than five years.'

'Is that supposed to make me feel better?'

She shook her head. 'Peg will do whatever you ask him to. But you shouldn't ask him to do this. It's too much. Orion can't be helped.'

'God, Lyra, you went out with Ryan for a year. You must have cared about him once.'

'Some people are a lost cause.'

I ignored her and strode back to my room, making sure she couldn't keep up. I didn't believe what she'd said about Peg. But even if it was true, I'd use anything I could to save Ryan.

'Do you promise to help me?' I asked Peg, as I came through the door, needing an answer before Lyra caught up with me.

'I already said I would.'

'But do you promise?'

'I promise.'

'Time to hit the road,' said Antoine, as Lyra walked into the room. 'I can give everyone a ride.'

'Go without me,' said Peg. 'My car is outside.'

Antoine nodded. 'Shall we meet here tomorrow afternoon? See what we have?'

'Meet at mine,' said Peg. 'Eden's checking out of the Lakeview tonight and moving in with me.'

'Moving in with you?' said Lyra.

Peg rubbed the back of his neck. 'Yeah. She's a minor. And – believe it or not – I'm now her legal guardian.'

'Antoine,' said Lyra. 'Please take me home.'

CHAPTER 16

As soon as Peg was done with work, we drove to the Institute. For the sake of appearances, we took a quick tour of the museum and purchased some gifts in the shop. Peg picked up a pen with the Space and Time Institute logo on the side and I bought a snow globe, with the Institute sitting in the middle of a big green lawn.

'Let's buy ice creams,' said Peg, as we set off across the real lawn.

All around us families were sitting in the shade enjoying picnics, while little children ran around pretending to be spaceships.

'I'm not hungry.'

'It will look more convincing if we're eating ice creams.'

I let him buy me a vanilla cone, though I was much too nervous to have an appetite. Slowly we strolled across the neat green grass, heading towards its outer perimeter. I took a quick lick of my ice cream, but it was sickeningly sweet. Peg was eating his in large bites. I watched him out of the corner of my eye as my ice cream melted and then dripped down my hand to my wrist and inside the sleeve of my shirt.

'You want mine?' I asked, as he shoved the end of his cone into his mouth.

He nodded, took the ice cream and waited while I wiped my hand clean on the grass.

'Once we get him out of the building, we have to get him off the grounds,' said Peg, looking around. 'We can't go through the main entrance because of the gate and security. We'd be stopped, obviously.'

I looked around. The Institute was surrounded on all sides by a vast lawn which was bordered by forest to the east and west, a small lake to the north and a car park and guarded entranceway to the south.

'It has to be through the forest,' I said. 'We can't escape using a pedalo!'

'Let's go and check it out.'

We continued walking across the lawn till the grass began to thin and we reached the edge of the forest.

'Won't it look a bit suspicious if we just wander into the woods?' I said.

'I don't think so. This area is open to the public so we're not doing anything wrong. We just have to look like we're having fun, not checking out the grounds for an escape route.'

The shade was a welcome respite from the thick humidity on the lawn. We walked deep into the trees until we reached a high metal fence and the lawn was just a hint of bright green in the distance.

'Damn,' I said, staring at the fence. 'This could be a problem.'

Peg leant close to it. 'It's electrified. Not good.'

'So even if we get him out of the Institute, we can't escape through the forest . . .'

'Maybe there's a break in the fence somewhere.'

I sighed. Now we were here, a rescue attempt seemed such a long shot. 'It's a boundary fence,' I said. 'Obviously designed to keep people out. We're not going to find a break in it.'

'Come on. Let's follow the fence towards the back of the Institute,' said Peg, striding ahead.

We continued north-west, heading towards the back where the lake and the service entrance was.

'It makes sense that the service entrance will be easier to escape from than the heavily guarded main entrance,' said Peg. 'Maybe we could bring in a laundry truck or something as our cover. Get Ryan out through the service entrance and into the truck.'

'There must be a particular company they use,' I said. 'For laundry. If we knew who they were, one of us could get a job as a driver with them and . . . damn! We need more time.'

'We have to work with what we've got,' said Peg. 'Let's see if we can get a bit closer to that service entrance.'

Silently, we made our way through the trees towards the building. The closer we were to the edge of the forest, the harder my heart knocked in my chest.

'This is close enough,' whispered Peg, when we were about ten trees' depth from the edge of the forest. Beyond the trees here was not lawn, but a yard. A lorry pulled up outside a loading bay and we watched as two men began unloading sacks of rice and crates of carrots.

'Looks like we've found the kitchen,' said Peg in a low voice.

'Maybe we could smuggle him out in a food delivery truck,' I said. 'What's the name of the company? I can't quite read it from here.'

Peg stepped forward a few paces, squinting into the distance. 'Norberry Foods,' he said.

'Can't we bribe a driver to let us make the delivery or something?'

'Maybe.'

He didn't sound convinced. I knew why. Even if we left through the service entrance, we'd have to drive through the security gate, possible roadblocks, not to mention a delivery driver who knew too much.

'What do we do now?' I asked.

'Back to mine to see what Antoine and Belle have managed to find out.'

Antoine and Belle arrived five minutes after we did.

'You find out anything useful?' I asked.

Antoine unfolded a map. 'Belle and I have studied the area. There's a Forest Service road that runs along here.' He pointed to a section of the map. 'It's about a mile away from the Institute. If we can get Ryan out of the building, through the forest to this track, one of us can be here waiting for him.'

'There's one slight obstacle,' I said. 'It's a two-metre high electrified metal fence.'

'Is it definitely electrified?' asked Antoine.

''Fraid so,' said Peg.

'Did you check to see if there are any gaps in the fence?' asked Belle. 'Or gates?'

'The only gap in the fence is where the forest meets the lake,' I said. 'So unless we want to escape using a pedal boat, or by swimming, we're all out of luck.'

'It's going to have to be the main gate then,' said Antoine.

'It's looking that way,' said Peg. 'I'm going to look into the companies that deliver to the Institute and see if we can borrow a truck.'

'And then what?' I asked.

'If we get Ryan to the shipyard, and on to one of the little space hoppers, we can take him far away. Outside of the Federation even. He could fly the ship himself.'

'And go where?' asked Belle.

Peg shrugged. 'Anywhere. I'd say that's the least of our worries right now.'

'OK, so we have a sort-of plan to get him off the Institute grounds and out of the Federation,' I said, 'but first we have to break him out of the Institute. Did you manage to get a map, Antoine?'

He closed his eyes and shook his head. 'I'm sorry, Eden. I tried. We both did.'

Belle held out her arms. She had a plaster around her left thumb, a bandage around her right wrist and another plaster on her elbow. 'I managed to burn myself twice and cut myself with a knife,' she said.

'Three times Mum left the office to see to Belle. Every time she locked her computer,' said Antoine. 'I tried to hack my way in. But I couldn't. I guess she's more careful than I thought.'

'We have to find a way to get a map of the inside,' said

Peg. 'Or something. Even a rough sketch would be something to go on.'

'Did you learn anything from inside the museum?' asked Belle.

'No,' said Peg. 'There were guidebooks, but they just had photographs of the public rooms. And you can't access anywhere else from the museum.'

'We need to find a way in,' said Belle. 'I wonder if we could get Lyra to interview a member of the kitchen staff? Maybe she could get a tour of the service level.'

The doorbell rang. Peg jumped off the couch to answer it. He came back a few seconds later with a parcel.

'It's for you, Eden.'

'What? Who would send me a parcel?'

'Delivery guy said he tried the Lakeview Hotel first, but they told him you'd moved here.'

'I left a forwarding address,' I said, taking the parcel.

I tore off the brown paper to reveal a white box with a lid. I lifted the lid. Inside was a long length of shimmering blue fabric, laid on a thick bed of white tissue paper.

'It's a dress,' I said, lifting it out of the box.

'God, it's beautiful,' said Belle, helping me hold it up.

It was pale blue silk with a beaded bodice.

'Who the hell would send me a dress?' I said, confused.

'There are shoes in here too,' said Belle, looking into the box. 'Heels.' The shoes were the same blue colour as the dress. 'And a letter,' said Belle, passing me a small blue envelope.

I ripped it open. Inside was a simple handwritten note.

Be my date for the Late Summer Ball? CW

I laughed. 'I can get inside the Institute.'

Everyone looked at me.

'If I go to the Late Summer Ball with Clarence Wolfe tomorrow.'

CHAPTER 17

Peg opened the door.

'Can I come in?' I heard Clarence ask.

'Sure.' Peg turned and winked at me.

Clarence was dressed in a cream linen suit with a silk bow tie the exact same colour as my dress.

'I knew that colour would suit you,' he said, running his eyes slowly up my body, from the blue heels to the plunging neckline.

'What time are you planning on bringing her home?' asked Peg.

Clarence raised his eyebrows. 'Pegasus, I know you're now her legal guardian, but that doesn't give you an excuse to act like her father.'

'If you touch her . . .'

'What?'

'She's sixteen.'

'Peg, I'll be fine,' I said, glaring at him.

'Last time I checked she was over a hundred years old,' said Clarence with a smirk.

He took my arm and we walked – slowly, me tottering, despite an hour of practice in the living room – down the stairs and across the street to the waiting car. Someone must have tipped off the press because the number of photographers was ten times the usual number that loitered outside the entrance.

'Just look down and let your hair fall in front of your face,' said Clarence. 'Don't let them get a good shot.'

He held the door open and then climbed in the back of the car with me. A driver in a white uniform and hat checked that we were ready to leave and then pulled out into the traffic.

'We'll have to do the red carpet,' said Clarence. 'It's just five minutes of posing for photographs and shaking hands. And then I'll introduce you to my family, because they'll expect to meet my date. But the rest of the evening will be fun, I promise.'

The car drove right up to the barricades around the red carpet. The driver opened the door for us, and Clarence – thankfully – lent me a hand so I could get out without revealing too much thigh. My shoes were pinching the skin of my foot, right where the ankle met the heel, so I walked slowly, clutching Clarence's arm and trying not to limp, determined not to broadcast my high-heel inexperience to the whole world.

After shaking hands with a few people, he guided me to the middle of the carpet to pose for photographs. He put an arm loosely around my waist. Cameras flashed from every direction, but the questions were gentler than what I was used to.

'Such a beautiful dress, Eden. Who is the designer?'

'Did you pick it yourself?'

'How long have you known Clarence?'

'The designer is Miller,' said Clarence. 'Eden and I met through mutual friends. I knew her friend Orion Westland.'

The main entrance of the Institute had been transformed. A wooden arbour had been constructed in front of the white stone doorway; hundreds of red and pink roses were twined around it. The scent from the flowers was overpowering.

Once inside, a welcoming party of the Guardians and their spouses – all except the Westlands – awaited us.

'It's OK, they won't bite,' Clarence whispered.

Clarence introduced me to just one couple: his parents.

'Mother, Father,' said Clarence with exaggerated politeness, 'may I introduce Eden Anfield.'

Clarence's mother – a petite blonde with bright red lipstick and unnaturally white teeth – almost curtseyed. 'How lovely to meet you in person.'

Admiral Wolfe shook my hand. 'I'm pleased to see you've settled into life in Lakeborough,' he said tonelessly.

I smiled at the man who had determined my life was nothing more than collateral damage. 'I've found the locals to be exceptionally friendly.'

We walked into the room. It was a formal hall, the sort of thing I'd only ever seen in stately homes in England, though they probably existed in palaces and official buildings all over the world. The ceiling was as high as three floors and the dimensions of the room were as big as a football pitch. The walls were the same white stone as most of the Institute, but tonight they glowed a warm pink – the result of thousands of fairy lights strung around the walls.

There were hundreds of people in the hall, and the

sound of their laughter and chattering bounced harshly off the cold floor and high ceilings. I was grateful to Clarence for quickly ushering me through the room – with just a few polite introductions – to the courtyard garden at the rear of the Institute. This, clearly, was where the real party was happening.

Under a gazebo at one end of the lawn an orchestra was noisily tuning up. We wandered across the grass to the other side where a lone harpist was plucking the strings of her instrument, creating a timeless, haunting melody. In between the two musical acts were dozens of food and drink stations, and ahead of us – on the lake – thousands of white candles floated and bobbed on the calm water.

'It's beautiful,' I said.

Clarence smiled. 'Isn't it? And everyone who matters in the whole of the Federation is here tonight. The Guardians, admirals, judges, film stars, musicians, diplomats, fuel tycoons, the young, the rich and the beautiful. And you.'

I bit my lip and tried to think of something to say. It was a genuinely stunning spectacle. And Clarence seemed all right to me, despite Lyra's warnings and Peg's obvious dislike.

'Is it true what you said about being Ryan's friend?' I asked.

Clarence smiled. 'Of course. We were in school together. Sat next to one another in Advanced Maths for Portal Creation.' He leant in and whispered in my ear. 'I stole the fuel that sent him back to 2012.'

'You did?'

'My family's filthy lucre comes from fuel,' he said. 'If

anyone can get their hands on large quantities of it without attracting attention, it's me.'

Peg and Lyra had never said anything about Clarence being one of the good guys, one of those who helped Ryan get back to me. Was it possible they didn't know?

'You were part of the whole plan?'

'Yep. Now this is your first Late Summer Ball. What would you like to drink?'

'Since it's a special occasion, how about a glass of your finest champagne?'

'We do have Canada's finest champagne. However, if you want to really celebrate in style, we could share a magnum of Alaskan beer.'

'Whatever you suggest.'

Clarence grabbed an enormous champagne-shaped bottle of beer and two tall champagne flutes from one of the drinks stations. He popped the stopper and poured us each a full glass with a frothy head that spilled over the top of the glass and all over our hands.

'Here's to the future,' he said, knocking his glass against mine.

I sipped, but got only a mouthful of froth. That was fine; I had to remember – whatever Clarence said about having helped Ryan – I was here for a reason, and I needed a clear head.

'Let me give you the low-down on some of these people,' said Clarence. He topped up his glass. 'That's Claudette Legrand, the president's daughter.' He pointed to a beautiful young woman in a silver ballgown. 'Terrible drug habit.

237

Started on opium at fifteen. Lucky for her she's exceedingly rich.' He pointed at another young woman. 'Juliette Bernard. Highest paid actress in Hollywood. And that's Simon Pratt standing next to her. He's dating her. He used to be her chauffeur.'

The orchestra began playing and men and women in ballgowns and suits of every shade of the spectrum moved towards the wooden dance floor that had been constructed in front of the lake. Clarence took my hand and led me to it. I remembered that he was a good dancer from the night I danced with him at the Watering Hole.

'I don't know any of the dances,' I reminded him.

'It's a simple four-step,' he said.

I watched his feet. It was a straightforward back and forth, left and right shuffle. I looked at the floor and copied his moves.

'You're doing great,' he whispered after a while. 'Now look at me and let your feet follow their instincts.'

I met his eyes, held on to him and tried to ignore the moves my feet were making. To my surprise, the combination of music, the atmosphere and Clarence's lead all conspired to make the whole experience a thoughtless, effortless event.

We were being watched and photographed, not only by the official photographers, but by many of the other party-goers as well. I closed my eyes to block them out and held on tight to Clarence, letting him guide me through the moves.

'You OK?' Clarence asked me.

'Just trying to pretend that people aren't watching us.'

'People are bound to be interested,' Clarence said. 'I'm the eldest son of one of the richest men on the planet. You're the first person to travel through time before time travel was invented.'

'When you put it like that,' I said, 'I almost understand their interest in us.'

The song ended and Clarence led me to a drinks table.

'Another beer?' he asked.

'Great.'

He unplugged another bottle and filled two glasses.

'Cheers,' I said.

Clarence leant across the table and tucked a stray strand of hair behind my ear. His hand lingered on the side of my face. Cameras clicked and lights flashed.

I shut my eyes and tried to hide my revulsion. 'Clarence,' I said.

'You're not just any old time traveller from pre-time travel,' he said, taking his hand back. 'You happen to be stunningly beautiful. Your face is selling millions of extra copies of magazines and newspapers. Do you have any idea how many women are getting their hair dyed red since you arrived?'

I shrugged, embarrassed.

'Not that I read the fashion pages,' said Clarence, 'but I flicked through my mother's port-com yesterday. And apparently early twenty-first century fashion is going to be the next big thing. All because of you.'

I laughed. 'I was probably the least fashion-conscious person I knew back in the twenty-first century. I practically lived in T-shirts and jeans.'

'That's what they were talking about,' said Clarence. 'Jeans.'

'I hope they do come back in fashion. I'm not wild about twenty-second century styles.'

'You'd look good in anything.' He was looking at me in a way that made me feel uncomfortable.

The band started playing a jaunty tune.

'Another dance?' I asked.

'You can't get enough of my smooth moves, huh?'

'This sounds like very danceable music. I'm determined to learn at least one dance.'

For the next two hours we danced. When we stopped for a rest – or for Clarence to top up his drink once again – he pointed out the rich, famous and infamous. He introduced me to his friends and only danced with other girls after ensuring I had a dance partner myself.

As Earth gently dipped away from the sun, the lights and candles grew brighter, the orchestra played louder, the guests laughed harder. Clarence had dispensed with his beer glass some time ago and was now swigging directly from the bottle, one arm around my shoulder, the other swinging the bottle by his side, his breath warm and beery as we danced.

'You having a good time?' he asked.

'I'm having a great time,' I said. 'But my feet are starting to hurt from all the dancing. How about you give me a tour of the Institute?'

He crinkled his forehead. 'Seriously?'

'You have a residence here, don't you? How about giving me the grand tour?'

His eyes twinkled. 'You want to see my apartment? Absolutely.'

I slipped off my heels and walked barefoot across the cool lawn, glad to feel the soft, yielding earth beneath my sore feet. Clarence grabbed another large magnum of beer – his sixth or seventh now by my count – and led me around the side of the east wing.

'If you want to see something really impressive, you should come up to Quebec and see our mansion up there,' he was saying as we approached the side entrance.

A doorman smiled at Clarence and held the door and just like that we were inside. When I'd visited the Westlands in their apartment, I'd assumed the lack of security measures was because I was with Admiral Westland. But even with Clarence, there was no security protocol, no X-rays or body scanners or handbag search. Clarence pressed a button for the lift and we travelled up to the top floor.

'They just let you in?' I asked. 'Why isn't there any security?'

'Don't worry – you're safe,' he said, his voice slurring a little. 'The doorman knows me. And you can't access the administration block from here so no one really cares.'

'Does this entrance only go to the apartments then?'

'Yep. It's completely self-contained.'

It suddenly dawned on me that I was going to be alone in an apartment with a very drunk boy I hardly knew. The lift door opened and we walked into a wide hallway.

'Welcome to the penthouse,' said Clarence. 'One of them, anyway.'

He gave me the tour. There was a formal sitting room and a dining room with shiny walnut floors and a chandelier the size of a small car. His father's office, which was adjacent to a large library, opened on to a roof terrace with views over the lawn and lake below. Clarence pushed open the glass doors and we wandered on to the terrace. The orchestra was still playing and the dancers were still dancing, and from this height – away from the spilled beer, the smell of flesh sweating in the warm evening air – the lawn looked like it was inhabited by hundreds of little flowers swaying and tumbling across the lawn.

Clarence lit a cigarette and leant out over the edge of the balcony. 'All the world's beautiful people gathered in one place,' he said. 'You can be a part of this set, Eden. You're unique. Everyone wants to know you.' He sucked hard on his cigarette and blew smoke rings into the air. 'You could come to Quebec with me for Christmas. It's the best place for parties. And then skiing in Alaska in February. Cruising the Arctic ocean in June – midnight sun and all that. It's not a bad life.'

'It sounds amazing,' I said. 'How do you fit in your studying?'

He laughed. 'I work hard and I play hard. It's what my father taught me. You want something, you have to work hard for it.'

'And what do you want?'

He flicked the butt of his cigarette over the balcony on to the lawn below and turned to me. 'You.'

I took a step backwards.

'Don't worry, I'm not going to hurt you,' he said with a laugh. 'I want you to fall in love with me.'

'What? Why?'

'Because you're one of a kind. No one else can be you. Money can't buy what you are. Surgery or fashion or connections mean nothing. You are the first person to travel through time.'

'So you want me because I'm a novelty?'

'Girls throw themselves at me all the time, Eden. They want to date me because I'm rich – obscenely so – and I know anyone who's anyone. You're different.'

'Well, I'm very flattered,' I said, backing into the library.

'Eden, wait.'

I hesitated.

'I probably shouldn't say this and I wouldn't be saying it if I wasn't very, very drunk. But I am sorry about Orion, you know,' he said. 'He's a good guy. I wish my father had let him go.'

'Me too.'

'He must have cared a lot about you.'

I said nothing.

'You must have cared a lot about him.'

'I still do.'

'Of course you do. I wasn't meaning to suggest . . . look, what I'm trying to say is, I don't expect you to be ready to move on yet. But when you are, I'll be waiting for you.'

I was speechless.

'In the meantime, I'd like to be your friend. I can introduce you to a lot of people.'

243

'I have friends.'

'Look, Eden, you're new to the twenty-second century and Lakeborough. But Pegasus Ryder is a nobody. He's a nice guy and all that, but he doesn't have two cents to rub together. Lyra Thornhill is a bitch, pure and simple. The Cohen twins are sweet, if you like bland and nerdy. You could have so much more than that.'

I said nothing.

'You're very quiet.'

'It's a lot to take in. This new world.'

He smiled and staggered across the terrace towards me. 'How about just one kiss?'

'I don't think so.'

'Aww, come on, Eden. Just a quick peck on the cheek. Then we'll go back downstairs and join the party.'

He hiccupped.

'Back in 2012 we don't allow boys to kiss us on the first date,' I said.

'So this is a date?' He smiled and lurched forward and the next thing I knew, vomit was spurting out of his mouth and all down the front of his shirt.

'Excuse me a moment,' he said, raising a hand and leaning over to heave.

I turned away from the sour smell of stomach acid and went back into the office. Quickly, I cast my eyes around. Surely there had to be something useful I could discover during my tour of his apartment. The desk was neat and tidy, just a translucent computer screen and a wireless headset. No folders or files I could take a quick flick through. I tried the top drawer of the desk. Locked. That had to mean there was something important inside. I looked around for an obvious hiding place for a key. Nothing.

I heard the lumbering foot shuffle that meant Clarence was heading inside. I moved away from the desk and pretended to be absorbed with a map of the world on the office wall.

'I am so sorry,' said Clarence, staggering, his words still clumsy in his mouth. 'There must have been something wrong with the shrimp tempura. Seafood never agrees with me.'

'It could happen to anyone,' I said.

'I'm just gonna brush my teeth.'

'Clarence, where's the kitchen? I'd like to get myself a glass of water.'

'We don't have a kitchen,' he said as he swayed towards the door. 'All our food is prepared in the Institute kitchens and delivered by the dumb waiter.'

'Oh, really?' I said, following him into the hall. 'Where is that?'

He pointed towards the dining room. 'Down there. A little alcove next to the dining room. Press the intercom and tell them what you want. I'll just be a minute.'

My bare feet slapped on the cold, marble floor as I made my way to the alcove. The dumb waiter was set into the wall, a touch screen intercom next to it. I pressed the open button. There was a quiet whirr and a click and then the door slid open revealing an empty box about the size of a storage trunk. Before I had time to think, I gathered up my dress and squeezed myself into the empty space. I pressed the button that said *Kitchen*, the door slid shut and then I felt the sensation of falling.

I took a deep breath and closed my eyes, somehow believing that if I couldn't see how dark and enclosed the space was, I wouldn't panic. My blood thrummed through my ears, a roar that drowned out my thoughts. And then I stopped falling, the door opened smoothly and I began to breathe.

Clambering out, I discovered I was in an alcove off the kitchen. I could hear the clanging and banging of pots and pans, orders being barked by one of the staff, the sizzle and spit of food cooking. I straightened my dress and peeked round the corner. Sure enough, the kitchen was a hive of activity.

I slipped out of the door and found myself in a corridor that led to a stairwell and a bank of lifts. This was the service level. Hallways led in all directions. I tiptoed further into the corridor.

I heard a hum and a ding and the lift door opened. A young woman dressed in a maid's uniform came out carrying a silver tray with a covered dinner plate on it. She jumped when she saw me.

'Madam! You shouldn't be here.'

'I'm sorry,' I said. 'I took the wrong door. I was trying to find my way back to the ballroom but I think I found the wrong stairs.'

'This is for staff only,' she said. 'But now you're here, the quickest way to the ballroom is to go up one flight of stairs and follow the corridor to the end.'

I thanked her and waited for her to leave. I had a hunch that if I was to find a way to get to the South Wing, where the offices and the Time Court – and presumably Ryan's cell – were located, it would be via the service level. Wishing I was wearing a uniform instead of my billowy gown, I headed quietly along the corridor.

I passed a suite of laundry rooms which smelt of sweet, fresh powder and hot ironing presses. Next up was a door simply labelled *Stores*. And then I saw something that made my heart beat faster: an old-fashioned analogue clock on the wall. The clock I had noticed on my way out of my cell, en route to the debrief with Admiral Wolfe two weeks earlier. I was close to the cells.

I shut my eyes and tried to remember which direction I had been coming from, which direction I was walking in, when Admiral Westland had escorted me to Admiral Wolfe. The clock had been on my right. I kept the clock on my left and headed down the next corridor.

I passed three empty cells, their doors open, before turning a corner and coming face to face with a guard. He was the only guard, standing outside the only closed cell. This had to be where Ryan was being kept.

'Don't move,' said the guard. He raised his gun and pointed it at my chest. I was aware of a red dot trained on my heart.

'I'm lost,' I said, hoping he wouldn't recognise me from the news. 'I was looking for the ladies' room and I think I took the lift to the wrong floor. Where am I?'

'You're in the lock-up, miss,' said the guard, lowering his

weapon. 'You need to turn around and go right back the way you came.'

Ten minutes later I was back on the lawn. I wished I had a pen and paper so I could map out the route I'd taken. But it wasn't so difficult to remember. The kitchen led to the service corridor which led everywhere. So long as I could get into Clarence's apartment, I could access the service area and the lock-up. We'd need to find a way to get Ryan out of his cell, but once we'd done so, we could get him into the service area and out through the kitchen. This evening hadn't been a complete waste of time after all.

'There you are!' bellowed a familiar voice.

There was a good chance I would need Clarence – or access to his apartment – to execute the rescue. So I gritted my teeth, turned on a smile and walked towards him, a fake stagger in my steps. Clarence opened his arms to receive me in a hug, and I was relieved to see he had changed his shirt.

'Where did you go?' he asked.

I shrugged. 'I couldn't work out the intercom so I came outside to get a drink.'

He laughed hard. 'You silly thing. Don't they have intercoms in 2012?'

I shrugged and smiled. 'No.'

He picked up a bottle of water from a table and we walked down to the lake's edge. A few candles still bobbed along the shoreline, though most had burnt themselves out by now.

'Stillwater Lake,' said Clarence. 'It belongs to the Institute. Families rent pedaloes here on summer afternoons, but they never go beyond the cove. If you paddle beyond the corner there, the lake opens up. It's twice the size it looks from here.'

'It's lovely,' I said.

'Give me a hand.'

Clarence pulled at a small rowing boat until it was freed from its protective covers. He dragged it to the water.

'Jump in,' he said.

I sat in the boat, while he kicked off his shoes and rolled up his trousers. Effortlessly, he pushed the boat down the beach and into the water, paddling up to his knees. Once it was floating, he clambered in and sat opposite me. He fitted the oars into their slots and began rowing us out beyond the cove. The orchestra had stopped playing, but the deep notes of a lone saxophone followed us across the water.

'Close your eyes,' he said.

I did as he asked and listened to the creak and groan of the oars, the slap of the water as the oars pushed it aside, the quiet rustle of leaves in the trees. I trailed one hand in the cool silk of the lake and focused on my own slow breathing.

The oars rattled in their rowlocks and we stopped rowing. I felt the tilt and wobble of the boat on the water.

'Open your eyes,' said Clarence.

I opened them. All around me was intense darkness. The water was black. The trees were shady silhouettes in the distance. But above was the most incredible show of glittering stars.

I gasped.

It was like magic. I might be living in a different country with different people in a completely different time, but some things hadn't changed. The constellations winked at me like old friends.

Clarence stopped rowing. He hoisted the oars inside the boat.

'Lie back,' he said. 'You can see the whole sky from here.'

I rested my head on the wooden bench and laid my legs across the bench by his head. He lay the opposite way and there we were head to toe, gazing up at the inky, star-studded night sky.

I found myself scanning the sky for Orion, but the constellation was nowhere to be seen. Still missing. Ryan had told me once that it was a winter constellation, that the days would be shortening before I would see it again. The first constellation I recognised was Cassiopeia, its w-shape a clear message in the sky. I navigated from there to Vega and then to the big square of Pegasus. Finally I found Perseus and fixed on Algol, the so-called demon star with its slow wink. The ancients thought it was bad luck, but I didn't think that. Luck was too close to Fate – and I didn't believe in Fate. I might not be able to influence the vast tides of time, but I would control my own destiny. A star shot across the sky, leaving a bright trail in its wake.

'Did you see that?' I asked.

'It's the Perseid meteor shower,' said Clarence. 'It peaked a couple of nights ago, but there should still be a few shooting stars.'

Before the words were out of his mouth, another star shot across the sky.

'This is so beautiful,' I said.

His fingertips brushed mine, an accidental touch, fleeting, like the stardust burning in the sky.

Another star grazed the night sky.

'Did you see that one?' asked Clarence.

'Yes.'

His fingers moved over mine and stayed there, the warmth of his hand now wilfully, knowingly touching me. I didn't move. I held my breath and reminded myself I was doing this for Ryan. Minutes passed. More stars tripped across the sky.

'They're not really stars,' I said. 'It's just dust burning up in our atmosphere.'

'I know.'

Clarence's fingers caressed mine. It was a light touch. But it was a step too far. I retracted my hand, curled it into a tight fist.

'I've always loved this lake,' said Clarence. 'I learnt to swim in it, I learnt to sail on it. I even learnt to scuba-dive here. It's much deeper than you might think.'

My heart jolted. I knew how we were going to get Ryan off the grounds of the Institute: under the water.

'But this is perfect, isn't it?' said Clarence.

It was perfect: the lake; the stars; the music.

And now I had the perfect plan.

CHAPTER 18

Trying not to jangle the key, I unlocked the door and tip-toed inside.

'It's three in the morning. I was getting worried,' Peg said. Empty coffee mugs and schoolbooks were spread across the table. He shut his textbook and came towards me.

'Everything's fine. I've got so much to tell you.'

'Tell me he didn't touch you.' Peg's voice was hoarse.

'I was fine the whole time,' I said, mentally brushing aside the moment I'd felt vulnerable, alone in Clarence's apartment. 'Although he did come close to throwing up all over me.'

Peg shook his head. 'What a charmer.'

I kicked off my heels. 'Help me with this zip.'

Peg's hands were cold against my skin. His hands shook as he struggled to unhook the catch at the top of the dress. When he pulled the zip down to my waist, I felt my whole body relax. Clarence had magically selected a dress in the right size, but the bodice was tight against my ribs. Now I could breathe.

I stepped out of the dress and threw it over the couch. 'I have a plan. I have it all worked out.'

'You wanna put some clothes on before you tell me about it?' He was looking at the floor.

I ran into my room, grabbed a T-shirt and tugged it over my head. 'He thinks I like him,' I shouted.

'Why does he think that?' Peg shouted back.

'Because I wanted him to think that,' I said, as I pulled on a pair of shorts. 'Actually, he doesn't seem so bad. A bit creepy and a bit pathetic, but not that bad, you know?'

'He *is* that bad. Don't let him fool you.'

I went back into the living room. Peg was tidying up his schoolbooks.

'Why do you hate him so much?' I asked.

'Because he's spoilt and arrogant.'

I perched on the edge of one of the couches. 'Clarence said he stole the fuel for Ryan's ship. Is that true?'

Peg nodded. 'Yeah. It's true.'

'So then why . . .'

'He didn't get Ryan that fuel because he wanted to help him. He got it in exchange for Ryan taking the blame for something. Clarence thinks he can buy his way out of trouble.'

'What are you talking about? What happened?' I asked.

'It doesn't matter.'

'Tell me.'

Peg rubbed his hands over his face and leant back against the table. 'A few months ago – it would have been March – Ry was completely stuck. He had a ship and he had a plan to save you, but no fuel. You can't just drive into a fuel depot and ask for a few tonnes of premium grade fuel without the right paperwork. We were all out of ideas. And then one night, we went to a party on the other side of Winnipesaukee. Me and Ry, Lyra, the twins.'

My stomach knotted at the thought of Ryan and Lyra going to a party together.

'Lyra hooked up with Clarence. She'd been on a couple of dates with him before, but they weren't together officially or anything. Anyway, they left the party before the rest of us.'

I tried to get it straight in my head. Lyra had been with Ryan for a year. Lyra dated Clarence five months ago. Ryan thought she liked Peg now.

'So what happened that night?'

'We left the party and drove home. There's no expressway around the lake unless you make a massive detour. Halfway home we found Clarence's car in a ditch. It had been raining heavily and the roads were slick. Lyra was injured, but he hadn't called an ambulance or anything because he was drunk.'

'Oh, God.'

'Driving under the influence would have meant immediate expulsion from the Academy and the end of any ambitions he might have for a career at the Institute. He asked us if one of us would say we'd been driving. Ryan was the only one who hadn't been drinking.'

'So he agreed?'

'Yeah. Ryan asked Clarence if he could get hold of five tonnes of premium grade fuel. He said he could. So Ryan took the blame. He was suspended from the Academy, but he didn't care. He had the fuel he needed and a way back to you.'

'And Lyra?'

Peg shrugged. 'Her leg and pelvis were badly damaged. She had three operations, but she'll always have a limp. She might have forgiven Clarence, but he never once called her to see how she was. Lyra was in hospital and Clarence was out drinking and partying with some other girl. Lyra had to let Clarence get away with it, because Ryan needed her to keep his secret so he could get back to you. So yeah – Clarence is right at the top of people I don't like very much.'

I ran a hand through my hair and exhaled. 'That explains a lot.'

'I'm gonna make some more coffee. You want some?'

Five minutes later, we were sitting together on one of the couches, each with a cup of coffee.

'You ready to hear my plan?' I asked, rubbing my eyes.

'Shoot.'

'I'm going to call Clarence and ask if I can come over tomorrow night and watch a movie with him.'

'I already don't like this. I don't trust him. I'm not saying he would be violent or anything, but he's . . .'

'Hear me out. I'm going to get him really drunk. And then I'm going to suggest we go outside and sit by the lake or something. You'll be waiting down by the lake.'

'How am I going to get through the security entrance? They count people in and out. By six o'clock the Institute is closed to visitors.'

'Do you still have Antoine's map?'

'Yeah.' He jumped up and snatched the map from the dining room table.

I opened it, resting it half on Peg's lap and half on my

own. 'The lake at the back of the Institute is called Stillwater Lake. It looks quite small from the back lawn of the Institute, but once you get beyond the cove it opens up.'

'How do you know this?'

'Clarence took me for a romantic boat ride under the stars.'

'What a creep.'

'He also told me that he learnt to scuba-dive in that lake.'

A smile crept on to Peg's face. 'I think I know where this is going.'

'If you came across the lake in a boat, you'd be seen. But if you scuba-dive from the far side of the lake, you can emerge in the forest this side of the fence.'

'Genius.'

'I need to get Clarence so drunk he passes out.'

'He's a big guy,' said Peg. 'That will take a lot of alcohol. Let me talk to the twins. Their dad's a pharmacist. They might be able to suggest something.'

I drained my coffee. 'Then we dress you as Clarence and we both go back inside and up to Clarence's apartment.'

'Don't they have security?'

'No. Not really. Just a doorman. I mean, he'd probably challenge us if he thought we were visitors. But if he thinks you're Clarence and I'm his friend . . .'

'That's a big "if".'

'I just walked in tonight. Clarence waved at the door-man and he let us in. It was easy.'

'Then what?'

'I found a way to get from his apartment to the cells.'

Peg swore. 'You're freakin' kidding me?'

I shook my head. 'These people can't even help them-selves to a glass of water without calling down to the kitchen. Can you believe that?'

'Actually, I can.'

'And everything comes up to the dining room in this dumb waiter.'

'What the hell is a dumb waiter?'

'It's like a lift for food. And it's quite big. I fit in it easily. It takes you down to the kitchen. From there you can access everywhere. We can get to Ryan's cell. Free him and then escape through either the service entrance or Clarence's apartment.'

'This is brilliant,' said Peg, grinning. 'You've figured most of it out. The only thing is getting him out of the cell.'

'I've seen where they keep him. I was standing outside his cell tonight.' I decided not to mention that the guard had his gun trained on my heart.

'How did you manage to do all this?'

'Good luck. There's just one guard outside the cell. And he has the key to the cell on his belt. He's armed – of course – but surely the two of us can overpower one of him.' I tried to hide the tremor in my voice. 'Especially if we play two silly, drunk kids who got lost.'

Peg chucked the map on the floor and reached over to hug me. 'I think we have a plan.'

CHAPTER 19

'Clarence, I'm going to turn in now,' said Mrs Wolfe. 'We have an early start in the morning. Don't be too late. I want us to be on the road by nine.'

'Don't worry. I'll be in bed soon.'

'Is Eden staying over? I can have Anna make up the spare room.'

'Oh no,' I said. 'I'll be heading back home in a few minutes.'

'OK, sweetheart. But if you change your mind, Clary will call Anna and have her make up a bed for you. You're always welcome here.'

'Thank you.'

Clarence waited till his mother left the room. 'She means well. Don't judge her too harshly.'

'She's lovely, Clarence.'

He smirked. 'She got extra helpings when God gave out enthusiasm.'

'I like her.'

Clarence put a hand on my arm. 'You know, I could arrange for you to have your own apartment in the city. I don't like you living with Pegasus Ryder in that run-down market area. It's not safe.'

'It's fine for now. In any case, he's my legal guardian; I don't have a choice.'

'I can be your legal guardian. Or one of my female friends. I don't like my girlfriend living with another man.'

'Am I your girlfriend now?'

'You're here, aren't you?'

I stood up. 'What time will your dad be home?'

Clarence shrugged. 'Don't worry about him. He seems fierce, but he's a pussycat really. Anyway, he's not coming home tonight. He had to head south to New Marseilles for work. He'll spend the night there. My mother and I have to join him tomorrow to help him with his campaign.'

'What campaign?'

'The election campaign. The date has been postponed until after the investigation into Admiral Westland. But it will still go ahead eventually. Dad's had some bad publicity with protestors outside Wolfe Energy in New Marseilles, so he's down there to deal with that. And then he's escorting Orion to the moon.'

I looked away.

'I'm sorry, Eden. I have to go with him. He's taking a film-maker and a load of journalists with him and using this as a publicity stunt. This isn't just the election; it's the whole of Wolfe Energy. A lot of people think the Lunar Facility is inhumane. He's using this as an opportunity to show that he's tough on crime and that the Lunar Facility is a good thing.'

'Great.'

'Don't judge me. He's my father. I don't have a choice.'

'I don't want to talk about it,' I said. 'Let's go down to the lake. I'd like to see what it's like without hundreds of party guests milling around.'

Clarence stood. 'If you want.'

'Do you have anything to drink?' I said. 'Maybe we could take some more of that beer with us?'

'This time traveller has expensive tastes,' said Clarence, winking.

We had already shared two bottles of beer, though in very unequal measures. I followed Clarence into the dining room alcove. He pressed the kitchen intercom and requested a magnum of Alaskan beer along with two glasses. Two minutes later the beer and glasses arrived on a heavy silver tray in the dumb waiter. Clarence shoved the bottle into one of his jacket pockets and hooked his fingers around the stems of the glasses.

'Come on then,' he said.

I snatched his big straw hat off the hatstand as we passed and pulled it over my head. It would help to cover Peg's dark hair later on. Clarence was bright blonde.

Everything outside was still, with nothing to disturb the quiet but the song of the cicadas and the gentle lapping of the lake against the sandy shore. The air had cooled; in the distance I could hear the low rumble of thunder.

'We need a storm to clear the air,' said Clarence.

'Let's just sit by the water's edge,' I said.

We both removed our shoes and walked barefoot over the cool sand.

'This OK?' asked Clarence, when we reached a sandy place by the shoreline.

'Perfect,' I said.

Across the lake, out on the Forest Service road, Antoine and Belle would be waiting in their car, ready to drive Ryan to the shipyard. The trees nearby rustled and I hoped Peg wouldn't do something premature. Clarence had a high tolerance for alcohol and the two bottles he'd drunk earlier had not dulled his senses in the slightest. The only way this was going to work was if I managed to slip the sedative Belle had given me into his beer without him noticing.

We sat at the water's edge, the lake water gently washing over our toes, two glasses of cold beer beside us. He was alert. Much too alert.

'I'm going to be a real pain,' I said.

'You are?'

'Do you think you could get a blanket? I want to lie back and look at the stars, but I hate getting sand in my hair.'

'You can use my jacket as a pillow,' he said, unbuttoning it.

'Thanks, but I want a blanket. I want to stretch out.'

Clarence sighed deeply and I knew I was pushing my luck. I reached across and ran my fingertips lightly up his left forearm. 'We can lie next to each other.'

He sighed again, but this time it was not annoyance I detected. 'I'll be right back. Don't go anywhere,' he said, leaping to his feet.

I heard him jogging up the beach and across the lawn.

'Hey!' came a voice from the nearby forest.

'We need more time,' I whispered.

'Have you slipped him the powder yet?'

'I'm just about to do it.'

I tore the packet of sedative open and sprinkled it into one of the beers. Using my index finger, I stirred it around. Bella had said it would dissolve within a minute or two and had no obvious taste.

A few minutes later, Clarence was back with a picnic blanket. He spread it over the sand close to the lake.

'Cheers,' I said, holding up my glass.

'To new friends,' he said.

He downed half the glass in one mouthful. I sipped at my glass, careful not to swallow any of it. Belle had told me the sedative took about five minutes to work once the full dose had been ingested. Clarence put his glass down in the sand.

'I'm not going to embarrass myself tonight by drinking too much,' he said. 'I like a few drinks but I'm completely humiliated by last night.'

'Don't be silly,' I said, touching his arm. 'It was a party and we both drank a lot of beer on empty stomachs. This is different.'

'Even so.'

I glanced at his beer. His glass still had half the sedative in it. Possibly more if it had sunk to the bottom.

'Let's play a game,' I said.

'I like the sound of this.'

'It's a drinking game. Do you have drinking games in 2123?'

He smirked. 'Of course we do.'

'If you get the answer right, you get to ask a question. If you get the answer wrong, you have to chug the rest of your beer.'

Clarence raised his eyebrows. 'Are you trying to get me drunk?'

'I might be. Just a little.'

He rested a hand on my knee.

'Who was the president of the USA in 2012?' I asked.

'What? How obscure is that? Not fair.'

'I could have asked you who the Prime Minister of the UK was, but I'm being kind.'

'I'm crap at history.'

'Oh, dear. Guess you're gonna have to down that beer.'

'Hang on a minute. I know. Barack Obama. First black president of the USA. Elected for two terms.'

'Congratulations. Your go.'

I heard a rustle from the treeline. I knew it was Peg, reminding me that time was short.

'Who is the current president of the USA?' asked Clarence.

I smiled. 'A trick question? The USA no longer exists.'

'Touché. Your go.'

'What was the name of the war that began in 1914 and ended in 1918?'

Clarence snorted. 'Another history question? Please.'

'Long before my time,' I said. 'Before my grandmother's time. It's a valid question.'

Clarence sighed. 'Korean?'

I shook my head. 'The Great War. Or the First World War. Either would have been fine.' I picked up his glass and handed it to him. 'Time to chug.'

Clarence leant his head back and poured the drink down

his throat. 'Something's wrong with this beer. It's all powdery at the bottom.'

'I might have accidentally kicked some sand earlier.'

He shrugged. 'My turn, right? I'm gonna ask you the name of the war that began in 2050 and ended in 2053.'

I racked my brain. Peg had given me a quick history lesson of the main events in the last hundred years. 'The Arctic War?'

'How the hell?'

'Lucky guess.'

Clarence rubbed his eyes and yawned. 'I don't know about you, Eden, but I'm beat. How about we head back upstairs?'

'In a minute or two. I'm hoping to see another shooting star.'

'Fine. You know, when I get back from this . . .'

He flopped on to his back and his eyes closed. It had only been about thirty seconds. Inwardly I hoped that Belle had been right about the dosage and the interaction between the sedative and alcohol. I didn't like Clarence especially, but I didn't want him to die.

I lay back next to him. Above us a meteor made a quick dash across the sky. I took that as a good omen.

'Clarence,' I said, touching his arm. 'Did you see that?'

'Hmm?'

'Never mind.'

The sound of a twig snapping told me that Peg was making his way towards us. A vice-like panic seized my chest. What if Clarence wasn't completely under? He could identify Peg and me later. He had to be completely unconscious.

I ran my fingers through his thick blonde hair. Nothing. No sigh or acknowledgement that I'd touched him. Not even a flicker of his eyelids. I shuffled down the blanket and began unlacing his shoes.

'Couldn't you have chosen a more hidden away spot?' asked Peg, as he approached. He looked like a ninja in his black wetsuit, his brown hair even darker than normal now that it was wet. 'Anyone looking out of the window might see us.'

'Clarence put the blanket here.'

'Let's drag him to the side. We'll blend into the shadows more if we move to the bushes.'

Together we pulled the blanket. Clarence rolled from side to side moaning gently.

'Have his parents gone to bed yet?' asked Peg.

'His mother turned in just before we came outside. His dad is out of town on an "important business event".'

'That's great news. Who's on the door?'

I shrugged. 'Clarence didn't speak to him. I'd guess it's not one of the doormen he knows well.'

Peg was busy pulling Clarence's jacket off his deadweight body. It was a light, green jacket that reached his hips. Underneath he was wearing a white shirt.

'Do you think you could finish undressing him?' asked Peg. 'While I take this wetsuit off.'

I nodded and looked away. Feeling slightly sick, I unbuttoned Clarence's trousers and pulled them down over his hips.

'Please tell me you don't want his underwear,' I said.

'I'd do almost anything to help Ry,' said Peg. 'But I draw the line at wearing Clarence Wolfe's underwear.'

I threw the trousers to Peg and started work on Clarence's white button-down shirt. Clarence moaned again and a tiny stream of drool made its way out of the corner of his mouth. Peg helped me prop Clarence up so we could pull the shirt off his back.

'How do I look?' asked Peg, as he tucked the shirt into his trousers.

Clarence's trousers were too short and too baggy for Peg, but with the jacket and straw hat, he might be confused for him. Anyone who knew Clarence well, however, would know at a glance that Peg was not him. Clarence was much broader.

I picked up the bottle and two glasses. 'Better look drunk,' I said.

Peg put an arm around me and held me close. 'OK, it's time for some role play. I get to be the loud-mouthed, alcoholic jerk. And you get to be the pretty girl.'

He kept his arm around me and I leant in close to him, but we stuck to the shadows as we made our way towards the residential wing. The first part of the operation had been a success, but we still had so much to do before Ryan would be free. Just before we reached the door, Peg stopped.

'He mustn't see my face.'

'Don't worry about that,' I said. 'Pull the brim of the hat down low and keep the bottle in your face.'

Peg held the bottle of beer up to his mouth and drank

from it. I wrapped my arms around his waist from behind and giggled loudly.

'Clarence, save some for me.'

As we walked through the door, I spun him around so he was facing me, his back to the doorman.

'Come on, my turn,' I said, reaching for the bottle.

I gave the doorman enough time to recognise me, smiled and waved, and steered Peg towards the lift. Peg pressed the call button for the penthouse. The seconds it took for the lift to arrive felt like minutes. If the doorman asked Peg a question, we would be caught. Even if Peg managed to run, they knew who I was. I knew enough about criminal law in 2123 to understand I'd be sent to the Lunar Facility.

The lift pinged to announce its arrival and the door slid open. Empty. I pushed Peg inside and pressed myself up against him, pretending to kiss him as the door shut behind us. As soon as the lift started moving, I took a step back.

'What if his mother sees me?' asked Peg.

'We have to turn right when we get out of the lift,' I said. 'The dining room is all the way at the end of the hall. If his mother shows up, Clarence's bedroom is the second door on the right. He has an en suite bathroom. Go inside and lock the door.'

'It disturbs me that you know your way around the inside of his bedroom.'

The lift arrived. I quickly checked to make sure no one was in the hall, put my arm around Peg and headed towards the dining room. Once we were in the alcove, we were out of sight unless Mrs Wolfe decided she needed something from the kitchen. I opened the door to the dumb waiter.

'Jeez,' said Peg. 'I have to squeeze in that?'

'It's bigger than it looks. You should go first in case Mrs Wolfe wakes up. When you climb out at the bottom, make sure to send it back up for me.'

'Where does it go?'

'To the kitchen.'

Peg swore. 'What if someone sees me climbing out of it?'

'The Wolfes are the only family who live here all week. The other Guardians go home for the weekend. And it's late. There should only be a skeleton staff on duty, so unless someone orders a late-night snack from the kitchen, we shouldn't run into anyone.'

'But if I do get seen?'

'You're Clarence Wolfe. You're a stupid drunk boy doing a dare or something. Just keep that hat tilted over your face.'

Peg wedged himself into the dumb waiter and tucked his knees under his chin.

'Take the bottle. We'll need it to hit the guard,' I said, passing it to him.

I pressed the button and watched as the door of the dumb waiter closed. It was only about a five-second journey, plus climbing in and out time. I counted silently in my head. On twenty, the dumb waiter whirred and began its return journey.

I yanked open the door and squeezed myself in, bottom first, then legs and finally arms. It wasn't until the door opened again in the kitchen, that I realised I'd been holding my breath.

Peg was waiting for me. 'Just one woman in the kitchen,' he whispered. 'She's watching a soap on the com-screen.'

I spun my legs out of the dumb waiter and slipped out. 'Let's go.'

I peered around the corner into the corridor that linked the various service areas. Nothing. We started along the corridor. There were no sounds from above or below us, just the patter of our footsteps on the marble floor.

'If someone sees us?' he whispered.

'We make it look like we're trying to find somewhere private to make out.'

'If you wanted to kiss me so bad, you should have just said. There was no need to go to such elaborate lengths.'

I shushed him with a finger to my lips. I knew he was just trying to lessen the tension, but this was no time for jokes. I needed to focus all my attention on finding my way.

We passed the sweet-smelling laundry rooms and the storeroom. I turned down the next corridor, my heart beating faster when I saw the analogue clock at the end.

'This is it,' I whispered. 'Follow me to the end of this corridor, but don't come any further. When you hear me cough, you know the guard has his back to you. Ryan's cell is about ten metres down the corridor.'

'He might hear me coming.'

'There are two of us. He's not expecting anyone. We can do this.'

Peg nodded.

'You OK?' I asked.

'Terrified. I need to knock this guy out, but I don't want

to kill him. If I don't hit him hard enough, he'll have time to raise the alarm. I've never done any kind of hand-to-hand combat training.'

'It's going to be fine,' I said.

I took a deep breath, but nothing would calm my jittery pulse. I knew my story; I'd practised it many times. I was playing hide and seek with Clarence Wolfe. If he found me, I had to let him kiss me. Please let me hide here for a couple of minutes. He wouldn't agree – I knew that – but it should be enough to distract him. I would get him to face away from Peg, but if he did see Peg approaching, he would assume it was Clarence come to seek me. All I had to do was play the role of a silly drunk girl.

I passed the three open cells and turned the corner towards Ryan's cell.

No one was there. I was definitely in the right place. But if there was no guard to knock out, there was no key to steal. Perhaps there was a shift change and the new guard hadn't shown up yet. I ran along the corridor till I reached the cell where Ryan was being held. If I could talk to him, I could let him know what we were planning. His was the last cell.

Before I even got there, I knew something was wrong. The cell was unlocked, the door slightly open. I ran faster and pushed open the door.

Ryan wasn't there.

CHAPTER 20

Lyra was waiting for me halfway down the hill from the Institute. Her car was parked against the kerb, under a tree. A faint glow from her port-com lit up her face.

I pulled open the passenger side door and climbed in.

'Well?' she asked, leaning towards the retinal scanner on the dash. The car purred to life.

'He was gone.'

Lyra turned to look at me. 'What?'

'Everything went to plan. Clarence passed out, Peg and I got inside the Institute, but when we got to his cell it was empty.'

'Where's Peg now?'

'He's swimming back across the lake to Antoine and Belle. He couldn't walk out of the main gate because he's not registered as a guest.'

Lyra pulled away from the kerb. The avenue was empty of cars and pedestrians, but she drove slowly, her forehead creased.

'They must have moved him early,' I said.

'No shit.'

'I just don't understand why. It's only Saturday night now. He's not due to leave Earth until Tuesday. How far away is the nearest spaceport?'

'New Marseilles. It's about two hours south of here on the expressway. They might have moved him to the prison there, I guess.'

'Clarence said his dad was in New Marseilles tonight. That he'd gone there for work.'

Lyra shrugged. 'Might be connected.' She glanced at me. 'I don't know how you could stand to let Clarence Wolfe touch you.'

'He didn't touch me. Well, he held my hand, but that's all.'

She shuddered. 'You're lucky he didn't try anything with you. He doesn't think the usual rules apply to him. If he's spending time with you, it's because he thinks he can use you in some way.'

'His mother was in the room with us all evening. Until we went to the lake, anyway.'

'Good move.'

Light rain began to fall. Droplets dotted the windscreen until the world outside blurred.

'Wipers on,' said Lyra.

'Peg told me about you and Clarence,' I said.

'Told you *what* about me and Clarence?' She made no attempt to hide her irritation.

'About the accident. That he was drinking and crashed his car, but let Ryan take the blame.'

'He thinks his family's name and wealth can protect him. And he's right. If the world knew the truth about Clarence Wolfe, he'd be kicked out of the Academy and facing a trial of his own.' She gripped the steering wheel hard, her eyes burning with anger. 'I wish I could tell the world about Clarence Wolfe.'

'Why don't you?'

She flashed her eyes at me. 'Orion asked me not to. If I told about Clarence crashing the car, Clarence would tell about Orion travelling back to 2012. To keep one secret, I had to keep the other.'

'Ryan's not in 2012 any more. There's no reason to keep his secret.'

'I've thought about it. But I don't want Peg to be implicated. Peg helped Orion steal the time-ship.'

We were in the heart of the city now. We sped past the Lakeview Hotel and then Lyra pulled off the wide main street and into the narrower streets of the market district. The rain had thickened and the ground gleamed under the streetlights.

'Wipers full speed,' said Lyra.

The slow rhythm of the wipers changed to a furious slash back and forth across the screen. For a moment I felt bad about leaving Clarence passed out on the picnic blanket in the rain. But then I reminded myself of the way he'd treated Lyra. That was nothing compared to a broken pelvis and leg.

Lyra made abrupt turns, sounding her horn against a lone pedestrian making his way slowly across the road.

'Tell Peg to call me when he gets home,' she said, pulling the car alongside a skip just outside the noodle bar. 'I need to know he got out safely.'

★ ★ ★

I bought myself a tub of satay noodles and let myself into the flat. Before the rescue attempt, I'd been much too nervous to eat; now I was starving. I sat in the dark at the dining room table and shovelled food into my mouth with the cheap wooden chopsticks that came with the food. Through the windows, the last of the Saturday night party boats were sailing back to the dock. A bright half-moon floated in the dark sky.

My head spun with worries. So much planning had gone into this rescue attempt. There was almost no time left and I had to come up with a Plan B. How could I plan to rescue Ryan when I didn't even know where he was? What if Lyra was right and he'd been transported to the prison in New Marseilles? The advantage we'd had when planning to bust him from the Institute was that it wasn't a real prison. But the one in New Marseilles was the real deal. We'd need weeks or months to plan a rescue from a place like that. If he was even there.

I yawned and rubbed my eyes. I mustn't give in to sleep. It was now the early hours of Sunday morning. In just two days Ryan would be on the spaceport. If I was going to rescue him it would have to be either at the spaceport in New Marseilles or at the Inter-Planetary Spaceport between Earth and the moon. I knew nothing about the spaceport in New Marseilles. I knew two things about the Inter-Planetary Spaceport. First, Ryan would be there for twenty-four hours beginning some time on Tuesday. Second, my friend Ben was the captain of that spaceport. That was where I needed to be.

I flicked on all the lights. The flat was a mess. Peg's

274

schoolbooks were stacked haphazardly at one end of the dining room table, cast-off clothes were draped over chair backs and the floor, this morning's breakfast dishes and crumbs were piled high in the sink along with a dirty pan from the night before. He was usually neat and clean. I brewed a pot of coffee – I needed all the caffeine I could get – and started tidying things up.

Peg's clothes smelt of washing powder and cologne. I gathered them up and dumped them in the hamper he kept in the small bathroom. Lyra had seemed worried about him, but really there was no need to be. Ryan hadn't been rescued. There was no reason for anyone to alert security or search the grounds. I wanted him home, though. I wasn't sure how long I could bear to be alone with my thoughts.

I drank cup after cup of coffee, washed the dishes and swept the floor. Peg had done so much already. But I was going to need him to help me one more time if I was going to rescue Ryan from the spaceport. I couldn't do this alone.

I scanned my thumb across Peg's com-screen and typed in Ben's number. His face flickered on to the com-screen and once the connection was established he smiled.

'Eden. How are you? It's the middle of the night.'

'Did I wake you?'

'No. I'm working late tonight.'

'I need a job,' I said. 'On the spaceport. Right away.'

He frowned. 'Is everything all right? You seem –'

'I'm fine,' I said, interrupting him. 'You said you could probably get me a job on the spaceport and I would like to take you up on that offer. And I'd like to bring a friend as well.'

'There are vacancies for kitchen staff. But they tend to get filled very quickly. How soon could you start?'

'Right away.'

'Let me just check the transport schedule.' He moved away from the screen for a minute. 'This is probably too soon for you,' he said when he came back on-screen, 'but there is a transport leaving at four o'clock tomorrow afternoon. The next one after that will be in two weeks' time.'

Two weeks would be too late.

'Tomorrow is good.'

'You would need to be at the New Marseilles spaceport four hours in advance for medical clearance and security. And you'll need papers.'

'How do I do that?'

Ben scratched his head. 'I can get temporary papers for you. You'll be allowed to work for a couple of weeks until we get full security clearance. Kitchen work only requires low level security so it shouldn't be a problem. I'll ping the papers to New Marseilles for you right away. You'll pick them up at Customer Services. What's the name of your friend?'

'Pegasus Ryder.'

I thanked Ben and hung up. It was going to be a tight schedule. I searched through the one closet in the apartment until I found a suitcase. It was old and battered, hidden under a pile of racquets and sports shoes. I pulled it out and dragged it into the bedroom and on to the bed. My pile of clothes was pretty small. There was plenty of room for Peg's. Momentarily I considered letting him pack his own clothes, but I quickly changed my mind. He'd be exhausted by the time he got home. He'd want to sleep for a few hours before we drove down to New Marseilles. I'd need everything ready to go. I worked my way through his chest of drawers, blushing slightly when I reached his underwear, grabbing handfuls of clean clothes. I zipped up the case and left it by the foot of the bed.

It was three in the morning when Peg showed up. He stood in the doorway, his hair soaked, his clothes drenched. Water pooled on to the floor. The thin cotton of his white T-shirt was almost transparent; it clung to his skin so tight I could see the shape of his muscles beneath it.

'You waited up,' he said, a tired smile lighting up his face.

I nodded. 'Of course.'

I grabbed a towel from the bathroom and threw it to him. 'Dry off.'

Peg rubbed the towel over his hair and neck, then strode towards the bedroom, pulling his wet top over his head as he went.

While he changed, I paced the room nervously. He might take some convincing. My plan was sketchy at best. I wasn't sure how many more favours I could expect.

'Are you planning to kick me out?' said Peg, as he came back into the living room. He was shirtless. 'Or are you just stealing my clothes?'

'Guess again.'

'Well, my chest of drawers is empty and my clothes are in a suitcase by the bed. Are we going somewhere?'

'We are,' I said, trying to hide the smile from my face.

Peg looked at me doubtfully. 'So where are we going?'

'How would you like to work on the Inter-Planetary Spaceport?'

Weariness was written all over his face. 'It's the middle of the night. We just failed to rescue Orion. Why are you talking about jobs on the spaceport? Can't we just sleep?'

'There's no time for sleep. We have to move on to Plan B. Ryan's going to be transported to the moon via the spaceport, so we have to be on the spaceport if we're going to rescue him.'

Peg sighed. 'You don't just show up at the spaceport and ask for a job.'

'I have temporary work permits for you and me to work in the kitchens. And I have reservations for the two of us on a transport ship leaving New Marseilles this afternoon.'

'Are you serious? How did you do that?'

I smiled. 'I told you I have a contact on the spaceport. I asked for a favour. I thought our angle could be that we're a new couple and we want to start over somewhere new where I won't get hounded by the press all the time.'

He ran a hand over his face. 'You don't give up, do you?'

'I'll never give up.'

'Why are you doing all this?' he asked, his voice low. 'Because you love him or because you think you owe him?'

'Both.' I bit my lip. 'I don't expect you to come with me. I just know I'll have a bigger chance of success with you there as well. You said you wanted adventure.'

Peg collapsed on to the couch. 'Tell me your plan.'

CHAPTER 21

Sunday morning at the Peacock Feather in Lakeborough. Exactly two weeks since my first meal there. I was jittery from too much coffee and not enough sleep, so I ordered an orange juice and a plate of potato cakes to settle my stomach.

I sat in the same seat as last time, one by the window with a clear view over the streets outside. The storm had passed, but the sky was still low and threatening. A dozen paps were gathered outside the diner, attempting to film me through the window, but I knew the smoked glass would make their pictures pretty worthless. Clarence had said he would meet me at eight. By nine o'clock he would be on his way to New Marseilles to help with his father's election campaign. By nine o'clock, Peg and I needed to be on the road too, if we were to get to the spaceport in time to clear the medical and security checks.

I checked the time on the clock by the front door: eight fifteen. I hated relying on other people, but I couldn't do this on my own. For the hundredth time I wished I'd got round to buying a port-com; I had no way of contacting Clarence to find out why he was running late and he had no way to contact me.

The waitress brought me a plate of potato cakes – thick pancake-shaped discs flecked with browned onions and oozing with oil. I ate quickly, checking for signs of Clarence between bites. Outside, shopkeepers were pulling up the metal shutters on their storefronts and turning on the lights inside their shops.

Eight thirty. At four o'clock, when Peg had gone to bed, I'd made him set his alarm for now. Half an hour to dress, grab something to eat, convince Lyra to help us and pick me up. He'd been exhausted. What if he slept through the alarm? We couldn't afford to lose an hour. It was a two-hour drive to New Marseilles if the roads were clear. We had to be there by noon at the latest. I should have borrowed his port-com; I could have called him to make sure.

I finished my potato cakes and pushed the dirty plate to one side. Time was moving too fast and too slow. I ordered another juice. The diner was beginning to fill. The oil had clogged the inside of my mouth, but the juice was too sweet to be refreshing. I longed for a toothbrush and toothpaste to scrub away the stale coffee taste. I wanted to shower. Most of all I wanted to sleep.

A sleek black limousine pulled up outside the window and Clarence climbed out of the back. He was wearing a pale grey suit, freshly pressed, and his hair was neatly slicked back. Dressed for the campaign trail. I checked the clock: eight fifty-five. He was nearly an hour late. The car stayed put. My guess was that Mrs Wolfe was in the back, waiting for her son before they both headed for New Marseilles.

'I'm sorry,' said Clarence, sliding into the seat next to me.

'My mother made me wait for her. It's a big day for Dad. I've only got a few minutes.'

'I wanted to apologise for last night,' I said. 'I left you on the beach. I didn't know what to do.'

'I should be the one apologising,' said Clarence. 'I have no idea what happened. I just passed out.'

'If I'd known it was going to rain, I would have asked someone to help me bring you inside,' I said. 'But I thought you'd probably just sleep it off.'

He rested his hand on my arm. 'As soon as I get back from the campaign trail, I'll make it up to you.'

'That sounds great.'

'I should go,' he said, taking back his hand and pushing himself up.

'Clarence, wait. I have a favour to ask you.'

He sat back down again.

'My friend Lyra is going to the University of New Hampshire in a few weeks as a journalism major. Right now she's interning at the *Lakeborough Times* and trying to write a story about the rich kids of Lakeborough.'

'Yawn.'

My stomach twisted. 'I know. So, last night I told Lyra about your dad's campaign and the trip to the moon with Ryan. She'd love to be able to go along too. It would make a great story.'

'You spoke to Lyra last night?'

'She drove me home from the Institute.'

Clarence began inspecting his fingernails. 'You may not know this, Eden, but Lyra Thornhill dated Orion for a year

281

or more. Has it not occurred to you that she may still have feelings for him?'

'It has occurred to me.'

'You don't mind?'

'Ryan and I were friends. But . . . well . . . some people are a lost cause.'

A lazy smile spread slowly across his face. 'You're right about that. Now I really have to go.'

My throat clenched. 'I told her you probably couldn't make it happen.'

Clarence looked at me, his eyes blazing confidence and arrogance. 'I *could* make it happen.'

'Really? Your dad would listen to you if you asked?'

'Of course. But why would I want to do anything to help Lyra Thornhill?'

'Because her other idea is a bit ordinary. She was telling me she had some information about a drink–driving cover-up. Someone well known.'

He drummed his fingers on the table and frowned. 'She said that?'

'Yeah. But I think she'd do better to write about Ryan. I mean, his story is much more interesting. I think that if she had access to a story like that, she'd drop the other one completely.'

He narrowed his eyes. 'I'll do it. I'll call my father's personal assistant from the car and get Lyra's name added to the passenger list. But make sure she knows I helped her out.'

'I will.'

He leant forward and smoothed my hair. 'If I do this for you, what are you going to do for me?'

I blinked slowly and forced myself to smile. 'What do you have in mind?'

'When I get back from the spaceport, I'm taking you to my family's home in Quebec for the weekend. Just the two of us.'

'Can't wait,' I said.

The wipers whipped across the windscreen, but they couldn't keep up with the water pouring from the sky. Thunder rumbled from the other side of the mountain.

We were on the expressway just outside Lakeborough and the traffic had slowed to a crawl.

'We get a lot of localised thunderstorms here in the mountains,' said Peg. 'Once we get past the rain, things will speed up a bit.'

'How long a drive is it?' I asked.

'Two hours on a good day. Bad weather, traffic, it'll take longer.'

The battery on my old phone had long since died; I had no way of knowing the time. I couldn't see a clock on the dash.

'It's half nine,' said Peg. 'We'll need to be at the check-in by noon. So we're cutting it fine.'

'We have to make it,' I said.

Forked lightning split the sky and thunder bellowed overhead. Why couldn't Fate just work in my favour for once? The cars ahead of us slowed down even more. There were six lanes on the expressway, but each one was solid with nose to tail traffic, crawling along at twenty kilometres an hour.

'Can't you just drive on the hard shoulder all the way to New Marseilles?' I asked.

Peg pulled a face. 'You can't drive manually on the expressway. We just have to be patient. When the storm passes, traffic will speed up.'

'What if it doesn't pass in time?' I said.

He scanned on the traffic news and we listened as the announcer reported on all the lane closures, accidents and heavy traffic in the area.

'Do you think the weather will delay the flight?' I asked, groping for a glimmer of hope.

He shook his head. 'There's no weather in space. Not the sort of weather you're talking about, anyway. And we'll be portalling off the planet.'

We inched forward, close to the next exit off the expressway.

'Is there an old road? A road used before this one was built?'

Peg shrugged. 'I suppose there might be.'

'Have you got a map?'

He reached across me to the passenger glove compartment, pulled out his port-com and dragged a few icons across the screen. 'Here you go.'

It was open to a page that showed our location in relation to Lakeborough. I zoomed in close and searched for smaller roads. It looked like there was one. It ran almost parallel to the highway, though it was less direct.

'Take this exit,' I said.

'An old road might be longer and slower,' said Peg. 'If we stay on the expressway, eventually traffic should speed up.'

'You can drive manually on the old road, right?'

'Yeah.'

'So let's go.'

He took the exit and followed my directions to a narrow road with just one lane in each direction.

'This road will take us all the way to New Marseilles,' I said.

The rain was still heavy, the storm circling overhead, but there was no other traffic on the road. Peg increased his speed, hurtling round the corners and racing down the hills so rapidly I thought I was going to be sick. I focused on the small flashing dot on the map that showed where we were.

'Was it difficult to convince Lyra to help us?' I asked.

'No. This story will be a real coup for her. A trainee journalist with the inside story. Orion will talk to her in a way he won't talk to a journalist he doesn't know.'

'Fingers crossed that Clarence manages to sort things out at his end,' I said.

If he did, she would be on the same ship as Ryan. She would get to speak to him and spend time with him. The thought that I might never see him again if I didn't make this work tore at my insides.

'Where will she meet us when she gets to the spaceport?'

'Apparently there's a bar that's open to residents and visitors. She'll meet us there as soon as she's allowed off the ship and let us know where he's being held.'

'When I said goodbye to Ryan at the Institute, he asked me if you and Lyra were together yet,' I said.

Peg glanced at me sideways, before turning back to the road. This was not the sort of road where you could afford to lose concentration, even for a moment. Especially at this speed.

'Did he?' It wasn't really a question.

'He said he wants you to ask her out.'

Peg laughed.

'He thinks you like her. And that she likes you.'

Peg said nothing.

'You do like her, don't you?'

'Yeah, I like Lyra.'

'And he said he's not going to be around so it wouldn't be weird. I think he wanted you to know that.'

We rounded a corner and were met with clear blue skies. Bright sunlight glared from the wet tarmac.

'You were right about the weather,' I said.

'You were right about the road.'

'Peg?' I said. 'Do you think we can pull this off?'

'Ordinarily, I'd say no. No way. You'd have to be crazy to even think it. But I have the feeling you're gonna make it happen.'

We made it to the New Marseilles spaceport with five minutes to spare. The port was shaped like a clock: a large round central building with twelve smaller round buildings ringed around it.

'What are they?' I asked Peg.

'Each one is a spacedock. Some are for freight, some are for cruise liners, some are for workers. We're employees of the spaceport now, so we'll get the cheap seats.'

'What does that mean?'

'They won't be offering us peanuts and drinks or allowing us to unclip and enjoy the experience of weightlessness.'

My insides began swimming around as we walked through the main entrance into the terminal building. What if Ben hadn't managed to send our papers? What if I didn't pass the medical exam? Or clear security? I looked around me. The other passengers were a mixture of men and women, all dressed in uniforms of various styles.

'All employees of the spaceport,' said Peg quietly. 'Back from shore leave probably.'

He pointed towards the Customer Services desk. 'You go and get our papers. I'll check in our luggage. I'll meet you by the entrance to security, OK?'

I nodded and strode over to the desk, trying to look as though I travelled through space all the time. There was no need to be nervous. We hadn't done anything wrong. Yet.

The assistant handed me two cards: one with Peg's details and one with mine. Easy.

'We go through security now,' said Peg, 'and then we'll be separated for our medical exam.'

'What sort of things do they look for in your medical?' I asked as we joined the line for security.

'Simple things. Cardiovascular health is the main one. They'll also check you for any signs of infectious diseases. Check your bone density – that sort of thing.'

'What if I don't pass?'

'Then we don't get on the flight. But you're not feeling sick, are you?'

'Only sick with nerves.'

Peg's fingers found mine and he gave my hand a gentle squeeze. 'I'm kind of nervous myself,' said Peg. 'I've never been further than low Earth orbit.'

'Is it dangerous?'

We shuffled forward in the queue.

'It's the safest form of travel there is. Statistically. Still, there's something a bit unnerving knowing that you're surrounded by the vacuum of space.'

I gripped his hand tighter. 'I wouldn't know what to do in an emergency.'

'Relax. Travelling through time is much more dangerous and you survived that.'

We reached the security checkpoint. I handed over my paperwork from Ben and the flexi-card the Institute had given me when I'd arrived.

'Eden Anfield?' asked the emigration officer.

'Yes,' I said.

'Says here Eden Anfield is a minor,' said the emigration officer. 'Sixteen years old. We'll need authorisation from your parents for a trip into space.'

'I'm her legal guardian,' said Peg, handing over his port-com.

The officer looked doubtfully at Peg, but scanned through his details. 'OK,' he said eventually. 'Males that way, females over there.'

'See you on the other side,' said Peg, finally letting go of my hand.

I was directed into a cold, curtained-off cubicle that smelt of antiseptic and metal, and told to strip down to my underwear and lie on the trolley. I folded my clothes up and placed them in a neat pile on the floor. There was nothing to cover myself up with – no gown or sheet. I sat up on the trolley in my bra and pants, my arms cradling my body to keep warm.

The curtain snapped back and a nurse came inside, pushing a small trolley filled with bottles, a stethoscope, a port-com.

'First trip into space?' she asked, staring at my records on her port-com.

'Yes.' Now didn't seem like a good time to mention my time-trip or that Peg had taken me into low Earth orbit.

'You will probably experience nausea for the first twenty-four hours.' She met my eye with an unsmiling face. 'Most people do.'

I lay shivering on the trolley as she checked my heartbeat and blood pressure, took several swabs from the inside of my nose and my throat and made me breathe into an inflatable bag.

Through the flimsy divider, I could hear other women undergoing the same procedures in the cubicles either side of me.

Finally, she handed me two plastic bags. One was empty; the other contained a bright orange outfit.

'Put your own clothes in the empty bag and dress in the

flight suit,' she said. 'When you're done, leave the curtain open and go to the departure lounge.'

'Have I passed?'

The curtain clanged as she pulled it to one side, revealing me in my underwear to the passengers waiting for their medical. 'You're free to fly.'

Embarrassed, I pulled the curtain shut quickly and tore the plastic wrap from the flight suit. It was a thick, tight-fitting boiler suit with a high collar that reached to just under my chin. Immediately I felt too hot. I stuffed my own clothes in the other bag and left the cubicle.

Peg was waiting for me at the entrance to the departure lounge. He was dressed the same as me.

'Nice clash,' he said, picking up a strand of my hair and holding it against the flight suit.

'Why on earth would you choose orange?' I said, looking around. 'Anything would be better than orange.'

'Easier to spot you in the event of a self-eject,' he said.

'Why would anyone self-eject?' I couldn't disguise the tremble in my voice.

'If there was a problem with the ship and we had to eject, the bright orange is easier for the rescue crews to see,' he said. 'It's just a health and safety thing. Don't worry. We'll be safe.'

'How come we didn't wear them when you took me up before?'

'Strictly speaking, we should have. But it was only a quick flight and I wanted to show you a good time, not scare you to death.'

An electronic voice announced that our flight was cleared for boarding. We walked down a tunnel to the spacecraft. It was much the same as the shuttle Peg had taken me joyriding in. There were seats for fifty, laid out in wide rows just like on a bus except that the space around each seat was much greater.

'It's a Westland Shuttle,' said Peg. 'About twenty years old. These ships were designed for short distances. Utterly reliable. This one is a more recent model than the one I took you on.'

We found our seats on the back row.

'How long will this take?' I asked, as I strapped myself in.

'Twenty-four hours.'

'Really. It only took two minutes to get here from 2012.'

'That's because you portalled all the way,' he said. 'Uses a lot of fuel and is much higher risk. Like I said, we're in the cheap seats. We'll portal to just beyond the reach of Earth's orbit and then cruise towards the spaceport.'

The cabin crew came round with small glass bottles. They passed me a green bottle and gave Peg a blue one. 'Please drink all of your medicine right away,' said the flight attendant. 'We will be attaching helmets ready for portal in five minutes.'

'What was that all about?' I asked.

'It'll send you to sleep,' he said. 'When we wake up, we'll be at the spaceport.'

'Do we have to drink it?'

'Yes. It's not a cruise ship, it's a bus. They don't want to deal with people unstrapping to go to the toilet or experiencing motion sickness or having to feed us in a weightless environment. Much easier to send us all to sleep, strap on our helmets and go.'

Peg unscrewed his bottle and downed it in one.

'Why do we have to wear helmets?' I asked.

'Safety precaution in case of eject. The cabin's pressurised.' He leant across for my bottle and untwisted the top. 'Drink up.'

I swallowed the contents. It was a clear, sweet liquid that made my throat sting; like so many medicines it had been over-sweetened in an attempt to disguise its bitter taste.

'Thank you for coming with me, Peg,' I said quietly.

'I wouldn't have missed a trip to the spaceport for anything.'

My tongue felt thick in my mouth and my eyelids were growing heavy. 'If we have to eject, will you hold my hand?'

'I'll hold it now,' he said, his fingers intersecting mine.

'Don't let go.'

'I won't let go.'

I had a sudden desire to tell him how much his friendship meant to me, but my mouth couldn't form the shapes, and then I was gone.

CHAPTER 22

Inter-Planetary Spaceport

Ben was waiting for us on the other side of the security checkpoint. 'Welcome aboard,' he said.

'It's an honour to meet you, Captain,' said Peg, shaking Ben's hand. 'I've read about your missions.'

'Call me Ben, please. Come on, I'll show you to your quarters.'

The central section of the spaceport was spherical and the corridors were coiled and twisted like intestines. I quickly became disoriented. Peg, I noticed, was looking around carefully.

'It's like a rabbit warren,' I said.

'It is a bit,' said Ben. 'Don't worry. There will be an induction at nine in the morning for all new employees. And I'll give you a map. You'd be surprised how quickly you'll learn your way around. Within a week you'll know this place like the back of your hand.'

A week was too long.

We got into the lift down to the deck below. 'Civilian

living quarters are down on B Deck,' said Ben. 'The berthing areas are pretty basic, but you'll only use it for sleeping and washing.'

We reached a door, which Ben opened with a swipe card. 'This is your berthing area, Eden,' said Ben. 'Men and women have opposite sides of the passageway.'

He held the door open for me. Peg waited outside. Inside was a wall of tiny sleeping areas, no larger than coffins, stacked from the floor to the ceiling. On the wall opposite was a row of lockers.

'Like I said, nothing special,' said Ben. 'Choose a rack. You're the first of the new arrivals to get here.'

I placed my bag on the lowest rack.

Ben handed me a map. 'This will help you find your way around. Downstairs you'll find the library, gymnasium, cinema, stores, canteen and bar. Up on A Deck, where you arrived, are the landing bay, security and temporary accommodation for visitors. Also the Space Bar and the Officers' Club.'

I decided to risk a question. 'So a ship travelling to the moon would stop here and the people on board would sleep in the temporary accommodation upstairs?'

Ben nodded. 'Maybe. Depends on their schedule.'

'What about prisoners?' I asked.

'Prisoners would be taken to the holding cell on A Deck.'

'When will Ryan's ship arrive?'

'Tomorrow morning. They'll dock at eleven and leave at two.'

'I thought they got to stay overnight?'

'No. This is an expedited transfer. Ryan will only be

aboard the spaceport for three hours. Long enough for the prison transport to refuel and for a crew change. I'll do my best to arrange for you to see him, Eden, but I can't promise anything.'

He opened the door back into the hallway where Peg was waiting.

'Pegasus, your berthing area is directly across from Eden's,' said Ben. 'I'd be delighted if the two of you would join me at my table for dinner tonight in the Officers' Club on A Deck. Shall we say seven o'clock?'

'We'll be there,' I said, waving the map, 'so long as we can find it.'

'We don't have much time,' said Peg quietly, as soon as Ben had left. 'It's nearly five o'clock now. Dinner with Ben at seven. That could run till nine. Then we have orientation at nine in the morning. Ry's ship arrives at eleven. If we're going to explore this spaceport before he gets here, it's going to have to be at night.'

'I think Ben's trying to help us, Peg. He told me what time Ryan's ship will arrive and the time the prison ship will leave. He told me that Ryan would be escorted to the holding cell on A Deck.'

Peg shook his head. 'I think you're wrong. Ben's the captain of this spaceport. Anything that goes wrong is going to reflect badly on him. I think he's deliberately trying to keep us busy.'

The Officers' Club had a very different feel to the rest of the spaceport. Where the other rooms were bare and functional – all metal and strip lights – the club was wood-panelled with dim lighting. The captain's table, which was covered with a heavy, white tablecloth and laid with silver cutlery, was placed next to a large window that looked out into the darkness. Through the window, more stars than I had ever seen made patterns in the sky, their light brighter and steadier than they were on Earth. The bright blue glow of the Earth was just beyond the reach of the window.

Ben was already seated when we arrived, as was another man, younger than Ben, dressed in a smart uniform covered with insignias and badges.

Both men stood as we approached. Ben made all the introductions.

'This is my first officer, Milo Jackson. This is Eden Anfield, a colleague from a time mission and her friend Pegasus Ryder.'

We all shook hands and sat down. I was disappointed; I had hoped to probe Ben to see if there was any chance he would help us. With the first officer present we were going to have to be careful.

Within seconds of sitting down, a waiter appeared with a bottle of champagne. Our glasses were filled and Ben proposed a toast.

'To old friends,' he said. 'And new beginnings.'

We clinked glasses, the pleasant tinkling throwing me back to a different time, when Ryan and I had sat on a beach with glasses of champagne, toasting his return to 2012. Then it had seemed as if we had for ever stretching ahead of us. We'd had just six days. I pretended to sip my champagne, but

I swallowed nothing. If Peg and I were going to come up with a plan, we needed to keep our wits about us.

'As first officer, I am in charge of the welfare of all the crew aboard this spaceport,' Milo was saying. 'Since you are good friends of the captain, I will take a personal interest in your careers. Please let me know if there is anything I can do to assist you.'

'Thank you,' said Peg with a broad smile. 'I was training to be an engineer back on Earth. I worked in the repair yard in Lakeborough. Shuttles mainly. I'd love to get back into that field again if any openings become available.'

This was clearly an area of interest to Milo Jackson. While the soup – something green and minty – was served and eaten, they talked about different classes of shuttles, favourite ships, engines, fuel efficiency, the virtues of Icelandic engineering over Burmese.

'We have a small shipyard on the spaceport,' said Milo. 'Perhaps, after we finish dinner, I could show you around it.'

The main course was served, a savoury pancake filled with green sludge I now knew was a popular seaweed, served with carrots and cauliflower on the side.

'Is all the food transported by ship?' I asked. 'It must be very expensive.'

'Much of our food comes on supply ships,' said Ben. 'But on the lowest deck of the spaceport we have a large hot-house for growing fruit and vegetables. The sun's energy keeps it at a constant temperature. It supplies ninety per cent of our produce.'

'We even have an artificial sea,' said the first officer. 'It's small of course, but large enough to grow seaweed. Our kelp grows at an average of two metres a day.'

'That's incredible,' I said.

'Kelp is one of the fastest growing plants in the world,' said Ben. 'But it does especially well here on the spaceport.'

I had nothing against seaweed in general – but the fishy green sludge on my plate was not remotely appetising.

'After your induction tomorrow, I can give you a tour of the spaceport,' said Milo.

I smiled, but that was the last thing we needed. Peg and I had little enough time to devise an escape plan and put it into action.

'Are there any time-ships docked at the spaceport?' I asked.

'Time-ships go straight to Earth,' said Ben, catching my eye. 'Most of the ships that dock here are shuttles and cargo ships.'

'That's too bad,' I said. 'The only time-ship I've ever seen is the one I travelled on.'

'Four-dimensional travel is very dangerous,' said Ben. 'You're best off staying well away from it.'

'If Admiral Wolfe wins the presidency of the Space and Time Institute, all time-ships will be decommissioned,' said Peg. 'There will be no more time travel.'

Ben shook his head. 'That would be a great pity. I believe there's a place for carefully regulated time travel.'

'Talking of Westland,' said the first officer through a mouthful of green sludge, 'weren't you involved with his son?' He was looking at me.

I shrugged. 'We knew each other. We were friends. Nothing more.'

'But on the news they said . . .'

'All lies,' I said, reaching across the table for Peg's hand. 'A way for Admiral Wolfe to discredit the Westland family.'

I watched Milo Jackson notice our joined hands.

'That doesn't surprise me,' he said. 'Wolfe is an ambitious man. He'll stop at nothing to win the presidency and shut down Westland Shipyards. He's even using the Westland boy's transport to the moon as a campaign opportunity. He's coming along himself, together with his son and a host of reporters.'

'Really?' I said, feigning surprise. 'I don't suppose I would be allowed on board to say goodbye to him?'

'I doubt that very much,' said the first officer. 'Tight security. Admiral Wolfe wouldn't allow it.'

After dessert and coffee, Peg went off with Milo Jackson for a quick tour of the shipyard. Ben walked me back to my quarters.

'Eden,' he said as we took the lift down to B Deck. 'I don't know what's going on in your head, but I hope you don't think you can rescue Ryan. It's not possible. The spaceport has tight security and if you were caught trying something, security would shoot first and ask questions later.'

'I understand. I'm not trying anything.'

He placed a hand on my shoulder. 'You can make a good life here. Work your way up. Make good money.'

'That's all I want,' I said. 'To live a good life.'

★　★　★

There were two women in my berthing area now, both undressed and in the process of washing their faces.

'Hi, roomie,' one of them called, waving a hand in my direction.

I waved back and counted silently to twenty, long enough for Ben to get back to the lift. I opened the door. The dimmed lighting that signalled night-time cast a warm pink glow on the walls, so that as I stumbled along the curved passageway, I had the strangest impression that I was walking inside a blood vessel. Peg had the map Ben had given us, but I had carefully memorised the route from my room to the lifts. I passed dozens of slim doors that led to tiny berthing areas just like mine, but not a single person.

I reached the lifts and pressed the call button. With no map, I wasn't sure what I should do, but I wanted to locate a few key places. Ryan's ship would arrive at the landing bay on A Deck. Temporary accommodation was also on A Deck. With the little information I had, it seemed Ryan's entire stay aboard the spaceport would be centred on A Deck.

The lift arrived and the door opened. No one was inside. I pressed the button for A Deck and concocted a cover: I'd left my handbag in the Officers' Club. No one would know I'd never owned a handbag in my life.

The curved passageways of A Deck were equally deserted. I walked straight ahead, trying to commit the layout to memory. I counted twenty-four doors before I reached the entrance to security and the landing bay beyond. The walk between security and the lift had taken me about two minutes.

'Can I help you?' asked a tall female security officer.

'I'm trying to find my way back to the Officers' Club,' I said.

'Keep walking,' she said, pointing along the passageway I'd been following. 'It's a little way along there.'

I thanked her and continued. I passed a holding cell with a bored-looking security guard sitting at a desk reading something on her port-com. Someone had handwritten a sign that said *Vacancies* and stuck it to the door. I kept walking. I passed toilets and a store cupboard, a cleaning cupboard and then came to the double doors that led into the club. Just as I was about to push the door open, it swung out and I came face to face with Ben.

'Eden?' he said, the surprise clear in his voice. 'What are you doing back up here?' The door swung shut behind him and latched with a faint hiss.

Somehow I didn't think he would believe I was looking for my handbag. 'Looking for Pegasus.'

'Milo was taking him for a quick tour of the landing bay,' said Ben. There was a touch of impatience in his voice. 'He's probably back in his berth by now.'

I took a step backwards. 'I'll go back down and see if he's there.'

'It takes a few days to get used to the rhythm of life aboard the spaceport,' he said. 'The central section of the port rotates on its axis every twenty-four hours to help with circadian rhythms in our workforce, but even so, most people take a while to adjust. You should try to sleep.'

I strode quickly back along the passageway, past the

security checkpoint to the lift. Peg was there, touching the call button.

'What are you doing here?' he asked.

'Exploring.'

'And?' He looked at me expectantly.

'I bumped into Ben and he told me to go back to my berth. How about you?'

'I have good news,' he said quietly.

The lift arrived. Peg waited until we were inside before telling me. 'He took me out on the landing bay where we arrived. There's a small shipyard there and he wanted to show me some of the things they're working on.'

He touched the button for C Deck.

'What about security?' I asked.

'Milo was with me so it wasn't a problem that I didn't have ID yet. But that's not the good news.'

The lift doors opened on to C Deck.

'What are we doing down here?' I asked.

'That's just it,' said Peg, taking my arm. 'Milo told me that there's a small boat deck on C Deck where the evacuation craft are kept. They're like lifeboats. You only use them if there's an emergency. I want to find them.'

He let go of my arm and walked out into the lobby.

'Peg,' I whispered, half running to catch up. 'What if someone sees us? It's ten o'clock at night. We shouldn't be here.'

'We say we're lost.'

Unlike the twisting guts of B Deck, C Deck had a large central lobby with four passageways leading off it, like the spokes of a steering wheel. There were no signs pointing the way.

'Choose a passageway,' said Peg.

I turned in a circle. 'Wait. If these shuttles are for emergency evacuation, there must be directions to them. You don't hide the lifeboats.'

There was a noticeboard by the lifts. A laminated sign at the bottom of the board gave instructions for evacuation.

'Found it,' I said. 'First left and follow the fluorescent green arrows.'

The left-hand passageway took us past a library and a storeroom. The boat deck was at the end. Although the hatchway to the deck was sealed, there was a reinforced glass panel in the hatch. Peg pushed his face against the glass to peer in.

'Can you see anything?' I asked.

'Not really. It looks like there must be several shuttles inside, each within their own airlock. But I'm not sure.'

'How do we get in?'

He stepped back from the glass. 'There's a swipe machine by the door here. I guess you swipe your ID card.'

'We get our ID tomorrow. Do you think our cards will open this hatch?'

Peg shrugged. 'No idea. There must be a way to trigger the hatch, though. If it's for emergencies, it needs to be accessible.'

'Assuming we can get inside, do you think you could fly one of the shuttles?' I asked.

'I can fly anything.'

'You're so modest,' I said, nudging him. 'If you're so good at flying, how come you're not on the Elite Pilot Program Clarence and Antoine are on?'

'I can't afford it. The Elite Program is for rich kids. I'm doing it the poor kid way: work your way up from the bottom and squeeze in a few flights along the way.'

'Can we get to Titan in one of these lifeboats?'

Peg shook his head. 'We'll have to go back to Earth. We need to think of a secluded place where no one will see us arrive.'

I knew where we would go. I'd had it in mind all along. The farmhouse at the bottom of Trenoweth Lane was well above sea level and I doubted it had seen much development in the past hundred and eleven years. Both Ryan and I knew the area well.

I heard a door hiss open further along the hall. 'Let's go,' I whispered. 'I don't want to get caught down here – it's a big giveaway.'

We walked back along the hall to the lifts, as silently as our shoes allowed on the metal floor.

'So we have to find a way to get Ryan out of the holding cell, across the port to the lifts, down to C Deck and along the passageway to the boat deck,' I said. 'Then we have to find a way to open the hatch and fly the shuttle.'

Peg raised his eyebrows. 'Is that all?'

CHAPTER 23

Induction took place in Conference Room Four, on C Deck. As well as Peg and me, there were two other new recruits, the two women sharing my berthing area: Nikki and Becca. They were both teachers.

'This place has a school?' I said, surprised.

'There are two thousand residents on board the Inter-Planetary Spaceport,' said Milo. 'Including two hundred and fifty children. We have a suite of twelve classrooms to accommodate their education.'

I couldn't imagine how awful it must be for those children to grow up on board a spaceport. To live their young lives in an artificial atmosphere. To never swim in the ocean, or run through the trees.

'You'll see the schoolrooms during the tour,' said Milo. 'But first we need to run through the Health and Safety policy.'

We were shown a short film and given a lecture on what we were and were not allowed to do on board the spaceport.

'And now for perhaps the most important part of your induction,' said Milo. 'Emergency evacuation.'

Peg caught my eye, a fleeting glance.

'In the event that the spaceport needs to be evacuated,'

Milo continued, 'emergency lighting will illuminate. If you follow the green arrows they will direct you to the emergency shuttle bay.'

Milo led us from the conference room and along the passageway to the shuttle bay, the same one we'd followed the night before.

'How do you get inside?' asked Peg when we arrived.

'Only those with high level security clearance can get inside,' said Milo, waving his ID. 'Except in an emergency. When the spaceport is on a Code Red, the hatch opens automatically.'

'I don't suppose there's any chance we can take a look inside?' asked Peg.

'Not today. There isn't time.'

'If I saw a fire, how would I operate the alarm?' I asked.

'Good question,' said Milo. 'There are alarms all over the spaceport. You simply break the glass to sound the alarm and then head to your nearest muster station.'

From the emergency shuttle bay, we were shown the sick bay, the mess rooms, the kitchens and the stores. Milo took our photographs and issued basic ID cards. And then we moved on to the other things we would need to know. I tried to hide my impatience; if everything went to plan we wouldn't need to know how to log an accident or where to go to get a burn treated.

'Before we head up to A Deck, let's go over to the laundry room and pick up some uniforms for you,' said Milo.

Peg was talking to Milo about what sort of clearance we would need to access each area. I wanted to listen in, but didn't want to seem too obvious, so I fell into step with Nikki and Becca.

'Why do you want to work up here?' I asked Becca.

She looked at me like I was stupid. 'For the pay of course. My salary here is four times what they pay back on Earth. My boyfriend and I are saving for a house.'

'Is he here too?'

She shook her head. 'He was hoping to get a job in the kitchens but apparently all the posts were filled.'

I smiled at her. 'I bet a position will open up again soon.'

We reached the laundry room. 'Every Friday you must bring your clothes to be washed and pick up new uniforms for the week,' Milo told us.

We were each given five tunics and loose trousers, a pair of shoes and a sash. Mine and Peg's were green for the kitchens. Nikki and Becca had purple.

'We will complete your induction in the Landing Bay,' said Milo, glancing at his wristwatch. 'We'll need to make this quick; there's a scheduled arrival at eleven o'clock.'

When we had first arrived, Peg and I had to go through the rigorous security procedure for visitors. Now that we were residents with identification cards, we were able to take the much faster route through residents' security.

'You won't spend much time in the Landing Bay,' said Milo as we walked out on to the docks. 'But every time you have shore leave, you will embark and disembark the spaceport here. And it's imperative that you understand how dangerous the landing bay really is.'

I looked around. The landing bay was a busy area, with

307

dockers unloading cargo ships and cleaners working on the shuttles. It smelt like a poisonous mix of hot metal and welding fumes.

'The cargo docks are at the far end,' said Milo, pointing to the other end of the landing bay. 'Shuttle craft dock as close to security as possible.' He checked his watch. 'Any moment now, you will hear an alarm. It consists of five long blasts. That's the ten-minute warning.'

'Warning for what?' asked Becca.

'Warning that the hatch to the landing bay is about to be opened. If you find yourself in the landing bay when that hatch opens, you'll get sucked into space. You'd be surprised: it does happen. You either need to get out of here within ten minutes or stay inside one of the ships. The ships are all clamped down. Don't leave until you hear the all clear. That is three short blasts of the alarm. Don't take any chances out here.'

The alarm sounded. Five long blasts, so loud that any conversation was impossible.

'That's the alarm,' said Milo.' He escorted us back through security. 'Work starts tomorrow,' he said. 'Kitchens at seven. Schoolroom at eight. Make sure you show up on time and in uniform.'

We were dismissed. I checked my watch: eleven on the dot.

'How long do you think it will take for them to transport Ryan from the ship to the holding cell?' I whispered to Peg.

He shrugged. 'It took us thirty minutes to clear security.'

My arms were aching with the weight of five uniforms.

We followed Nikki and Becca back down to B Deck to hang up our uniforms and work out our next move.

'Nikki and I are going to freshen up and go to the Space Bar,' said Becca. 'Do you want to join us?'

'Maybe later. My friend Peg and I are going to go and check out the library.'

Nikki pulled a face that evidently summed up her opinion of the library, and the two of them went into the bathroom.

I pulled the plastic wrap off one of the kitchen tunics and put it on. It was made of a soft green cotton and hung to just above my knees. The sash that went with it was a darker green. Quickly I tied it around my waist. The final part of the kitchen uniform was a hat designed to cover your hair. I bundled my hair into a ponytail and coiled it on top of my head, pulling the hat over it to hold it in place.

I was just about ready. All I needed to do was put on my necklace – the one with my mum's wedding ring attached – for good luck. Rummaging through my backpack for it, I noticed the penny I'd found, seconds before leaving 2012. I tucked it into my tunic pocket; I'd need all the luck I could get.

Peg was waiting for me out in the passageway. He smirked. 'You look lovely in a utilitarian sort of way.'

I looked up and down the passageway. There was no one around. 'I have an idea,' I said in a low voice. 'I'm going to head down to the kitchens and say that I've been sent to get lunch for the prisoner. I'll take it up to the holding cell.'

'That might get you in,' said Peg. 'Then what?'

'You'll be waiting outside. Last time I passed, there was only one guard. As soon as she unlocks the cell to let me deliver the food, you come in. I'm going to try and get something hot – soup maybe – to throw in her face. Between us we can overpower her and free Ryan. Then we dress him in one of your uniforms, hit the alarm and head for the evacuation shuttles.'

'It could work,' said Peg, unravelling the map. 'There's a restroom close to the holding cell. I could wait in there with a spare uniform for Ryan. Why don't I head up to the bar to meet Lyra and find out if Ryan's in the cell yet?'

'Good idea. I'll meet you in the restroom in twenty minutes,' I said. 'Wish me luck.'

The kitchens were down on C Deck. I smelt them long before I reached them. Steam and grease, the lingering fishiness of seaweed. Then came the clanging of pans and the clattering of dishes, voices calling. Lunchtime. Everyone would be busy. Perfect.

'Are you the new girl?' a red-faced woman barked at me. 'You're late.'

I was about to tell her that I wasn't scheduled to begin until tomorrow, but she thrust a platter of steamed rice into my hands and ordered me to deliver it to the canteen. I carried it swiftly to the serving table, feeling more and more like a worker and not an imposter. The canteen was already busy with workers in for the early sitting. I squeezed the platter of rice on to the end of the table, next to a tureen of steaming hot soup.

At one end of the table was a pile of plates and bowls.

The workers each picked up a plate and shuffled along the line, buffet style, helping themselves to what they wanted. I grabbed a plate and spooned some rice onto it.

'Hey, you!' said one of the kitchen staff, a young boy with a face full of spots. 'What do you think you're doing?'

'The captain asked me to bring a plate of food to him,' I said.

'The captain doesn't eat down here. You get the captain's food up on A Deck.'

'He specifically asked me to come down here and fetch him a bowl of the soup. It's his favourite.'

The spotty boy accepted my explanation. I filled a bowl with soup, placed it on the tray next to the rice and put a cover on top. Then, to make it look realistic, I added a bottle of water. I walked carefully, wishing I hadn't filled the soup bowl so high, out of the canteen and down the passage to the lifts. Thankfully the lift was empty. I plastered a bland, bored look on my face and pressed the button for A Deck.

The lift opened with a ping on B Deck and Nikki and Becca came in. Nikki had changed into a dress and was using her hands to explain to Becca all the different ranks on board the spaceport. My heart began to race. They knew I wasn't due to begin until tomorrow. I ducked my head and turned away, staring down at the tray.

'There are ten men for every woman on the spaceport,' Nikki was saying. 'The officers all eat and drink up on A Deck.'

'OK,' said Becca. 'I'll come with you just this once. But I'm here to save money, not to spend it.'

The lift slowed and stopped and the door slid open. Keeping my head bowed, I let them leave first. I pressed the button to hold the door until I heard their voices fading as they made their way towards the bar, and then took the other direction, towards the restrooms and cells. Just before I reached the holding cell, a door opened a crack and a voice hissed at me. 'Hey! Eden!'

I stopped. It was Peg. 'I'm in here. OK?'

I nodded and used my hip to open the door fully.

'Did you see Lyra?' I asked.

'No. She's not there yet.'

'We must be too early. I should wait. What time is it?'

'Half eleven.'

'I'll give it ten minutes,' I said. The tray was heavy; I put it on the floor and stretched my arms.

'There's always the possibility that she won't be able to get to the bar,' said Peg. 'Milo said it was an expedited transfer. They're only here for three hours. They still have to have security clearance and clear quarantine. That doesn't leave a lot of time for anything else.'

'She'll do everything she can to help us, though?' I said.

'Of course she will.'

Hanging around in the restroom, just waiting, wasn't helping my nerves. 'I'm going to go now,' I said.

Peg picked up the tray and put it in my arms. 'Good luck.'

I edged out of the restroom and continued on my way, fear trickling through me as I approached the holding cell. The door was open just as it had been the day before. The same security guard was sitting behind the desk, reading something on her port-com. Using my elbow to push the door open wide, I took a deep breath and stepped inside.

I scanned the room quickly. There were four barred doors, each leading to a cell. Now that I was closer to the guard, I realised she was solid-looking, all muscle. She probably had a weapon on her somewhere, but for now she was sat behind the desk.

'Yes?' she asked, without looking up from her port-com.

'I have lunch for the prisoner Orion Westland,' I said. My voice was too thin, too feeble.

'He's not here.'

I cleared my throat. 'Then I'll wait. The captain ordered me to hand his meal directly to him.'

The guard finally tore her eyes away from her port-com. 'Wait as long as you like. I have no prisoners scheduled to arrive today.'

'But the captain told me that he would be arriving this morning. He insisted I hand deliver his lunch.'

The woman shrugged indifferently. 'You want me to page the captain?'

'No! He'll kill me for messing this up.'

The woman squinted at me. 'Who are you? I don't recognise your face?'

'I'm new,' I said, backing out of the room. 'I made a mistake. Sorry.'

I hurried out of the prison office and down the corridor to the restroom where Peg was hiding.

'What happened?' asked Peg.

'He's not there. The guard said she has no scheduled prisoners today.'

Peg sighed. 'Why can't something go our way just once?'

I put the tray on the floor. 'What are we going to do?'

'Just leave the tray here. Change out of your uniform and we'll go to the bar. Perhaps Lyra will be there by now.'

The Space Bar was shaped like a wedge of pizza, with the entrance at its narrow pointed end, and windows on the curved wider edge. The bar itself bisected the room. Although it was daytime, the sky outside was as black as night, the stars steady and unblinking. Two men were sitting alone at the bar. There were a couple of pilots sitting at a table by the window. At the end of the bar closest to the pilots, Becca and Nikki were each nursing a glass of wine and talking too loudly. But there was no sign of Lyra.

'Maybe his ship was delayed,' I said.

'Let's see if we can find a com-screen. If the ship's been delayed, it will be on the news.' He began walking towards the exit.

'Unless,' I began, grabbing Peg's arm. 'What if they bypassed the spaceport and went directly to the moon?'

Peg stopped. 'That doesn't seem likely. It's a long haul to the moon. There are rules about flying hours and scheduled breaks, not to mention security clearance.'

'What time is it?'

'Twelve fifteen.'

Nikki shrieked with laughter, a high-pitched, attention-seeking laugh. I turned to look at her. And that was when

I saw him. From behind I hadn't recognised him, probably because I wasn't expecting to see him here. But he had turned towards Nikki as well. His expression was one of pure irritation.

I grabbed Peg's elbow.

'What is it?'

'Clarence.'

We both stared. He had his back to us again and was tucking into a plate of food.

'If he's here,' I whispered, 'that must mean the ship has docked and the passengers have cleared security.'

'Let's go,' said Peg quietly. 'If he sees us, he'll know we're up to something.'

It was too late. Nikki laughed again and Clarence turned his head. Peg and I were just in his line of sight. He stared.

'Crap,' I muttered under my breath. 'We just lost the element of surprise.'

'Eden?' Clarence had hopped off his bar stool and was walking over to us. 'What the hell are you doing here? With him?'

'Good to see you too,' said Peg.

'I got Pegasus a job here on the spaceport,' I said, my brain rushing ahead of my mouth, pulling ideas from everywhere.

'She knows Benjamin Hansen, the captain,' said Peg.

'Peg's helped me out a lot. I'm just pleased I could do something for him,' I said.

'But why are *you* here?'

'Ben invited me to come along for the ride. Say hello and introduce the two of them.'

'Right.' He narrowed his eyes. 'Because the captain of the Inter-Planetary Spaceport has so much free time on his hands. I'm not buying it.'

'And I don't give a damn,' said Peg.

Clarence ignored Peg and stared at me. 'Is there something I should know about the two of you? I'm not going to be jerked around.'

I stepped between the two of them and lowered my voice. 'Peg has a thing for Lyra Thornhill. Is she here? I know he's hoping to see her.'

'Good luck with that. She got a nasty bout of space sickness on the way here. She's in the ladies' room cleaning herself up.'

'Which ladies' room?'

Clarence pointed behind him.

'I'd better check on her. Try not to fall out with Peg.'

Lyra was standing by the basins, splashing water on her face. Her skin had a yellowish tinge to it. I quickly checked the stalls to make sure they were empty.

'Clarence said you were sick,' I said.

'I'll live.'

'Where is he?'

She met my eye in the mirror above the sink. 'They're not letting him off the ship.'

'Why not?'

'I don't know. They brought the quarantine doctor on board to clear everybody. I think Wolfe wants to get this done as quickly as possible. Just a crew change and we're on our way.'

'We'll never get him through security,' I said. 'We need him in the holding cells for our plan to work.'

'That's not going to happen, Eden. Wolfe has about twenty reporters on board the ship with him. They're documenting the whole thing. Wolfe's been answering questions all morning. Posing for photos. It makes me sick.'

'How's Ryan?'

'He's scared. But he's also being incredibly stubborn. Refusing to answer all questions except mine.'

I allowed myself a smile. 'Good for him. Who else is on board apart from the media?'

'Just Orion, Wolfe and a security guard.'

'We have to get those reporters off the ship,' I said.

'You'll never be able to do that,' she said. 'Orion's story is huge. No one is going to walk away from that.'

'What if there was another story?' I said. 'A bigger one. A story about the son of a Guardian who crashed his car because he was drunk, let someone else take the blame for him and stole fuel from his father's depot? Do you think they might want to hear that?'

'What about Peg?'

'He's another witness. He'll back up your story.'

'That's not what I mean. Remember what I said to you about him getting into trouble for covering up the truth.'

'No one knows Peg helped Ryan but us. And we're not telling. Come on. He'd want you to do this.'

CHAPTER 24

Peg was waiting for me just outside the ladies' room.

'Where's she going?' he asked me, as Lyra rushed past.

'She's going to get all the reporters, and Admiral Wolfe, to come in here.'

'And how's she going to do that?'

'Tell them she'll be holding a press conference about Clarence Wolfe and how he helped Ryan with the fuel. Wolfe believes that the children of the rich and powerful shouldn't get special treatment, so it'll be interesting to see what he has to say when he finds out about his own son. I wonder if he'll choose to make an example out of him.'

Peg glanced at Clarence, who was back at the bar finishing his food. 'I almost feel sorry for him.'

'Don't.'

'Then what?'

'I'm going to put my kitchen tunic back on and try to deliver Ryan's food to him on the ship. If Lyra does her part, it will just be Ryan and his guard left on board.'

'How are you going to get Ryan off the ship and through security?'

'I haven't worked that part out yet.'

Clarence turned around then and saw me.

Peg pulled a face. 'You'd better go and cosy up to Clarence or he's going to know we're up to something. I'll get your uniform for you and meet you in the restroom where you left the food.'

I swung myself on to the stool next to Clarence. 'Peg's gone to take care of Lyra.'

Clarence finished chewing and put his knife and fork down on his plate. 'What are you really doing here, Eden?'

'I thought you'd be surprised,' I said, playing for time.

'You're right about that.'

'You're not pleased to see me?'

He dabbed at his mouth with a heavy cloth napkin. 'I don't trust you.'

I raised an arm for the waiter and asked for water.

'You have no idea how hard it's been for me, moving through time,' I said.

'What's that got to do with anything?'

'There are only two people alive that I've known for longer than two weeks. One of them is about to be sent to the moon for the rest of his life. And the other one is Ben Hansen, the captain of the spaceport. He's like a dad to me. When I asked him if he could offer Peg a job, he invited me to visit. I had to come, Clarence. I needed to see someone who knows me from back then.'

His expression softened slightly and I began to think I might have convinced him, but I didn't have time to find out because at that moment the door to the Space Bar opened and Lyra strode into the room, a line of reporters behind her.

'What the hell?' said Clarence.

Lyra stood by an empty table, one hand on her waist and waited while everyone filed in and found a space.

'I'd like to make a statement,' she said, her voice bright and clear over the clatter and chatter in the room.

'What is she doing?' asked Clarence.

'I don't know,' I said.

'As you all know, Orion Westland is being transported to the International Lunar Correctional Facility for breaking one of the Temporal Laws,' she said.

'Tell us something we don't know,' said one of the reporters.

Lyra ignored her and continued talking, her voice steady. 'He broke the law to save the life of an innocent girl.'

'That's not what the court said,' said the same reporter.

'If you're not interested in hearing what I have to say, I suggest you return to the ship,' said Lyra. She took a deep breath. 'Eden Anfield was killed by a mission cleaner, despite the fact that she had played a vital role in the mission. She should have been protected under the Clemency Protocol. So Orion went back to make things right.'

As the words left her mouth, I saw Admiral Wolfe walk into the bar.

'He took his case to the Board and was turned down,' said Wolfe. 'This is not news. The Westland boy broke the law for personal reasons.'

'We can agree to differ on his motives,' said Lyra. 'I'm more interested in how he made it happen.'

'That's a matter for the inquiry,' said Wolfe. 'Admiral

Westland has been arrested and the matter will be tried in the courts.'

'The thing is,' said Lyra, 'Orion Westland is a good friend of mine and I know how he made it happen.'

I slipped off my stool. Lyra had them captivated now. If I was going to sneak out of the bar without Wolfe seeing me, this was my best chance.

'Where are you going?' whispered Clarence.

'To find Peg. I'll be right back.'

I eased myself around the back of the reporters towards the door.

'Orion Westland is a pretty resourceful boy,' said Lyra. 'He found out that his old ship was going to be scrapped and worked out a way to get his hands on it. Within a few weeks of returning from his mission to 2012, he had a ship and a plan. The only thing he didn't have was premium grade fuel for a trip through time.'

'Are you suggesting you know where he got the fuel?' asked one of the reporters.

'That's exactly what I'm saying. But, for you to under-stand the story fully, I need to give you a little background.'

Lyra caught my eye. I needed to get out of there quickly and move on with my part. I slipped out of the door and ran down the corridor to the restroom where Peg was waiting.

'We have a couple of minutes,' I said, pulling off my shoes. 'That's all. Make sure no one walks in on me.'

There was no time for delicacy. I stripped off my clothes and pulled my kitchen uniform on.

'The soup is cold,' said Peg. 'It's no good to you. Let me come and help you.'

'They'll never let two of us through to deliver a meal,' I said.

I straightened the cap over my hair and pinned my identification card to my uniform. 'Give me your kitchen uniform and ID,' I said. 'I'll hide them under mine. Maybe I can get him through security dressed as you.'

Peg helped me wedge them around my waist, held in place by my belt.

'How do I look?' I asked.

'Well fed.'

A quick glance in the mirror confirmed that I looked like a plump kitchen worker. I picked up the tray.

'Hey,' said Peg as I was about to leave the restroom. 'Whatever happens. Good luck.'

'I'll meet you in the emergency shuttle bay,' I said.

I was trembling when I left the restroom and began the short walk to security clearance. I was running against the clock. Who knew how long Lyra would be able to keep Admiral Wolfe and the reporters entertained. And how was I to overcome Ryan's guard with nothing but a cold lunch?

'How can I help you?' asked the security officer at Residents' Clearance.

'I have lunch for the guard on Admiral Wolfe's ship.'

'Your card?'

I passed it over and silently prayed that it didn't say anything about my employment status not beginning until tomorrow. He scanned the card and handed it back, without looking at either the screen or me.

'C Dock. You can't miss it. It's the only one there. But you'll have to be quick. We're opening the airlock to let a supply ship dock in ten minutes.'

'Thanks,' I said, and hurried past him.

A white ship with the logo *International Lunar Correctional Facility* was the only vessel parked at A Dock. I shuddered and hurried past. B Dock was busy with small vessels and people hurrying to and fro. Ben had said there were two thousand full-time inhabitants on the spaceport, but obviously there were many visitors too. And then I was at C Dock. Just the one ship. Admiral Wolfe's official spacecraft. I paused for a second to gather my courage. The last time I'd seen Ryan I'd told him, 'This is not goodbye'. What must he have thought when I hadn't rescued him from the Institute? Did he think I'd given up on him? Moved on with my life?

I hurried up the gangway towards the open hatch, aching to see him again, my heart beating so loudly it drowned out the sound of my shoes on the metal stairs.

I was only halfway up the stairs when the guard approached the opening, his gun at the ready.

'Permission to come aboard, sir?' I said, keeping my head bowed. 'I have your lunch.'

The guard indicated his assent with a nod of his head. I continued walking up the steps, holding the tray steady, begging my knees not to buckle. I glanced at Ryan who was handcuffed and slouched in his seat. He was pale, the set of his mouth hard. I willed him to look at me, but he just stared at his hands.

The guard sat down just across from Ryan and lowered his tray table.

I placed the tray on the table in front of him and lifted the cover off the rice and seaweed.

'Today's special is seafood soup and rice and wakame stir-fry,' I said, noticing that he had rested his gun on the seat to his left, out of my reach.

'Terrific,' he said sarcastically. 'You can leave now.'

'Let me,' I said, reaching for the napkin that held his knife and fork.

I had some vague notion that I could stab him with the fork. But before I had the chance to remove either utensil, the guard wrapped his burly hand around mine.

'I can manage my own silverware,' he said.

'Then let me pour your drink,' I said.

The soup was cold and I had lost my chance to use the fork. The water bottle was my last chance. It was small, but it was glass. I made as though to twist off the lid and then quickly smashed it over the back of his head. It thunked against his skull, but the bottle didn't break. The guard yelled out and his head fell forwards. Desperately, my eyes searched the cabin looking for something hard to break the bottle.

'Here!' yelled Ryan, holding out his hands.

Our eyes locked and for a split second I was lost in their deep bronze warmth. He didn't seem surprised to see me. He seemed relieved. And proud. As though he'd known I would come through for him. As though he believed in me.

The look was quickly replaced by one of panic. 'Break the bottle against the handcuffs.'

I smashed the bottle hard against the ring of steel around one of his hands, shattering glass and spilling water all over Ryan's lap.

The guard was reaching across the seat for his gun. Adrenalin and instinct took over. I whipped around and held the jagged bottle edge under his throat. I had no idea what to do next. He stilled, but I could tell he was sizing me up, deciding whether he could risk throwing me off him.

And then I heard footsteps clanging rapidly up the steps.

'Put the bottle down,' said the guard, 'and no one needs to know any of this happened.'

I didn't know what to do. A figure appeared in the doorway. I risked a look. It was a man silhouetted against the open hatchway.

'Don't come any closer or I'll go for his jugular!' I shouted, trying to hide the quiver in my voice.

'It's me – Peg,' said the figure.

'Thank God!'

Peg ran down the aisle. He was wearing a set of cleaner's overalls. He reached across the guard for the gun and pushed the nozzle into the side of his neck. 'Where's the key for the handcuffs?'

The guard lifted a bunch of keys hanging around his waist. I took the key from his belt and started unlocking Ryan's handcuffs.

'What's the plan?' whispered Ryan.

'We have an escape shuttle on the other side of the space-port,' I said, unlocking the handcuffs. I pulled them free of Ryan's wrists. Underneath, his skin was pink and raw. I ran my thumb over the tender spot and felt the throb of his pulse against my skin. He moved one hand and tilted my chin so that our eyes met.

'Put these on,' I said, pulling the kitchen porter's uniform out from my waist.

A loud screech, urgent and insistent, began to sound.

'Oh God,' said Peg. 'Security alarm. They must be on to us.'

'It's not that,' I said. 'It's the ten-minute warning for the airlock. There's a supply ship coming in. We have to get off the dock within ten minutes.'

'Or stay on the ship,' said Ryan.

'By the time the airlock is shut again, Wolfe will be wait-ing for us at security,' Peg said. 'We'll never make it.'

'Why don't we take this ship?' I said. 'If they're opening the airlock, we could just fly out. It'll be a lot easier than trying to cross the spaceport to the emergency shuttle bay.'

'This is a little trickier to fly than a space hopper or escape shuttle,' said Peg.

'I thought you said you could fly anything?' I said.

Ryan laughed sharply. 'Did he really say that?'

'I might have exaggerated a little,' said Peg.

'We have about nine minutes,' I said. 'So make up your minds right now.'

'Does this ship have an escape pod?' Peg asked Ryan.

'It has two. One right through that door.' He pointed to a doorway with a green arrow above it.

'You've got thirty seconds to get in that escape pod,' said Peg to the guard. 'Or I'm gonna be forced to shoot you.'

He held the gun to the man's neck and pushed him towards the door.

'Do you think you can fly this?' I asked Ryan.

'I'm going to give it a try.'

'That doesn't fill me with confidence.'

'There are flight suits in that locker,' said Ryan. 'Put one on. And a helmet. Just in case.'

'What about you?'

'There's no time.'

Peg shoved the guard through the doorway. Ryan opened the locker and chucked me an orange flight suit.

'I can't believe you're here,' said Ryan as I ripped the plastic off the suit. 'How the hell did you manage to get to the spaceport, get everyone off the ship and then show up just as they're about to open the hatch for a cargo ship?'

'It's a long story,' I said, as I stripped off my kitchen tunic. 'And – for the record – this is Plan B. The first one didn't work so well.'

Ryan helped me with my flight suit, pulling up the zip that ran from the waist to the neck. He rested his hand on the side of my neck. 'Kiss me?' he said quietly. 'Just in case Plan B doesn't work well either.'

I reached up and brushed my lips against his. Ryan wrapped his other arm around my waist and pulled me closer to him.

The door to the escape pod slammed, making us both jump. We pulled apart.

'He's in the pod,' said Peg. His eyes swept across mine and then continued to the hatch.

'Thank God you showed up,' I said.

'I had a hunch you'd need some help in here.' He met my eyes again, but fleetingly. 'You did great.'

Ryan dragged another flight suit from the locker. 'Peg, you want to put this on while I start the engines? We need to go right now.'

Peg looked from me to Ryan and back to me again. 'I'm not going with you.'

'What?' I said. 'You have to come. You'll never make it off the landing bay in time.'

'I will.'

'You might never get another chance to fly a Guardian Class ship,' said Ryan.

'I thought you wanted an adventure,' I said.

He pushed his fingers through his hair. 'You two need to make this journey on your own.'

Ryan and Peg locked eyes for a second and then Ryan backed into the cockpit.

'Please come with us,' I said.

Peg shook his head and made for the metal stairway. 'I need to make sure Lyra's OK.'

I followed him to the hatch, wishing we had more time. In a different time, a different timeline, our paths might have crossed and led us to a different destination. But in this lifetime, this place in the universe, this was where our paths diverged. I followed him halfway down the stairs. 'None of this would have happened without you,' I said. 'Thank you, Pegasus.'

He nodded. 'Say goodbye to Ry for me. We sort of ran out of time up there.'

'Look up Penpol Cove in Cornwall one day,' I said, my throat constricting.

'Penpol Cove?' he repeated.

I nodded, not trusting myself to speak. Peg kissed my cheek, turned and clattered down the stairway.

'Come on, co-pilot,' Ryan called from the hatch. I ran back up the stairs. Ryan pressed a button and the metal stairway slowly retracted. 'We have four minutes.'

I followed him into the cockpit. It was no bigger than the cockpit of the space hopper Peg had taken me in. I strapped myself into the co-pilot's seat. In quick succession, he tapped a grid of buttons on the panel.

'You realise I'm not going to be any help to you,' I said.

For a second, Ryan stopped tapping buttons and looked at me. 'I can't believe you did all this. You're crazy.' Then he was back at work on the screen. I heard a hiss and felt a jolt as the ship freed itself from its constraints.

The alarm stopped sounding.

'Hatch is opening,' said Ryan. 'We're going to have to slip through the opening at the same time as that cargo ship comes in. It's going to be tight; our ship isn't exactly small either.'

'Have you ever flown a ship like this before?'

'Only simulations,' said Ryan.

The ship slowly backed away from the dock.

'What do you know about security?' asked Ryan.

'Nothing,' I said. 'We didn't have the chance to check it out. I didn't notice any security shuttles on the docks, so I'm guessing they're on another part of the spaceport.'

'They'll probably be waiting for us on the other side of the hatch then.'

'What are we going to do?'

'I'm going to fix a portal while you fly us through the hatch.'

'Ryan . . .'

'Just take the controller for a minute. You're going to fly under that cargo ship. It's just a matter of steering. Like driving a car.'

I wrapped both hands around the controller in front of me and Ryan pressed a button to transfer the control to me. The controller vibrated in my hand.

Ryan went back to tapping away on the screen in front of him. I watched through the window before me. The hatch was fully open now and a ship – a mammoth ship ten times the size of ours – was slowly floating through it.

'What's the destination?' I asked.

'I'm gonna set the coordinates for Titan,' said Ryan. 'It's the obvious choice.'

'If it's that obvious, won't they follow us straight there?'

'It's the first place they'll look,' said Ryan. 'They'll portal there and try to intercept us. Everyone goes to Titan.'

'Then why are we going there?'

'We need a decoy. Something to throw them off our real

destination. And once we get beyond the asteroid belt, our portal signature will be harder to trace.'

We were approaching the cargo ship now. Its colossal bulk almost entirely filled the window in front of us.

'Coordinates are set,' said Ryan. 'The portal should be ready in sixty seconds. I'm going to transfer the controller back to me now.'

The cargo ship was completely inside the airlock. I held my breath as its shadow passed over us and the doors to the outside came into view. They were closing, but slowly. Ryan accelerated the ship and swore. 'Come on, come on,' he muttered. 'The acceleration on this ship is a piece of shit.'

Frowning, he bit his lip and moved the controller abruptly to the right, turning the ship on to its side. I could see the doors to the hatch closing faster. We would make it. But only just. Then there was a ping on the side of the ship, followed by another.

'They're firing on us!' shouted Ryan. 'We're not even through the freakin' hatch and they're already on us.'

Something hit the side of the ship hard. We jolted sideways.

'Oh God,' I said.

'It's a Guardian Class ship,' said Ryan. 'Reinforced hull. It can take a little damage.'

Another blast of something jolted our ship once again.

'They're targeting our portal drive,' said Ryan. 'We still need ten seconds for our portal to stabilise. Hold on.'

Ryan began tapping rapidly on the screen. A third jolt flung our ship sideways.

'Amber alert,' said the computer. 'Danger of hull breach.'

'Hold on,' said Ryan.

He spun the ship in a three hundred and sixty degrees roll. My stomach leapt into my throat and a shiver of nausea rippled through me.

'Portal stabilised,' said the computer.

That now-familiar sense of moving backwards gripped my stomach. I held my breath until the blackness outside the window formed a tunnel shape with a bright yellowish hue at the far end. We began to race through the tunnel.

'We're going to Titan first,' said Ryan. 'Let them think that's where we're headed. Just before we arrive, I'm going to set new coordinates.'

'You're going to create a portal from within a portal?' I asked.

'It's going to be OK. Trust me. We're going somewhere no one goes. Somewhere no one knows about. The portal will hold.'

Ryan started tapping in a new set of coordinates. The yellow moon curved off to one side.

'I've set up the new portal,' said Ryan. 'We'd better release our passenger. It will look like we had to do an emergency eject.'

The ship jolted forwards as the escape pod was released.

'Get ready for portal number two,' said Ryan.

Another narrower, blacker tunnel emerged within the first one. A faint blue glow shone through it. Ryan flew straight towards its narrow entrance. Curved around the outside of the larger tunnel, I could still see the spaceport, the yellow hue of Titan, and the frisbee-shaped rings of Saturn. Ahead, growing rapidly brighter, our destination glowed blue.

'They'll probably think our portal collapsed,' said Ryan. His eyes were glued to the screen in front of him. 'All they'll be able to find is one of the escape pods. With a bit of luck they'll assume we were in the other one and didn't make it.' He almost laughed. 'No one is crazy enough to portal into the unknown.'

We entered the smaller tunnel. The Inter-Planetary spaceport had now disappeared. Titan and Saturn were still within view, but elongated and distorted into thin sausage shapes. Other moons were alongside them, but I had no names for them.

'Ten seconds,' said Ryan.

Titan disappeared. Then Saturn.

'Three,' said Ryan. 'Two. One.'

The tunnel vanished. In our window were two moons, one larger than the other, but both white and pockmarked just like Earth's moon. Ryan eased the controller to the right until a planet, a blue-green and white, Earth-like planet, floated in the velvet darkness in front of us.

'Welcome to Eden,' he said.

Twilight was rapid. First, the halo of light over the planet turned copper, then it deepened to scarlet. Seconds later it had gone and we were plunged into darkness. There were no artificial lights on the planet's surface to show the shape of the continents. It was as though there was nothing but this ship and the eternal blackness of space.

Ryan had put us in a stable orbit above Eden, from where we saw the three suns rise and set every ninety minutes. He explained that trace signatures of our portal could be discovered for up to an hour after we'd closed it. Five hours later he was still scanning the space around us for incoming ships.

'No one knows we're here,' I said, unstrapping my seatbelt. The cockpit was cramped and my muscles felt tight. 'It's been hours. You said yourself they probably think our portal collapsed.'

'But what if they did catch a trace of our destination? I'd have risked everything just to save myself.'

'But they didn't.'

'I shouldn't have brought us here. I panicked.'

'Of course you panicked. You were under fire,' I said, standing up. 'But no one has followed you. And no one will because no one else knows this place exists. No one except Cassie, Ben and your dad. But they're not going to risk telling anyone about this planet. They know the consequences.'

'Let me run one last scan,' he said, dragging an icon across the control panel.

'Fine. I'll give you ten minutes. And then I want you to come out into the lounge area with me.'

I left him frowning at the control panel and went to explore the rest of the ship. There were a couple of rows of airline-style seating just behind the cockpit, and then the body of the ship opened out into a lounge area with white leather couches, a bar and a massive window. Right at the back of the ship was a small galley with a fridge and an oven. I opened the fridge and squatted down to look inside. There were a number of pre-packed meals that had probably been brought on board to feed the admiral and the journalists on the trip to the moon. I counted them. Forty-four. I opened cupboards and pulled open drawers, locating plates and utensils, condiments and napkins. We wouldn't go hungry for a few days.

Next I located the bathroom – an airline-style toilet and sink – and unzipped my bulky orange flight suit. I assumed that we were safe now we were in orbit. In any case, Ryan wasn't wearing one so if anything happened to the ship, there would be no one left to rescue me. I'd prefer to die quickly if death was inevitable. I dressed in my green cotton kitchen tunic and adjusted my hair in the mirror.

When I got back into the main cabin, Ryan was standing at the bar, untwisting the wire top of a bottle of champagne. He smiled, but his eyes looked tired and the prison clothes he wore were hanging off him.

'Nice outfit,' I said.

'You too.'

I looked down at the frumpy tunic I was wearing and laughed.

'I never thought I'd see Eden again,' he said, his thumbs pushing out the cork. 'Not the planet and not you. I can't quite believe we're here.'

'Nor me.'

He poured the champagne into two crystal glasses. The bubbles caught the light and twinkled like stars.

'A toast,' he said, passing one of the glasses to me. 'To Eden.'

I wasn't sure whether he was referring to me or the planet, but I tipped the glass against my lips and bubbles shot up my nose.

'If it wasn't for this planet, we wouldn't be here,' I said. 'You'd never have travelled back to 2012 to stop it being discovered. I'd never have met you.'

'I always wanted you to see the planet that was named after you.'

'I'd love to land on the surface. See it up close.'

'We could do that.'

'What about the parasite?'

'We'd have to stay away from the infected continents. But we could visit one of the small desert lands; it's safe there.'

I wanted to do that so much. Space scared me – the endlessness of it.

'What about where you lived when you were a boy? Can we see that?'

He shrugged. 'Sure. We can do anything. But if we went there, we'd have to stay on Eden for ever. That's where the parasite lives. We'd never be able to return to Earth.'

'What do you think we should do?'

'Dance,' he said. 'I think we should dance. Everything else can wait.'

He put his glass on the table and went over to a small com-screen. Seconds later, music began playing softly.

'Come here,' he said. He took my hand and led me towards the window. 'Lights off.'

The inside of the ship was thrust into a darkness so intense, even the outlines of furniture were invisible. I stepped forward, lost my balance and fell against Ryan.

'I'm sorry,' I said.

'Don't be.' His hands wrapped around my waist and pulled me close to him.

There was nothing but blackness and starlight. Through the window, the ship turned in its orbit, and then we were dancing, chasing stars across the sky.

EPILOGUE

The Southern Desert of Eden, three days later

'I promise it's worth it,' he says.

I nod; my mouth is too dry to waste words. We've been walking across the desert for about an hour by now, only it's not like the endless sand in the deserts of my imagination. Here the desert is bare, brittle rock. Thin sliver of rock upon thin sliver of rock. It snaps and splinters underfoot, like walking across thin ice. I peel my shirt from my damp skin and squint against the bright sunlight, wishing I had sunglasses or sunscreen. Or both.

And then, abruptly, the rock turns to sand. We turn a corner and I see why. We've reached the ocean; its surface is like blue silk.

'It's so still,' I say, as I unscrew the lid of my water bottle. The water inside is hot and offers almost no refreshment.

'Perfect for swimming.'

'We're going to swim?' I say, looking down at my kitchen tunic. I've cut off the sleeves, but they're still kind of heavy to swim in. Beneath, I have nothing but the set of underwear I've washed overnight every day for the past three days.

'Yes, we're going to swim. There's something I want to show you.'

He pulls his green prison shirt over his head and I'm glad to see that he's already filling out again, that the sunlight is washing away the grey pallor that comes with being locked inside for three weeks.

'So you know this place?'

'Dad used to bring us here every year for a vacation,' says Ryan.

I peel off my tunic, feeling the sun leaching the moisture from my skin.

'It was different then of course. Not as mind-blowing as this.' He sweeps his arm, encompassing everything in its arc: the spires and towers of pink sandstone that rise like petrified trees from the ground; the flat expanse of ocean ahead of us; the vastness of blue sky above.

'How was it different?'

'Well, there was a huge hotel at the top of the bluff behind us,' he says, turning back and pointing at the stone cliff. 'A thousand suites. Eight restaurants. Three swimming pools. Utter luxury.' He looks at me. 'Water piped in from the oasis, seventy kilometres away. A big white blemish on the landscape. And then down here on the beach there were hundreds of loungers for sun-bathing and moon watching. Stalls selling cold drinks and snacks. You could rent all-terrain vehicles to go and destroy the desert. They took an unspoilt paradise and turned it into a beach resort just like everywhere else. It was pointless.'

I wouldn't mind a beach shack selling cold drinks and snacks right now, but I get what he's saying.

We're walking across the hot sand to the water's edge when something occurs to me. 'How could your dad bring you here to a hotel when you were a child, when that hotel never existed?'

Ryan shakes his head rapidly, like a dog shaking off water. 'I still have memories from the original timeline. But I have new memories too. Like, I remember spending my childhood on Eden, but I also remember spending it on Earth.'

'So it's like you're two people?

'Sort of. I've had two different sets of experiences, but those different lives are beginning to converge.' He dips his foot in the sea, sending ripples through the still water. 'I wish I could explain convergence theory to you, but it's a really tricky concept.'

'Are you saying I'm not smart enough to understand it?'

He shakes his head, laughing. 'I'm saying *I'm* not smart enough to understand it. It messes with your head. Come on – let's swim.'

The water is much warmer than the sea at home in Penpol Cove or the icy lake water in the mountains of Lakeborough. It coaxes you in, slips over your skin, relaxes your muscles. I lie on my back, letting it hold me, watching the sky turn bluer.

'We're gonna swim over to the rocks,' he says.

He swims ahead of me, his arms and legs streamlined, his

movements clean, unlike my splashy attempt at front crawl. He waits for me by the rocky headland, reaching out for my hand.

'Follow me under the water,' he says, 'and open your eyes.'

Maybe the sea is less salty on Eden, because it doesn't sting my eyes at all. The sunlight reaches deep below the surface, giving the underwater world its colours. The pink rock of the desert is a deeper rose down here, the weeds that sprout within its cracks as green as English grass. But it's the fish that are most captivating. There are blue and yellow stripy fish, no bigger than goldfish. Black and orange fish the size of small sharks. Fish every colour of the rainbow, darting in and out of the rocks.

I surface for air. Ryan shoots up next to me.

'Are they . . .' I begin.

'All safe,' says Ryan. 'Nothing predatory here.'

We stay in the water for what feels like hours, swimming through arches of pink rock, around spires that point up from the ocean bed like wrinkled fingers. We spot hundreds of different fish, weird turtle-like creatures with large curious eyes, fat black animals that look something like a cross between a dolphin and a cat. By the time we decide to head back to camp, my skin is puckered and white and the suns are low on the horizon.

Back at camp, Ryan heads into the ship to sort out something to eat while I finish building a fire with the small pile of dead leaves and twigs I've managed to scavenge. There's not a hell of a lot to burn out here in the desert. Once I've got the fire in a rough pyramid shape, I strike a match to the dry grass and leaves at the base. It crackles and spits, quickly catching the small twigs. Smoke coils upwards into the empty sky, smudging its clear blue with grey.

Ryan comes back out carrying two foil trays of food. 'I think it's some sort of mashed potato thing,' he says, passing one of them to me.

By the time we've eaten, dusk has fallen. Purple shadows race across the ground, swallowing up canyons and spires in mere seconds. The second sun sinks below the horizon and the safe blue sky disappears, revealing the enormous immensity of space. The first of the stars peeps from the darkness.

'That's Eden's third sun,' says Ryan. 'It's much further away than the other suns, but it's still technically a part of this solar system.'

'This is how we first began,' I say. 'Alone on a clear night – you teaching me about the stars.'

'There's one more I want to tell you about.'

'Yeah?'

'Lie back. This constellation is high in the sky.'

I do as he asks, lying there while my eyes adjust.

'You're looking for a square with a triangle above it,' he says. 'Like a child's drawing of a house. You see it?'

At first I see nothing. And then pale stars emerge from the blue-black sky.

'Do you see the one that forms the apex of the triangle – the roof?' asks Ryan.

'I see it.'

'That's our sun. That's home.'

I can't say anything. I fix my gaze on that one yellow star and think of all the people back there on Earth circling it. All the people we love. I think of Pegasus and Ben. Ryan's mother and father, his brothers and friends. And before them, in a different time, Miranda and Connor and Megan. I think of all that empty space between us, all those burning stars scattering their light across the universe.

'It's ninety-three light years away,' he says softly. 'You know what that means.'

I do. The light we see now actually shone on the Earth ninety-three years ago, when Miranda and all my friends were still alive. I'm looking into the past and we are connected by this beam of silvery light.

'I'll be right back,' Ryan says.

He gets up. I hear his footsteps crunching over the ground towards the ship.

Seeing our sun so many light years away makes me think about all we've been through. How we've stepped through time again and again. Together. We changed our Fate – if Fate is nothing more than the passage of time – and made the world a better place. On Ryan's first trip through time, he and I prevented Connor from discovering this planet with its deadly parasite, and the destruction of Earth. On his second trip, he saved my life. When I jumped through time, I saved him from spending the rest of his life on the moon. We've both given up so much to be here. Me: my time. Ryan: his home.

Yes, we've given up a lot, but we've gained more.

343

Ryan sits back beside me on the ground, two glasses of champagne in his hands.

'More champagne?' I say. 'We've been celebrating a lot since we got here.'

'Every day we're together is a reason to celebrate.'

'Actually, I think I'll just stick to water tonight,' I say, sitting up. 'I'm kind of dehydrated.'

'That's something we need to talk about,' he says. 'We're down to our last six litres of water. We can't stay in the desert any longer. It's decision time.'

I've thought about staying here. I really have. The whole time Ryan and I have known each other, we've been told we can't be together or we've been forced apart. Now we have a whole planet to ourselves. We could travel to the place where Ryan spent his childhood, in a wooded valley surrounded by pink mountains and four converging rivers, and build a treehouse. We could forage for food and tell stories around the fire at night. We could swing in hammocks and swim in warm seas and just be together. A little part of me wants to do just that.

But I'm too much of a pragmatist at heart. I'm much too used to indoor plumbing and buying my food at the shops to be comfortable spending eternity in paradise. Eden is beautiful, but it's a wild, untamed planet. Ryan has told me stories of lizards the size of dogs and birds with wingspans the breadth of pterodactyls'.

We have discussed the possibilities of course. We've imagined living here or back on Earth. Not present day Earth of course; that would be much too dangerous. But if

344

we jumped well into the future or into the past, where no one knows us, we could start again. Neither of us has stated a preference. He looks happy – hopeful – but I have no idea what he's hoping for.

'So,' he says. 'Where do you want to live?'

'What do you want to do?' I ask.

'I asked first,' he says, smiling and shaking his head. 'Tell me where you want to live.'

I take a deep breath. 'I really like it here,' I begin. 'It's the most beautiful place I've ever seen.'

'OK.' He's holding my gaze, as though trying to read my thoughts.

'But I think I'd like to go back to Earth.'

His eyes close and my fears are realised. 'I do love it here,' I say, trying to reassure him. 'It's just, you know, what if one of us got sick?'

His eyes flick back open and he smiles. 'I was terrified you were going to want to stay here. I love a good meta-phor as much as the next guy, but the thought of the two of us alone, like Adam and Eve in paradise for ever . . .'

'It would be pretty intense,' I say, relief flooding through me.

'And it would leave our children in a sticky situation, genetically speaking.'

'Our children?' I say, raising my eyebrows.

He smirks. 'How else would we pass the time? There's no com-screen in paradise.'

To my amazement, I'm not blushing. 'So it's Earth,' I say. 'I know a little farmhouse by the sea.'

'I'd like that. I never did get to finish decorating that place. And I know a loose floorboard with a whole wad of cash hidden underneath it.'

'So the question is, when. In the past? Or in the future?'

'You decide. Either choice is fine with me. But whatever we choose, we stick with it. I'm done jumping back and forth through time. Like I said, it messes with your head.'

I stand up and stretch. It's such a big decision. And yet – and yet, no one knows what might lie ahead of them. I thrust my hands into my pockets and one of them bumps against something small and warm. And then I know exactly how I'm going to decide. I take out the lucky penny I found just before leaving 2012 and turn it between my fingers. 'Heads is the future. Tails is the past,' I say.

Ryan stands up next to me. 'Are you serious?'

'This seems as good a way as any to decide.'

He takes a deep breath and nods. 'Let's do it.'

He's still holding my gaze, still waiting to see where fortune will take us, as I flip the copper coin into the air and leave our destiny to chance.